WHEN SKIES ARE GREY

Fran Clark

ISBN: 978-0-9933381-6-8

When Skies Are Grey
Island Secrets Series Book 4

Also in the series:
Holding Paradise Book 1
A Prayer For Junie Book 2
The Long Way Home Book 3

Also by Fran Clark
Lovers

*For Pete
And this time next year...*

Part One

Then and Now

1

The pub door flies open and a man staggers out into the still evening, only to land at Rayna's feet and she freezes. The door closes slowly on the busy pub and Rayna is alone in the dark street with a man who appears to have passed out in front of her. She looks up, sheepishly, when the door opens again with a yawn that emits the fug of cigarettes, jazz music, the chatter of rowdy voices and a woman with red hair. Rayna stares at her and notices the man at her feet is regaining consciousness. He staggers to a semi-vertical stance and sways towards Rayna, whose shoes stay stamped to the cold paving stones.

'Get on with you, George,' the redhead says, arms folded across her thin blouse, goosebumps visible on her freckled skin. 'You've had a skinful and it's time you were home. Go on. Get off.'

He mutters one or two unintelligible syllables and heads towards the bridge that will take him over the rail tracks. The redhead turns back to face Rayna, whose heart beats like thunder.

'Were you about to cross the bridge?' the redhead demands. White vapour clouds her breath and vanishes seconds after leaving her lips.

Rayna nods. She wonders if the woman can read her thoughts.

'You come in with me until George finds his way back to his Missus, then. That's this week's wages down his gullet – again.'

Rayna has no time to protest before she is pulled into the pub by the elbow, warm air brushing the chill from her cheeks. She'd heard the jazz band play every Friday evening when she walked home from work. The music was unlike anything she'd experienced. She had never heard it from the radio back home, nor from the one in the factory where she sews dresses all day, sitting in a row of seamstresses, their voices as loud as their industrial machines. You can scarcely make out a conversation, let alone hear the radio. In the evening, though, when the factory staff leave for home, Rayna turns the radio up. She dons an apron and starts to brush away the waste and debris from the factory floors and polishes every surface. Then she cleans the offices and the lavatory and washes her hands before sinking them into her coat pockets as she heads home.

Rayna has dreamt of shirking her second job, just once, to arrive early enough at the pub to listen to the band playing for longer. She'd imagined spending the whole evening wrapped in the vibration of sound. In reality, she only dares to hover outside The Pelican for a few seconds before crossing the bridge over the railway tracks that leads to the row of terraced houses on the other side.

'You look like a frightened mouse,' the redhead says as they stand just inside the saloon door. 'Don't worry, they won't bite.'

The redhead folds her arms and partially blocks Rayna from the revellers. No one notices her, but she notices the men on stage who play the music that speaks to her in ways she can't explain. Not once did she imagine the musicians were black. Not that Rayna would have entered the pub had she known this. The Pelican is no place for a single black woman, so small and quiet – though the redhead thinks otherwise.

'You ought to make this your regular if this is your kind of music. You'll get on famously with this lot. Not to mention Terry.'

'Terry?'

'Landlord. I don't think he'd survive a week without the band playing.' The redhead stops throwing this dialogue out of the side of her mouth and turns fully to look at Rayna. 'What the hell is a little lamb like you doing out so late on her own, anyway? Shouldn't you be at home?'

Rayna nods and collects herself to leave, but the sound of the saxophone piercing through the cloud of cigarette smoke turns her head back to the stage.

'Don't rush off,' says the redhead. 'Wait two minutes while I get my coat. I'm going over the bridge. We can walk together. I'm Sandra by the way.' She swiftly elbows through the crowd, mostly men, all ages, all working class, and they happily step aside for her. Rayna is conspicuous, now, without Sandra as her guard. Eyes turn towards her, bodies turn, too, and she can feel the musicians glaring at her, even while they continue to play.

'Shall we?'

Sandra is back, wearing a black, three-quarter length faux fur coat. Her hat matches but her handbag is shiny and tan with a large brass clasp. The freezing air outside makes Rayna's skin tingle, and she is shocked to feel Sandra's arm link hers as they walk towards the wooden steps of the footbridge. Rayna looks down at the delicate pink hand in the crease of her elbow, at the brazen red nail polish and a large gemmed ring. She slows her pace.

'What's the matter?' Sandra asks.

'No white woman has ever been this friendly to me,' Rayna whispers with a half smile on her face. 'In fact, no one been friendly all the time I'm here.'

'I haven't got anything against coloureds. I had a black boyfriend when I was about your age.' She squints as she looks Rayna up and down. 'Or thereabouts. A soldier. After the war, he never came back. If he survived, he probably went home to Barbados. Probably married, anyway. Though he kept me in the dark. Men are men. People are people. Colour don't matter. And I'm Italian. When the war broke out, half of this lot thought I was a flaming spy. Tossers. The lot of 'em.'

Rayna giggles, a small hand over her mouth as she and Sandra climb the steps. A train explodes through the night across the tracks below the bridge and both women shudder.

'Last one of the night,' Sandra says, her voice raised. The train thrums and hisses into the distance.

'You finish work early?' Rayna says.

'I was only filling in while it was busy. Someone was off with flu. It was supposed to be my night off.' They descend the steps into St Ervan's Road. 'Not that I've got anywhere to be tonight but, Friday's are loud and my head hurts, so I'm glad to get home. A hot toddy and bed for me. I'm on the Golbourne Road. What about you?'

'Just up here at number four.'

'The Chamberlain's.'

'You know them?' Rayna turns to Sandra, remembering the frosty reception she got from Mrs Chamberlain when she came about the room, the landlady constantly reminding her that letting in black lodgers was her husband's idea and if Rayna put a foot wrong, she'd be out on her ear.

'Everyone knows them. Only place down this end that lets your lot in to board. Mind you, with so many of you in Notting Hill now, I don't know how they're going to stop you.' Sandra throws back her head to laugh. She makes a throaty sound and coughs several times before regaining composure.

'I suppose we are outnumbering your lot around here,' Rayna says and chances a look at Sandra to make sure her companion takes her comment in good humour. Sandra laughs again and slows down.

'What do they call you, anyway?' Sandra asks.

'I'm Rayna.'

'Rayna, I like you. You ever need me, you know where I work and I'm at number one six three over the greengrocer's if you need a friend.'

Rayna's cheeks grow warm at the sound of that word. Since she'd arrived in London, she had not had a single friend. "If you need a friend." *If*, Rayna thinks, *if*. She'd needed a friend to cry to when she spent years at the East London hospital, mopping up sick, blood and excrement. The only tasks she was deemed worthy of carrying out on the wards, though she had been employed to train as a nurse. When winters were too long and summers were too stifling, she would have stopped for a drink with her friend. She looks at Sandra now and wonders if she can ever tell this friend about the island she has left behind, the secrets that remain there and the lies she's had to tell. There had been tears, too, plenty of them, shed by Rayna and her mother. She'd had to leave when she did, and with every year that passes in this grey city, her pledge to make a success of her life has waned. Her rent has increased and her job at the factory is about to end. Rayna can't tell Sandra any of this. Not unless she can trust her, and Rayna doesn't know who to trust anymore.

'So goodnight, Rayna.' Sandra's voice stops her train of thought. 'Mind how you go.'

Rayna nods before finding the front door key. One quiet turn of the lock and Sandra's heels disappear off into the night and the smell of corned beef hash invades as Rayna tiptoes her way up to her damp single room at 4 St Ervan's Road.

2

Along the white, untroubled sand, Rayna's feet left deep imprints, the grains finding their way into her canvas shoes as she gathered her pace and ran towards the sea. The water, she knew, would be cold because the sun hadn't been up long. She should really go home. To safety. On the lonely beach, apart from the vast aqua sea and the trees that lined the edges, the only things visible were silvery crabs and washed-up seaweed. But Rayna's thoughts, after rushing away from the big house, were not of company but of escape, shame and anger. It had all happened so fast and at first, seemingly, not to her but to someone else. Not her. Not her body.

Rayna was knee deep in the water, not having felt the smack of coolness on her feet and then her legs. She clung to the front of her cardigan and pulled the side panels around her body as she stumbled on the sand, further into the water. Her lips tasted salty before she'd even entered the water and she couldn't understand why until a big heave of breath told her she'd been crying all the way from Madame St Jean's house. The water was up to her waist, and she sank into the giving sand beneath until the water foamed at her nose. It tickled, made her splutter as she inhaled tiny splashes. Then she closed her eyes and sank in deeper, the waves way above her head, her eyes shut tight.

With a gasping exhale, Rayna splashed to the surface, not sure how long she'd stayed beneath the clear water. She should have taken her clothes off first so that the sea could wash the contact of his skin from hers and for her to be cleaned of his grasping hands, sweaty skin and the pain inside her. When she thought that all traces of him had run from her body into the water, Rayna turned towards the shore and glided back to it. Her drenched clothes drew her downwards as she tried to wade onto the sand. It was then she realised she was not alone. A small boy with mahogany skin sat on a fallen log in the sand. His eyes grew larger as Rayna emerged more fully, as if she were a foreign creature rising from the sea. He ran away when she stopped to stare at him and disappeared through a small gap in the trees leading to one of the wooden beach dwellings. Rayna knew the boy and his family, so she scampered out of the sea and across the cool sand before the boy could call his father.

Rayna's shoes were lost in the waves somewhere and the road home was stony and rough under her bare feet as she hurried home. She stopped and stood at the front of her house. Her mother was there, pulling the door closed, about to leave for work. Their eyes met across the gravelled road and they stood in silence for several seconds. Her mother went back inside as Rayna slowly crossed the road. She wondered if her mother knew what had happened to her, or at least understood that something was not right, that something terrible had just happened. Her mother emerged from the house without her basket for work but carrying a blanket. Without uttering a single word, she wrapped the blanket around Rayna's shoulders. The girl tried to stop herself shivering but it was as if the blanket had reminded her that she was soaked through and cold.

If only she had been home last night. If only Daniella hadn't taken ill last night then Mrs St Jean wouldn't have asked her to stay over and keep an eye on Daniella. Then none of this would have happened. In her bedroom, she undressed. Her mother threw the wet clothes aside and inspected her daughters body as she helped her into a long nightdress and tied a thick scarf around her wet hair. Her mother pulled back the spread on Rayna's bed and gestured for her to climb in. She tucked the bedclothes right up to her neck.

'The sea can wash away a lot of things but you will never wash this away.'

'What can I do, Mum?'

'Only pray. For now. We'll see what we can do.'

Rayna knew that the St Jeans had money and the police would not listen to her claims. She felt powerless but she was so weak from such little rest the night before, to sleep was all she wanted. She didn't even want to cry.

'You can go to work,' she told her mother. 'I'll be fine.'

'You sure? You sure you don't need anything?'

'Only sleep. And to never wake up.'

3

Sandra's smile shines white through the hazy atmosphere, her red hair superimposed against the brown gloom of the bar. The only sounds are of the squeaking tea towel Sandra rubs on the pint glasses and the dull chatter of five men in dark jackets sitting on a row of bar stools, caressing pint glasses at different stages of consumption. Tables and chairs sit neglected from wall to wall in stark contrast to Rayna's first venture inside The Pelican. Rayna isn't here by chance, this time. She has gone to great pains to initiate the interview with Terry, the landlord.

For two weeks, Rayna has been out of work. All the dressmakers at the factory she worked at had been warned about cutbacks in staff numbers, and she was one of many who had been laid off. The company had hired a firm of cleaners which stole away her second income, too. Rayna was desperate. Her landlords were not aware of her situation because Rayna left the Chamberlain's house as normal every day and did not return until a reasonable hour, being as quiet as she could when she entered on a Friday evening when rent was due. Barring prostitution, the whole of West London was devoid of any job opportunities, but she remembered she had a friend in Sandra and she could ask her if she knew of anything going. Too shy to call on Sandra at her flat or to walk into the pub without a chaperone, she spent long hours looking into shop windows on the Golbourne Road,

11

hoping to run into Sandra. Rayna even stood at the greengrocer's downstairs from Sandra's flat, looking at apples and potatoes until the greengrocer frowned and looked at her suspiciously. She heard Sandra call her name out of the blue one afternoon, and her shoulders sagged in relief when she turned to see her friend smiling, her coral lipstick bright on a cloudy day.

The men at the bar stop talking and turn to see the young woman Sandra is waving to.

'Come over, love. I'll let Terry know you're here.' Sandra opens the door behind the bar and calls towards the upstairs. The landlord appears seconds after her call of 'Terry, love, she's here.'

Terry is shorter and slimmer than Rayna imagined. He has a wide smile, friendly. His dark hair is greased flat to the sides of his head, making his ears and nose appear too large for his face. He must be in his thirties, a good ten years older than Rayna, but his features are boyish and it's hard to tell his exact age.

'I'll come round your side,' Terry says. His trousers are wide fitting and his hands sink into his pockets as he walks to a table by the window, all the time looking over his shoulder as Rayna follows behind.

He stops, abruptly, and pulls out a chair. Rayna swallows, unfamiliar with this sort of etiquette, and sits with her eyes on the wooden table.

'Rayna, Rayna, Rayna.' She likes his voice, his smile and his easy movements, the cream colour of his hands and the neatly cut fingernails. 'Ever worked in a pub before?'

'My father had a liquor bar back home.' This is another lie she feels she has to tell. In truth, her father has sat in a liquor bar, several times and for several hours, but he has never worked in one, let alone owned one.

'Where's back home?' Terry still smiles.

'I'm from Dominica, it's in the West Indies.' She fiddles with her handbag, places it on the table and then shifts it back to her lap. Hunching her shoulders, she sits forward in the chair, her coat tight under the arms.

'Well, I guessed you must be from over there. Anyway, Rayna, I can teach you how to pull a pint, work the cash register and all that. You know it's just Thursday to Sunday? Nights. Maybe a weekend afternoon if I think we might get busy. Can you do that?'

'Yes, I can.'

''Course you can. It isn't so hard. If I can do it and if she can…' He nods his head towards Sandra and winks.

'Cheeky,' Sandra calls from across the room.

Terry places his elbows on the table. It creaks with age. 'I have to tell you, though, love, not one coloured person is likely to come in here of a night for a drink. Only coloureds here are my jazz band. They've played every week for … well, ages really, and not a single West Indian's been in to see them. I don't have a problem with them, but mainly they drink at the place in Powis Square. You know it?'

'No, I don't go out drinking and I don't know no one round here.'

'But the band are only in on Friday night,' says Terry. 'Will that be a problem?'

'No. Will I be a problem for your customers?'

'That sodding lot don't care who serves 'em so long as they get served. 'Scuse the language.' Terry blushes and Rayna turns her eyes away.

Next to the bar is a poster of a black woman, broad and big breasted, singing to a doubtless enthralled crowd. Eyes closed, mouth open, the singer's head tips away from a microphone on its stand. Her long earrings have caught the flash of the camera.

'Ella Fitzgerald,' Terry says. 'You like her music?'

Rayna shrugs and notices a far-off look in Terry's eyes as he admires his poster.

'You see my stage?' He points to the raised platform along the back wall. 'Built it the day I heard Nat King Cole sing *Return To Paradise* with Nelson Riddle's Orchestra. 1953. They all thought I was doolally 'cause it was years before I booked anyone to perform on it. Had to find the right ones, didn't I?'

Rayna nods.

'You got a bit of time on your hands, Rayna?' Terry stands, putting his hands back into his pockets. 'I'll show you the ropes.'

'You mean, that's it? I get the job?' Rayna jumps to her feet and has to catch her handbag before it slips to the floor.

'Why not? We'll try each other out. See if it fits. Follow me.'

Behind the bar, Rayna feels all eyes on her. She sets down her handbag and removes her coat to reveal a small frame inside a sweater and calf-length skirt.

She paces up and down behind Terry as he describes the workings of the bar. Her arms crossed, she watches as he demonstrates the pulling of a pint.

'You try.' Terry stands back. Rayna, who has been following everything Terry has shown her with a nod and occasional 'Yes, I see,' lets her arms fall to her sides and steps forward to pick up a bulky pint glass. She places it under the nozzle and rests her hand on the beer tap handle. She turns to look at Terry who encourages her with a smile. Sandra nods with enthusiasm from behind him. The men at the bar lean forward in unison and stare at the empty pint glass.

'Just nice and slow and remember to tip the glass first,' Terry says.

Rayna pulls on the handle. The honey-coloured fluid trickles in. She pulls faster. A white foam gathers above the beer. The men inhale and she looks at Terry.

'Slowly.' He knots his brow. Rayna releases the pressure on the beer tap, beer flows evenly into the glass. The head, a little deep perhaps, settles as she pushes the lever back up. The men at the bar look to Terry for his verdict.

'Not bad at all, love,' he says.

In the silence of the saloon bar, Rayna holds the overfull glass. Without hesitation, she takes several continuous sips before looking up with a smile. She rubs away the froth, which has gathered on her top lip and at the tip of her nose, with the back of her hand and puts down the glass.

Sandra shrieks with laughter. 'I like your style, my girl.'

'Just make sure you're selling more than you're knocking back.' Terry chuckles and touches Rayna's shoulder. She looks down at his hand, which rests there only briefly, until she notices how quiet the bar has become again.

'All right, lads, what you having?' Sandra's voice breaks through the silence. One man waves an empty glass at her.

'Well done, Rayna,' Terry says. 'Not bad for a first attempt. You'll be an expert in no time. See you Thursday, six p.m?' Terry picks up Rayna's coat and helps her on with it.

'Thank you so much, Mr...?'

'Collins. But you just call me Terry.'

'I'll be here Thursday, six on the dot. And thank you.'

Outside, Rayna fastens her buttons and makes for the bridge. It is dusk, the wind's cold fingers run themselves into the gaping collar of her coat. When she is at the top of the bridge, two trains pass in opposite directions, their engines booming below her. She grips her handbag and runs the rest of the way to her lodgings.

4

Rayna left school when she was fifteen. She wasn't given a choice in the matter. She hadn't known her father to have worked a day in her lifetime, and her mother had been left with the burden of keeping food on the table and paying her husband's liquor bills and going to vouch for him when she fetched him home from the police station at least fortnightly on a Monday morning. Rayna's older brother had never come back from fighting in the Second World War. The family had heard no word from him for at least a year, and when the war ended, her mother, Urma, wouldn't admit he was gone. She'd spent months seeking help in finding him at the government offices in Roseau. An endeavour that lasted almost a year until no one in the department would speak to her. She aged several years and her husband's drinking got steadily worse.

Urma cleaned houses, washed sheets, cleaned the rooms at the Portsmouth Hotel in town and looked after a little white boy all day Saturday while his parents sailed over to Martinique to have lunch with friends. Sometimes she had to keep the boy over night and fed him fried plantain in the morning until his father arrived smelling of cigars and alcohol to collect him.

Urma knew where a good, hard-working girl like Rayna could find employment, she'd told her daughter, and with her beauty and poise, she might be lucky enough to find a good man to marry her, too. A businessman, perhaps, who could help Rayna's family because Urma didn't know how long her poor back would hold out if she continued to work as hard as she did, her fingers calloused, her skin dry, her knees aching and her mind so jumbled she couldn't think straight at church or stay awake during the sermon.

Rayna went to work for the St Jean's, a rich black family who owned a big house about a thirty-minute walk away. Rayna knew nothing about the family apart from what her mother told her. Mr St Jean was a businessman who owned a large grocery store in Portsmouth and one in Roseau. His wife, Amelia St Jean, was a sickly woman. Urma said she spent most of the day in bed so there would probably be a lot of carrying food and drink up and down stairs.

From a comfortable chair in the living room, Mrs St Jean beckoned Rayna to her.

'You are so pretty,' she said to Rayna. 'What can you do?'

'Do?' Rayna was puzzled. 'I cook and clean.'

'Such a dear little thing,' her mistress said. 'Listen, if you pay close attention to my guidance and teachings, you could marry well.' She coughed, and Rayna had the urge to adjust the cushions that surrounded her and hand her the full glass of water that sat on the oak table next to her. 'Maybe even someone like my son.'

'You have son?' asked Rayna. 'How old?'

'Oh, he's a grown up young man. A gentleman. Darius is so handsome. But I don't want him to stay in New York and get married to some American girl. He is away at university.' She pointed a finger to a framed photograph on the upright piano by the window. 'That's him, that's my Darius. What do you think?'

Rayna stared at his picture. It was true, he looked very handsome wearing a suit and tie. He didn't smile into the camera, he looked bored.

'Pick up the frame,' Mrs St Jean encouraged. 'Take a closer look and tell me what you think.'

It seemed like something of a test. Tentatively, Rayna picked up the heavy frame and stared at it for several seconds. With each second, he seemed to grow more handsome.

She placed the silver frame back, carefully, and nodded.

'You are very lucky to have such a good-looking son.' In the silence, Mrs St Jean admired the photograph. 'What would you like me to do today? Where should I start?' asked Rayna.

'Can you read?

'Yes, I like to read.'

'Good. Then read to me every day,' said Mrs St Jean

'And the house?'

'Do the best you can but don't be noisy and have a large meal ready for Mr St Jean when he comes home in the evening.'

'Yes, of course.'

It had been the strangest encounter of her life. As vague and listless as Mrs St Jean seemed, she was a very nice woman. She was kind to Rayna and had her read to her for hours when Rayna thought she should be dusting or washing clothes. Mrs St Jean went about everything in an unhurried fashion, leaving the house once a day with Rayna supporting her as she walked a few paces in the garden. She showed Rayna a large box in a drawer in her bedroom where she kept her jewels. She told Rayna they were very expensive and that she should try them on. It made her uncomfortable

at first, but she liked the cool, heavy feeling of the neck-
laces, the earrings that pulled her earlobes and the rings that
were too loose but looked beautiful all the same.

By the third day, she had not met Mr St Jean. He left very
early and was home late. She left his meal on the stove, covered with a silver bowl and left a silent house at six thirty
each evening.

In the late morning one day, Rayna left Mrs St Jean's bedroom where she'd been reading to her for an hour or more
after a large breakfast she had insisted on having but had
eaten very little of. Her mistress had complained of a sick
stomach and had no intention of leaving her bed. Rayna left
her to sleep and decided to do some light cleaning downstairs. As she descended the stairs, she heard the piano in the
living room and hesitated at the living room door to listen.
She wondered if Mr St Jean had not gone to work or if Darius had made a surprise visit from New York. The door was
slightly ajar but she couldn't see the musician. She heard a
wrong note and then a loud cuss. A female voice. She pushed
the door open and the young girl at the piano turned swiftly.

'What do you want in here?' she asked, sharply.

'I'm sorry,' said Rayna. 'I heard the music and…'

'And what?'

'I just didn't realise anyone else lived here.'

The girl turned back to the piano. She was a few years
younger than Rayna. About thirteen. She was plump, her
dress was tight on her and her hair was short, brown and
tufty. She cracked her knuckles and leant her nose close to
the sheet music in front of her before picking up a pair of
glasses and easing them onto her face.

'Are you going to stand there and stare all day?' She kept
her back to Rayna.

'Oh, no, miss. I … *do* you live here?'

'Of course I live here. I'm Daniella. The daughter. Didn't she tell you about me?'

Rayna shook her head. 'I'm so sorry I haven't met you.'

'It's not your fault. No one cares that I'm here. Why should you?'

'You play very well.'

The girl shrugged and played a few more bars of Strauss before looking over her shoulder at Rayna.

'Well?'

'Can I make you some lunch? I'll be cooking for your mother when she wakes up. She didn't touch her breakfast.' Rayna looked at the tray she was still carrying, the china and cutlery clinking as she adjusted it.

The girl shrugged again and continued to play the piano.

Rayna left the room. After taking the tray to the kitchen, she tiptoed upstairs to look for evidence that this girl was who she said she was. Rayna had only seen photographs of Darius on the living room wall and the one on the piano. She had assumed *he* was the musician. The only other photograph was the sepia one of her master and mistress' wedding. Nothing of a girl or even her as a baby come to that. She must have a bedroom here, one of the rooms Rayna had not been inside. She wondered why she hadn't been told about her. She wondered why the girl looked at her as though she hated her.

5

Over her nightdress, Rayna wears a thick cardigan in bed. The bathroom on the landing below had been cold, the hot water had run lukewarm and turned to ice on her face and neck. She'd run to her room and danced around it several times to warm her body before she was brave enough to get into her nightdress. She had pulled on some thick woollen socks before jumping into bed and throwing the candlewick blanket over her head. The window, though it was bolted shut, did nothing to keep out the draught.

From a troubled sleep, Rayna wakes at six a.m. It is still dark and she prays once again for the miracle of warm water in the bathroom. It is Thursday morning; her first night at The Pelican is not for another twelve hours. Until then, she'll have to keep up the pretence of going to her job at the factory, wasting time for hours all day either in the library or walking in and out of the department stores in Oxford Street and Regent Street. For weeks, Rayna has avoided having to pay the rent.

Stretching, she hears three light raps on her door. Taking the blanket down to her neck, she yawns and imagines a twirl of vapour leaving her mouth. There is another knock. Just one but deliberate this time.

Clearing her throat, she calls. 'Who's there?'

'Chamberlain.' Her landlord's voice is deep and coarse.

'Just a minute, please.'

Rayna wraps the blanket around her shoulders and tiptoes to the door. Under socked feet, she feels the carpet cold and clinging. She unlocks the door, holds it open a few inches and pokes her nose outside. The light in the hallway makes her wince.

'You know why I'm here?' Mr Chamberlain looks at Rayna from under heavy eyelids, jowls drooping and his chin unshaven. Wearing his pyjamas and a dressing gown, the cord tied under his stomach, he does not wait for an answer before pushing his weight forward and entering Rayna's room.

'Mr Chamberlain!'

He looks around the shadows, his eyes circling the room until they come to rest on Rayna. She stands with the door held open, one hand clutching the blanket.

'You can't just come in like that,' she says. 'It's not right.'

'Right? Don't talk to me about rights, my girl. It's my right as your landlord to demand my rent money. You've been short for over three weeks now, and you know how many people there are in need of a room like this?'

Rayna smells the coffee on his breath as he shuffles closer.

'You see, Mr Chamberlain, I get a new job but they haven't pay me yet.' She holds her neck in a proud position.

'What new job? Thought you had a job already,' Mr Chamberlain says.

'That job was too far. This one closer, just over the bridge. I can pay you the full amount every week when I get pay.'

'And the arrears?'

He makes another step towards her, forcing Rayna to release her grip on the door handle and back up to the wall. From behind the door, the light from the corridor casts a thin strip down the side of her face, the rest of her is in shadow.

'I can find the money I owe,' she stutters. 'I'll work extra. I promise.'

'And you keep your promises, do you?'

He moves closer still. Rayna puts a hand up against his chest and immediately her delicate fingers are surrounded by his doughy grip.

'Mr Chamberlain, please.'

Rayna sidesteps her landlord, moving swiftly around him and into the open doorway.

'Just what will you do if you can't come up with that money?' He lowers his voice to a rasp and brushes past Rayna. She feels the weight of his stomach but holds firm. The landing light flickers and goes out so they stand in the dark, his breath vibrating the hairs in his nostrils.

Downstairs, the Chamberlain's living room door opens and the floorboards below creak just as the light comes back on.

In a loud voice, Rayna says, 'Mr Chamberlain, I have to get dressed now.'

'First wage packet in this new job of yours … we get that money. You understand?' Mr Chamberlain makes for the stairs. Before she goes into her room, she can hear Mrs Chamberlain chastising her husband for not having already evicted her.

Rayna dresses quickly, wrapping up as warm as she can. Picking up her handbag, she is aware of the last few pennies she has left to her name, jangling in her purse, before leaving the house. She spends most of the day in the gardens around Powis Square, listening to her stomach complaining of hunger. The cold becomes a constant companion and she shakes it by the hand because it is hours until she starts work at The Pelican.

6

Daniella was smart. Rayna hadn't ever seen her leave for school or seen a teacher come to tutor at home and wondered how it was she sounded so educated. Her glasses looked heavy on her small, round face and her dark brown eyes were magnified into sullen, sometimes expressionless mirrors of her inner thoughts. She didn't speak much to Rayna at first. Rayna did everything she could to win her over, treating her like a small child, baking cakes, offering to brush her hair or sit and listen to her when she played piano. Daniella would give replies to these suggestions: No thank you; Mother says I eat too much; Do I look ugly to you; I prefer the peace. She might add, 'If you don't mind,' but that was rare.

One morning, Rayna walked out of Mrs St Jean's room carrying her breakfast tray. Her mistress had been feeling faint and wanted something light served in her room. It was at the tip of her tongue to ask Mrs St Jean if she should make something for her daughter and perhaps Daniella might want to keep her company in her room while she ate. But as her daughter's name had so far, after two weeks, only come up in conversation once, when Rayna had tentatively mentioned she'd met Mrs St Jean's youngest, Rayna thought it best not to disturb the strange interactions of this family. Especially when Mrs St Jean told her not to over feed Daniella. She was an ungrateful girl and Mrs St Jean had suffered all the way

25

through a pregnancy she neither expected at her age nor welcomed.

'But you must be very proud of the way she plays piano.'

'Yes, she's very smart,' Mrs St Jean had said. 'She's had the best tutors. Up until her bad behaviour drove them all away. But after she was born, my body became weak and so frail I was bedridden for six weeks.'

'I'm sorry.' Rayna had looked away.

'Don't be sorry. I was fine because my husband found a wet nurse and I didn't have to have anything to do with her. If you could have heard the way she cried. Like a dying lamb. I've never been the same again.'

Rayna hadn't known how to take that. Her mother ex-plained that having a baby can make a mother mixed up and sad, and even the baby crying can be unbearable. But Mrs St Jean had had thirteen years to learn to love her child. Rayna felt sorry for Daniella and forgave her surly moods.

She had seen Mr St Jean twice. She'd arrived early enough to catch him before he left for Roseau, and both times, he had looked Rayna up and down as if she'd been served to him for breakfast.

Daniella stood outside her bedroom door and Rayna closed her mistress' room, balancing the tray on her hip. Daniella beckoned to her.

'Good morning,' Rayna said and Daniella quickly put a finger on her lips. Inside her bedroom, she tutted at Rayna.

'Why do you have to be so loud? So cheerful?'

'I'm sorry,' said Rayna. 'You didn't want your mother to know you are awake?'

'I don't care. She doesn't care about me.'

Rayna shook her head and smiled. 'That can't be true. She's your mother.'

'She doesn't act like she has a daughter. Does she?'

'Well…'

'So, you see. I'm nothing to her. Nothing to anyone in this family. I hate them and they all hate me.'

'A mother can never hate her daughter.' Rayna repositioned the tray. She would have liked to have put it down, carried on a conversation with Daniella, but she waited to be invited. It was clear Daniella wanted to talk.

'You don't know anything, Rayna. You don't know who hates me in this house.'

'Who?'

'You said you would brush my hair.'

'And I will. Let me put this tray aside.'

Daniella sat on the chair in front of a cluttered dressing table, the window above it open wide, and the chatter of birds flying over the tall hedges outside echoed into the silence of the room. Rayna looked at the thick and knotty ball of hair on Daniella's head. She had tied a silk ribbon around her crown and Rayna gently removed it.

'I think perhaps we should wet this.'

Daniella shrugged.

A few moments later, Rayna returned to Daniella's bedroom with a bowl of warm water. She shifted aside the books, brushes, skin creams and dress-up jewellery on the dresser and put the bowl down. Draping a towel around Daniella's shoulders, she began sectioning a sodden piece of hair and combing it with a wide-toothed comb from the tips to the roots. She twisted each wet piece into a coil and tucked it away while she tackled the next section. Each time she pulled on the knotted snags of Daniella's wild hair, she apologised. Daniella winced but made no sound, apart from to sigh when Rayna held up a mirror to show her how far she'd got.

Rayna took each section again and uncoiled it. Then she dampened it and spread in a generous amount of bergamot and plaited the section until there was a network of neat plaits springing from Daniella's head.

'I look like a *ladjalblès*,' said Daniella.

'No you don't. No she-devils look like this.'

'You ever seen a devil?'

'No.'

'I have.' Daniella leant forward to view herself without her glasses. She took in the sideways views of her neat hair.

'I could tie your ribbon in again.'

'Only don't make me look like a baby.'

'I won't.'

Rayna tried to pull the short plaits together and pin them into an upward style before placing the ribbon around Daniella's head and tying the bow at the back because she thought that would look more grown up. She thought for a second she caught a glint of approval on Daniella's face but it disappeared as quickly as it showed itself.

'There,' said Rayna.

As Daniella drew close to the mirror again to inspect her appearance, a horse and wagon pulled up to the front of the house. Both girls looked outside to see a shabbily dressed man guiding the horse to stillness. There was a young, smartly dressed man sitting beside him. The smart man pulled some coins from his front pocket and dropped then into the other's hand before jumping down and pulling a leather holdall from the back of the wagon which was piled with gardening tools.

Daniella sank back and went to sit on her bed. She hugged her knees to her chest, her face disappearing into her skirt.

'You all right?' Rayna asked her but Daniella would not speak or move. 'You not happy to see your brother is here?'

'I'm never happy to see him just like he's never happy to see me.'

'Shouldn't he be in New York?'

'How should I know?'

The door to Mrs St Jean's room rattled open and Rayna heard her slippered footsteps on the wooden stairs. She opened the door to the landing to see Mrs St Jean grinning widely, her hand on her chest as she moved quickly down the stairs. Rayna hadn't imagined her mistress could move with speed of any kind.

'Close my door.' Daniella's voice behind her came like a whisper.

Rayna came back in and closed the door with her back to it.

'Is that the devil who come?' she asked Daniella.

The girl nodded, rolled onto her side and faced away from Rayna.

'But I have to go down.' There was no sound from Daniella, so Rayna took the bowl of water, the towel and the knotted balls of Daniella's hair and went to wash it all away in the kitchen.

From the living room, she could hear Mrs St Jean laugh and she could hear the American-sounding voice of Darius St Jean speaking loudly without pause and she could see his tall and handsome outline through the gap in the door.

7

Rayna's hands stop shaking the moment Sandra puts a cloth into them and tells her to wipe down the bar. So far, the pub is quiet and Sandra talks about her week, her shopping, her ex-boyfriend, stopping often to fire a question at Rayna.

'But don't you get lonely?' she asks Rayna. 'How come you're here all on your own, anyway?' Sandra leans an elbow on the bar as Rayna wipes away spilt beer.

'I came to train as a nurse but I didn't like it and I give up.'

'So why not go back home?'

Rayna glances briefly up at Sandra only to see a look she interprets as suspicion but she reminds herself that Sandra is a friend and she's just being curious.

'After the hospital, I was lucky to get a job in a factory and learnt to do piecework. Sewing. That was in East London. But when that job pack up, another girl told me about the factory here in Notting Hill Gate. I been there a year and now it pack up, too. Redundancies.' She shrugged, hoping that would be the end of the interrogation.

'Everything packs up in the end,' Sandra says, reaching for her packet of cigarettes from under the bar. 'But at least you're here and I got to meet you. Mind you, it's getting a bit touch-and-go around here these days.'

'Touch-and-go?'

'You know? You must have felt it. Those lunatics out to fix up the black people and wanting you all to go back home.

30

Can't you sense the agitation?' Rayna only shrugs and Sandra lights up a cigarette. She squints through the smoke, her eyes still on Rayna. 'How old are you?' she asks.

'Twenty-two.'

'Ever been married?'

'No.' Rayna's answer is curt and she turns her back to put away the cloth.

The door opens and a couple walk in. Rayna smiles at them, eager to serve. The woman ignores her and looks directly at Sandra from whom she orders two half pints of bitter.

'You take this one, Rayna,' Sandra says with a wink.

By the next evening, Rayna becomes aware of a change in mood at The Pelican. Terry barely looks at her, hardly smiles. He is busy polishing the upright piano in the corner after having moved the tables and chairs off his 'stage'. Rayna also notices a young woman with blonde hair who sips a half of shandy at the bar and, once in a while, smiles over at Terry. Rayna can't help noticing the look of curiosity on Sandra's face as she pulls pints, one eye on the blonde girl.

'What's happening?' Rayna asks Sandra. A couple of men needing drinks are trying to get her attention.

'It's band night, Ray. You'd think it was Duke Ellington coming the way Terry carries on.' Rayna looks over at Terry and back at the blonde. 'Oh and looks like Terry got himself a girlfriend,' Sandra continues. 'Said he met her in one of his jazz clubs up the West End. Maggie or Mandy. I don't know.'

Sandra places a pint of Guinness on the bar in front of an old man with no teeth and holds out her hand for payment, her eyes still on the blonde. Rayna, while taking drinks orders, can't help but notice Sandra's constant glances at the blonde.

'Sandra?' Rayna says in a soft voice after closing the till. 'Were you and Terry ever...?'

Sandra tosses back her head and laughs. 'Don't be silly. He's like my little brother. I can't help being protective. He's a big softy, see? And on the rare occasion he has a woman in tow, I've got to make sure they ain't just here to get their hands on this place.'

They continue chatting in short bursts between serving, the pub steadily filling with customers. Eventually, a member of the jazz band arrives carrying a case in his hand. He wears a long raincoat over his suit, his fedora hat worn at an angle. Rayna recognises him as the saxophonist.

'Hello Eddie!' Sandra calls over. He tips his hat but looks straight at Rayna.

The rest of the band, wearing dark suits and ties, follow behind, all of them carrying cases of various sizes. They load in drums and a small amplifier and begin to set up their instruments on stage. An invisible mist of merriment and flamboyance surrounds them, their movements as loud as their chatter and laughter. Just like the drinkers, Rayna watches the activity as the stage begins to overcrowd; the saloon is transforming into the smoky, relaxed bar she remembers from the first time she walked in.

Two microphones appear on stage from nowhere. The guitarist and brass players warm up, their cases laid open on a nearby table. Sheet music is shuffled into place on music stands, and random notes strummed, hooted and tapped begin to reverberate around the room.

Rayna notices how Terry's Maggie or Mandy sits beside him as he chats to the musicians who have now huddled around the small table by the stage.

'Rayna!' Terry calls to her. When she looks up, he flaps his hand, beckoning for her to come over. The musicians stand when Rayna arrives at the table. Terry follows their lead after a short pause.

'These gentlemen are all from the West Indies, like you. Not a single Yank in this band,' Terry proudly announces.

Eddie, the saxophonist, is tall with a thin moustache and hazel-coloured eyes. He snatches off his fedora and stares at Rayna. She sees the swirl of light browns that speckle his irises, at first unaware of his outstretched hand.

'I'm Eddie … Eddie Keane.' His hand is warm and soft but his handshake is firm. He holds Rayna's hand as he turns to the others and points with his hat in turn as he announces them. 'Let me introduce our drummer, Horace Cole, and this is Cedric Maynard, double bass. Both Jamaican.' Respectively, they bow and smile and take their seats. 'This is trumpeter, Hinton Beckles from Barbados.' Already seated, Hinton touches two fingers to his flat cap. 'Pianist, Truck Harrison from Jamaica.' The pianist nods from his chair. 'And our youngest recruit, Pearson Gladstone. On guitar. Jamaican born and bred and another Alpha Boys School protégé.' Eddie winks at him before both Pearson and Terry sit down.

Only Eddie, who still has hold of Rayna's hand, remains standing. Their hands, laced together, are the same shade of brown. Rayna's, small and girl-like within his, her narrow frame dwarfed by Eddie's.

'I'm from St Vincent,' Eddie says, gently releasing his grip. His voice is deep. 'And you?'

'Dominica,' Rayna replies.

Her announcement causes a buzz of commotion among the musicians.

'Nice people! They's nice people.' Truck Harrison nods his approval. 'And a beautiful island. I could even live there.'

'Truck, you can live anywhere they serve fish broth and curry goat.' Hinton Beckles wags a finger as the others all laugh.

'We have a Dominican trombonist joining us tonight,' Eddie says. 'Name of Cuthbert Goode. You might know him, Rayna.'

'I don't think so.' Rayna's shoulders tense and she turns to leave the table.

'Could you take some drinks orders, Rayna? There's a love,' Terry calls. 'All on the house.'

'We all are whisky drinkers, Rayna,' says Eddie.

'Not me,' Pearson says. 'You have a soft drink, Miss Rayna?' She nods and walks quickly back to the bar. As she prepares the drinks, Rayna watches Eddie. His suit is crisp, the creases of his trousers razor sharp. Truck undoes the straining buttons of his blazer and waddles over to the piano. The stool disappears beneath him and he plays a ballad while the rest of the band sit waiting for drinks. Terry twitches with excitement and the blonde girl rubs his arm before draining the last of her shandy.

Balancing a tray of whisky shots and a squash for Pearson, Rayna returns to the musicians' table.

'Here comes Cuthbert Goode,' one of the musicians exclaims. Rayna is motionless apart from her fingers pressing so hard into the empty tray she's holding, the tips turn white.

'Cuthbert,' says Eddie. 'Let me introduce this beautiful girl from Dominica.'

Cuthbert puts down his trombone case and extends a hand to Rayna. She reaches to shake his hand, her eyes moving slowly up from his shoes to his face. The tension leaves her shoulders when it's clear that neither recognises the other from home, but her hands still shake as she edges her way through the gathering crowd back to the bar.

Soon The Pelican is full to bursting. The level of conversation rises with the swell of the room. Cigarette smoke gathers above the heads of the punters and creates a seamless cloud that shifts in currents as people walk in from the street and move to and from the bar.

The excitement in the saloon is tangible. Drinks are sliding down throats at a faster rate than they had the night before. Rayna and Sandra run up and down the bar, bumping into each other and laughing loudly as they work. Rayna makes mistakes and several pint glasses are left abandoned, filled with just froth as she attempts another. Then, without warning, a warm, mellow voice pierces through the smoke and friendly conversations. The crowd stops talking all at once. The riff from Eddie's saxophone holds them captive, as an infectious rhythm from the drum and bass begins. His notes are joined by the piano and guitar. In seconds, Hinton Beckles' trumpet begins a dialogue with the saxophone.

Rayna has never heard applause so loud. She has seen music shows on television but never imagined that in real life the response could be as moving as the music itself. Rayna catches the look on Terry's face. He is miles away from whatever words the blonde is whispering into his ear and just as distant from the crowd. His body rocks in a steady pulsing movement to a bass drum in his mind alone. He has not touched the whisky she'd placed at the table for him. She follows his eyes to the stage. From there, Eddie Keane lifts

the mouthpiece to his full lips and winks with his whole face
at her before blowing long and seductively through the reed
once more.

8

It's Rayna's second Friday night shift at The Pelican. Eddie Keane's band pack away their instruments, but the pub is far from empty. Customers hover by the bar though Sandra called last orders twenty minutes ago. Some of them stop outside to chat and a few stragglers cling to empty glasses in the doorway. The band was hot again tonight, Terry had said in passing to Rayna as she collected glasses, putting them into a plastic crate before heaving it to the sink to drain out the dregs and swills of beer and spirits. Later, when all the punters have left the pub, encouraged by Sandra's loud cries of 'Haven't you lot got homes to got to?' Terry is talking to Eddie as Rayna puts her coat on.

'Rayna, love.' Terry walks towards her, shaking his head. 'I'm sorry. I been a bit busy and I haven't sorted your wages. Get off anyway. I'll have an envelope for you when you come in tomorrow.'

Rayna smiles, though her head bows to the floor. She has never forgotten Mrs Chamberlain's harsh warning about rent being due Friday, no excuses. Neither has she forgotten how deftly she has avoided the Chamberlains when her cash ran low. She reluctantly leaves, too embarrassed to say how much that wage packet is needed tonight, no excuses. The band members' call of 'Good night Miss Rayna' rings in her ears.

She takes a deep breath and climbs the footbridge steps. There's an unearthly silence as she hastens along the walkway. Her mind races with thoughts and excuses as she concocts ways to avoid her landlords yet again. Completely lost in convoluted and impossible scenarios, Rayna thinks someone is calling her name as she descends the wooden steps. A male voice. She doesn't look around because she can't imagine who could possibly know her name around here. Back home they say if a ghost calls you by name, you die soon after if you answer. The ghosts of her past haunt her day and night; she can do without meeting any others. The voice calls her again. This time, the ghost touches her arm. She pulls it away and she cries out, 'Please.'

'Rayna? Didn't you hear me call?' Eddie Keane stands at her side.

'Oh – Eddie. I thought…'

'I'm sorry, Rayna. I just wanted to make sure you got home safe.'

She smiles, her hand falling away from her chest which still heaves beneath her coat.

'Eddie, I … I just don't like that bridge.' A train goes by and swallows her words.

'I'll walk you,' Eddie says.

'Oh no. I'll be fine.'

'I insist,' he says. 'Truck is watching my horn, he won't mind. Just up here?'

Last Friday, Eddie had looked over at her a lot and she'd held his gaze a few times. At other times, she had been aware of his eyes on her as she nervously served drinks and gave change. Being around the musicians, especially Eddie, gave Rayna feelings of hopefulness. They all seemed at home at The Pelican, in London in fact, something she had yet to experience. So far, she had only been surviving, look-ing over her shoulder at a grim past or thinking forward to a time when her life could change. She wonders if Eddie is someone she will have in a future she dreams of but cannot yet see. He walks on the side closest to the cars despite there being no traffic at this time of night. He is fresh air caressing the right-hand side of her body as they walk. With him, she can let go of the past – even for the few yards to her room.

A few doors from the Chamberlain's, Rayna stops. The spell is undone.

'Here will do,' she says. 'You go back, Eddie.'

'This your door?'

She points towards the house. 'My landlord is a bit … well, I don't want him to get a wrong idea,' she says.

'Well then, I'll see you next Friday.'

'Thank you, Eddie.'

'My pleasure.' He tips his hat. His thin moustache curls up-wards in unison with his lips.

Without turning on the hall light, Rayna removes her shoes and tiptoes up the stairs. A tap drips in the little bathroom on the landing, there are deep voices coming from the neigh-bours above.

Across the high-backed armchair next to the bed, Rayna throws her coat and bag and begins to take off her headscarf when a knock on the door makes her jump. Her forehead against the door, she whispers, 'Eddie?' A foolish thought.

'Chamberlain,' comes the voice from the corridor. 'Open up.' Startled and without thinking first, she turns the handle.

'Friday. Rent.' Mr Chamberlain's thumbs are hooked into his dressing gown pockets. Rayna wrings her hands together.

'Mr Chamberlain, I'm sorry.'

He enters the room, pushing the door closed with his heel.

'I'm not sure we understand each other. Rent is due on a Friday. You still owe me and you promised me your new job was better paid. Haven't lost it, have you?'

'No, nothing like that.' She takes a step away from him. 'I'll have it tomorrow,' she says.

'Right, enough's enough. You pack your things and go. That's what happens when people don't pay rent. They get slung out.' He jerks a thumb towards the door.

She looks at him, pleading silently for one more day, but the expression in his eyes tells her she is wasting her time. Rayna kneels by the bed and pulls her suitcase out from under it. It is coated by a thin layer of dust. Tucked inside are her letters from home, all her important documents, her prayer book. Everything else she owns is in the single wardrobe: two skirts, a dress, two sweaters, a short-sleeved blouse and a few personal items.

She packs quickly as though glad to leave. In many respects she is, but where will she go? She closes the suitcase and goes to pick up her coat. Mr Chamberlain makes a grab for her hand. Instantly she recoils.

'Ever been homeless?' he asks in a low voice.

Rayna shakes her head.

'You could do something about it, you know?'

'I tell you, I will have money tomorrow.'

'Maybe you will, but what will I tell Mrs Chamberlain if I go down empty handed?'

'Tell her she can trust me. I have nowhere to–'

He places a hot finger on her lips and lets it trail across her cheek. Then, spreading his hand across the back of her head he grabs a handful of her hair, forcing her face into his chest. She tries to free herself but he is too strong.

'Shh-shh,' he whispers. 'I can convince her downstairs if you convince me I can trust you.'

Pushing Rayna down until she is on one knee, Mr Chamberlain keeps a grip of her hair. He opens the front of his pyjamas as she struggles to prise his fingers away, but he pulls her closer to his body.

'You have a choice,' he says between gritted teeth. 'To be in that bed tonight or out there in the cold. You choose.'

A memory floods her mind and blinds her. Grabbing hands, a strong body too close to hers and no chance of escaping what she knew was about to happen. She couldn't fight him back then, back home, but she has to try this time. Hot rage and humiliation runs through her body.

'Mr Chamberlain – please.'

'What's a couple of minutes of your time, anyway? Out there you might end up doing this for a living, like the rest of them.'

On both knees now, she looks at his abdomen protruding through his dressing gown, his pyjama bottoms wrinkled and stained. She screws her eyes tight and nods slowly up at him. She feels the release of his grip on her hair.

'That's a good girl,' he says. Rayna finds her balance, forms a fist and punches with all her might in an upward motion between his legs.

He yells and doubles over, staggering to get support from the chair. Rayna grabs her case, coat and handbag and stumbles down the stairs. Mrs Chamberlain has one foot on the bottom step but Rayna pushes past her and bolts for the door.

Clutching her belongings, Rayna runs all the way to the bridge. Heavy feet take her across it and down the other side. She stops outside The Pelican. There is a light on behind the bar. She rattles the door handle but it's locked. She knocks on the frosted glass panel of the door. A voice calls from within. 'We're closed.'

'Terry, it's me, Rayna.'

His footsteps are hasty across the wooden floor. He reaches for the bolt, throws open the door and pulls away the cigarette dangling from the side of his mouth.

'Rayna, love, what happened?'

The blonde, Mandy, comes into view from behind the bar, crossing her arms.

Rayna is breathless. 'The landlord, he … the landlord.'

Terry takes her case and sits her at the nearest table.

'Get us a glass of water would you, Mandy?' Terry says over his shoulder as he stubs out his cigarette in the ashtray. 'You're okay now, love. You can stay here. I got the spare room.'

Mandy puts the water on the table.

'Thank you,' says Rayna, but her nerves jangle and she can't hold the glass.

It is quiet for several seconds until Mandy says, 'Did 'e touch you?'

'No.' Rayna shakes her head slowly. 'He try, but I run.'

Mandy and Terry exchange glances.

'You're all right now, Rayna,' says Terry. 'Good girl.'

Her hands tremble in her lap as Terry places his over them.

9

The room Terry helps Rayna find is in a decaying, Victorian house on Basing Street. Steps lead up to the front door which is chipped and untidy unlike its shiny, new letterbox. There are bay windows on the ground floor with faded white windowsills. Though crumbling away now, they are ornate and probably looked quite stately at one time. A fat and tired grey cat sleeps outside in the corner by the front door. He never seems bothered by Rayna coming and going, only sometimes raising a yellow eye to glance at her but never rushing into the house. She wonders who owns the cat. She doubts it belongs to any of the other three lodgers because as far as she is aware, there are no pets allowed. Rayna's room is on the first floor, next to the bathroom and opposite another room.

There's a smell of home when she wakes up on Saturday morning after a dizzy night at The Pelican. The undeniable aroma of fried plantain wafts up from the kitchen. Someone in the house will eat well this morning. So far, Rayna hasn't met any of her neighbours. Not properly at least. She'd glimpsed the girl on the ground floor last Saturday evening. She had returned from the pub, watching over her shoulder as she always did, making sure there was no one there, that she hadn't been followed. The punters at The Pelican always hung around after closing. Even after Rayna, Terry and Sandra had cleaned up and cleared away, there were always one or two stragglers talking loudly on the street corner, throwing up, arguing, a wife screaming, 'That's it, I've had it with you,' but always managing to carry her staggering husband home when the fighting was over. Rayna had let herself in, quietly, so as not to disturb anyone. She had got to the foot of the stairs just as the door to the room on the ground floor was closing. Rayna had seen the back of a slim young woman, thick hair in a hairnet, a bright pink dressing gown and pink slippers. Another young black woman, she had thought at the time. Rayna had wondered then if she was also alone in London.

It must be the young woman from the ground floor room filling the air with her cooking, making Rayna's mouth water. She sits up and rubs her eyes, looking over at the cupboard in the corner where she keeps her food. A packet of Jacob's Cream Crackers and the last of her teabags. Sandra had told her to keep all of her food in the room rather than the shared kitchen where someone was bound to swipe it. A breakfast of dry crackers and black tea can hardly compare to one of fried plantain.

Rayna ventures into the kitchen in a housecoat and slippers.

'Morning,' Rayna says to her ground floor neighbour who turns from the stove and smiles at her. 'I was just coming to make tea.'

'This won't take long,' the young woman says.

'There's no rush.'

'You're from Dominca?'

Rayna sits at the folded table by the wall. 'Yes. You too?'

'Yes, but I been here a couple years now. I'm Junie.'

'And I'm Rayna. I've been here almost four and you are only the second Dominican I meet.'

'True? I believe there are quite a few more around Forest Gate. Places like that. What you do?'

'I work in the pub on the top of Tavistock Crescent.'

Junie's large eyes widen. 'A pub?'

'I know, but it's a nice place. I mean, they don't give me any trouble. I been there nearly two months and I get on all right with the landlord and Sandra who work there. You know they have a West Indian jazz band on a Friday night?'

'I heard, but I never been.'

Through the small kitchen window which looks out to a neglected garden, a sky the colour of smoke permits a hazy sun to shine through. Junie hasn't put on the light, and shadows gather in the corners of the small room. The little window above the door is open to let air in and out and the faint sound of traffic filters in, too. It will become busier once the Portobello Market is in full swing, but for now, the area is just waking up. One of the residents on the upper floor is playing a transistor radio.

'That will be the couple opposite you,' says Junie, turning off the cooker and moving the sizzling frying pan to a back burner to cool off. She has piled a stack of fried plantain onto a plate, the oil making each slice glisten. She pours whisked eggs into a saucepan then places several slices of bread onto a plate next to some soft butter on the sideboard.

Rayna's stomach lurches with sound.

'Hungry?'

Rayna nods, pulling the packet of crackers closer to her. Junie unfolds the table Rayna sits at and moves chairs, shrinking the small kitchen to half its size. Rayna wonders how this slender girl can eat so much. From the first floor, she hears a door open and noisy footsteps on the stairs.

'You are very welcome to join us for breakfast,' says Junie as she busily turns to the stove to scramble the eggs. She's putting on the kettle just as a young white couple walk into the kitchen.

'Morning, morning.' The young man is unshaven, his skin pale. His grey eyes penetrate Rayna's as he smiles with bold yellowing teeth. 'Tea, new girl?'

'Thank you,' says Rayna.

He pulls a teapot out of the cupboard as well as four mugs and begins preparing the drinks.

'You've done it all,' says the white woman. 'Thanks, Junie. I believe you are an angel, you know that?' She swings her fair hair off her shoulder and grins at Rayna. She looks at the crackers now cradled in the crook of Rayna's arm. 'Saturday morning we usually have a breakfast all together. I'm Sophie, that's my bloke, Patrick. You've met our angel girl here.'

Junie is dishing out plantain onto plates and serving scrambled eggs from the bashed-in saucepan.

'Help yourself to bread,' Junie says to Rayna while Patrick splashes milk into the four empty mugs he has already clattered onto the table and turns to get the teapot.

'Woah,' says Sophie. 'How do you know she ... what's your name again?' She nods to Rayna.

'This is Rayna.' Junie answers on her behalf.

'How do you know Rayna has milk?' Sophie continues.

They all stare at her now.

'I do. Thank you.'

'Sweet as a nut,' says Patrick and pours the brew into the mugs, whistling through his teeth while Sophie raises her eyes.

They begin to eat. Patrick is saying grace at the same time as chewing a mouthful of eggs.

'Are you religious, Rayna?' Sophie chuckles while cutting a slice of plantain. 'Don't answer that. You'll be the only one if you are.'

Rayna thinks back to the times she used to go to church with her mother. The times she prayed for forgiveness for the things she had done wrong and the things that were not her fault but that she'd blamed herself for, anyway. She had broken hearts. Was that a sin? Not to mention she had had hers broken, too. And her spirit. She had little or no trust left, and she lived in constant terror of her past reliving itself in a new place and with different people. She had allowed her heart to soften as far as Terry, Sandra and Eddie were concerned. Maybe that was enough and there was no room for these new people. It took one awful incident in her life to make her want to turn her back on God. He had forsaken her, so she had no room in her heart for Him.

'So this is a nice tradition you have,' Rayna says as she sips the last of her tea and replaces her cup. Still chewing, Patrick pours the last dregs of tea for her and pushes the milk bottle in her direction.

'It all started with Junie,' says Sophie. 'She moved in on a cold winter morning. Quiet as a mouse. One day she was making a cup of tea and I came in. I asked how she was and she burst into tears in my arms.'

Rayna looks at Junie who shakes her head.

'It wasn't like that.'

'It was. She never told me why she was crying and I thought she'd come out with it one day. But she hasn't so far. Anyway, time went on and I see she brings in another tiny little thing much like herself. Only it's a little Irish girl, face black and blue from a hiding her fella gave her. Junie made her breakfast and made enough for me and Patrick. I said if you're bringing in strays every Friday night, we can all help feeding them. But we can't keep them. The landlord would have a fit.'

'She fixes them up,' says Patrick. 'Like birds with broken wings and lets them fly. Well, some of them come back, battered again. She fixes them, we feed and entertain them and so on.'

'I don't know how but people have come to know me. Women,' Junie says. 'Come and tell me all about some of these men they take up with. London is full of them. I never seen so many.'

'That's a good thing you do, Junie,' says Rayna. She looks deeply at the diminutive woman beside her now. She has soft brown skin and soft brown eyes. Maybe she's a nurse and that's why she cares so much.

'I trained as a nurse once,' says Rayna. 'Is that what you do?'

'No. I have two jobs. One is in a hospital, the other is in a factory close by. I don't have the brains to train for nothing.'

'Don't sell yourself short,' Sophie puts in. 'You work wonders and you'll be rewarded for it.'

Rayna is very sure she can see tears clouding Junie's eyes. Whoever she is, she may well have stories just as big and just as painful as her own. She marvels at how she could meet someone so far from home with whom she feels such a connection. A woman who has mysteries behind her large eyes. She didn't confide in Sophie but will she ever speak of them to Rayna?

Sophie and Patrick get up and start clearing away.

'I'll clean up the kitchen,' says Rayna.

'I'll do it with you,' says Junie, standing now. 'As usual, these two are late and have to get to work.'

'You sure?' says Sophie, lighting two cigarettes and handing one to Patrick. 'We do need to rush.'

'Go,' Junie commands and the two vanish. Running up the stairs, they rattle the bannister. Doors open and close above, the floorboards creak and very soon Sophie and Patrick are leaving, shouting their goodbye's before they are gone with a slam of the door. Rayna stands with her hands soaked in the sink full of greasy plates and soap suds.

'They both work in White City,' Junie says. 'In the dog track. Someone have to give them a lift and they always late.' Junie dries the plates. 'I think I'm their alarm clock for Saturday morning. I'm the one who started the tradition to share breakfast.'

'So you really are an angel.'

Junie's back is to Rayna and she doesn't turn around, doesn't acknowledge her as she places the cups and crockery into the cupboard. Rayna wonders if she will be her angel. She needs one.

10

Darius had been home for three days. Rayna hadn't seen much of him because he'd slept for most of them and Daniella didn't leave her room at all. Mrs St Jean was up and about for a change, constantly fussing around Rayna, making sure she kept her back straight, checking her fingernails.

'And your hair, Rayna. What can you do about your hair?'

'My…'

'And do you have another dress?'

'No, Mrs St Jean. I wear this for work.'

'Well, never mind for today I suppose, but maybe you could find something smarter for tomorrow?'

'I really don't think I have anything smarter.'

'Maybe I could have something made.'

'Mrs St Jean, is there a problem?'

Her mistress put her finger over her lips and pulled Rayna by the hand into the living room. She had never known Mrs St Jean so animated. Since working for the St Jean's, a young woman had approached Rayna after church and told her that a lot of people thought Mrs St Jean drank a lot. She had waited for Rayna to confirm the rumour. Rayna had refused to comment and had walked away. She had known Mrs St Jean to become quite tipsy on occasion, very often drinking on her own and at various times of the day, but she felt disloyal about sharing this with anyone except her mother. She had told her mother it wasn't so much the drink but the strange way that Mrs St Jean could be full of joy and happiness in one moment and then lamenting her terrible lot in life the next. Sometimes she refused to poke her head from under her covers and at other times walked around the house not acknowledging any thing or any person. Not even her own husband. Rayna knew that the couple slept in separate rooms but she hadn't even told her mother that.

She wondered if maybe Mrs St Jean was still excited about Darius being home. She had made an enormous fuss of him and she hadn't taken to bed in the three days he'd been home.

Mrs St Jean pulled Rayna to sit with her on the sofa. She raised her hands as if she were about to start a speech.

'Now Rayna, I have this idea.'

'Yes?'

'I said to you that you were pretty and intelligent and that you could marry well if you listened to me.'

'You did.'

'And I've been thinking that perhaps you might even be able to marry Darius.'

Rayna was incredulous. She screwed her brow as if this was a joke. 'But Mrs St Jean … I mean … I don't know what to say.'

'Just looking at the two of you, you could make such a good couple. A very handsome one.'

'I don't think Darius…'

'The problem is he doesn't know what he wants. He doesn't know if he wants to finish school and that's why he's here. Considering it. I'm just worried that he might drift. What if he decides to stay in New York? Marry someone there?' Her eyes filled with tears. 'And Darius is all I have.'

Rayna held Mrs St Jean's shaking hands. She had seen her mistress like this. Soon she would be tearful and then she would have a shot of rum and then she would retire to bed for goodness knew how long.

'I'm sure Darius would marry a Dominican girl and maybe he has one in mind already,' said Rayna.

'He doesn't know his own mind. And I worry so much.'

'Please, don't worry. Give him time. Darius might surprise you. He's still young. Just be patient.'

Mrs St Jean kept on nodding but looked worried all the same. 'My head is beginning to hurt,' she told Rayna.

Rayna got up and swept Mrs St Jean's feet onto the sofa. She plumped a cushion and put it under her cheek.

'Just rest, ma'am. In a minute, I will make some lunch. Darius might be up and you can both talk.'

'You see what a good girl you are, Rayna?' She squeezed Rayna's hands. 'So good. Could you get me a glass of something to settle me? I think I need to sleep.'

'I'll get you something for now and I'll wake you up for lunch if you fall asleep.'

'God bless you, Rayna. I need you in this house.'

Rayna hurried to fetch some rum, to finish sweeping the front of the house, to start lunch for the three St Jean's.

For the rest of the day, she was completely distracted, thinking about Mrs St Jean's words and imagining a life living in this grand house. If she married a rich man, Mrs St Jean would not pick at her work clothes. She wouldn't have work clothes. She'd have dresses as expensive as Daniella's. She laughed at herself during each of her fantasies. She was not a St Jean. They were different and she really wouldn't fit in with them at all.

11

Rayna smiles, polishing the wobbly table by the bar, remembering last night, a hectic Friday evening when the crowd would not let the band stop playing and Terry had to pull the curtains across the windows in the hope that the Old Bill weren't about. The band were tighter than usual and they didn't mind playing on when the crowd shouted and hooted for more. Not once did Rayna notice the rumbling of the Metropolitan Line as a train rushed by under the bridge. Eastbound, westbound, they might never have existed.

There had been dancing, too. A woman was twirled over a man's head and a light fitting was knocked over sending splinters of glass across the room, but the dancing continued. The tables had been moved to the sides and some of the chairs had toppled over. An ashtray was turned upside down by the bar. Three gloves were found at the end of the night when Sandra and Rayna were clearing away, all from the left hand, as well as an earring and a shoe, but the most surprising of all was that four black people came to the pub. Three men in their best shoes and a woman, who smiled the whole night, nodding to Rayna.

'Well, I was wrong about no coloured people ever coming in here. Isn't it amazing, Ray?' Terry had placed his arm around Rayna's shoulder and squeezed her to him even though his girlfriend, Mandy, sat at the bar just inches away. Sandra had given Rayna a knowing wink, yet Rayna hadn't actually known why.

A fight had broken out at the door when time was called for a fifth time, and after half an hour of retrieving empty glasses, some of them having to be prised out of the hands of punters who had fallen asleep mid song, Terry had called it a night. When The Pelican was somewhere close to looking like itself, he'd sent Rayna and Sandra home.

They are back in early on Saturday morning to continue clearing up.

'My God, you're like a different person these days, Ray,' Sandra says. Rayna's smile is bright this chilly December morning. 'Hardly recognise you from what you were like when you first come in here.'

'I'm happier in my new place,' Rayna replies.

'That's good. Thanks to Terry, right?'

'Yes, thanks to him. He wouldn't take any money for the time I stayed in the spare room. Such a kind man.'

'Thinks the world of you, you know?' Sandra says. 'Always singing your praises. It's Ray this, Ray that.'

'Really?'

'And why not? You're a lovely girl, Rayna.'

The women keep busy as The Pelican starts to return to a cleaner, neater and more ordered version of itself. Glasses sparkle on the shelves behind the bar. Sandra starts to mop her way from the stage to the other end of the saloon. Rayna follows, straightening chairs and aligning tables along the way.

'How about a house-warming party, then?' Sandra stops mopping for a moment.

'In my new room?' Rayna shakes her head and giggles. 'It's too small. And who I would invite?' She thinks about Junie, Sophie and Patrick, but she mostly only sees them on a Saturday morning. Sometimes the couple have gone to work by the time she gets up and sometimes Junie is not home. If Junie doesn't start the Saturday breakfast, the four are not likely to see each other, coming and going as they do with odd shifts and more than one job to hold down.

'Well, maybe something more intimate between you and someone else, then.' Sandra gives a quick look over her shoulder at Rayna.

'What you talking about?' Rayna stops, placing one hand on her hip.

'A special someone. Who have you got your eye on?' Sandra turns to face her.

'No one.'

'Hmm. Interesting, since at least two people I know have got their eye on you. You can take your pick.'

Rayna doesn't respond.

'First Eddie, now Terry–' Sandra begins.

'Terry have Mandy.' Rayna interrupts her. She walks over to the bar and picks up a stack of ashtrays. She places them, heavily, onto a table.

'Terry and that blonde are never going to last,' says Sandra. 'Besides, I seen her flirting with Eddie, too. You want to watch her. She might just whip them both away.'

Rayna begins to polish the ashtrays one by one, placing each onto a table. She has tried not to think about the two men. She knows that in their way each of them like her, but so far, she has been careful not to show anything more than just friendship to either. For both Terry and Eddie, she feels a bond. Very different to the friendship she has with Sandra and nothing like the relationship she has with the lodgers at her house. With men, it's different. She hasn't met one she can trust but then she hasn't met one that stirs up these new emotions in her the way both Terry and Eddie do. Terry was her saviour: he gave her a job when she needed one, a place of refuge when she was desperate and tirelessly accompanied her in her search for a place to stay. Dependable Terry who barely questions her about her background in the pressing way Sandra does. It is as if he respects her boundaries and knows to wait until she is ready to share.

Eddie, too, asks her little to nothing about her life back home and what she's done since arriving in London up to the day she first walked into The Pelican Public House. Like Rayna, he is moving on from his old life. Eddie talks non stop about his music and his future plans, yet Rayna knows little about this handsome, intelligent man other than how he mesmerises her with his music whenever he plays or even speaks about it. She is in awe of Eddie. Eddie is the storm that whirls her up into the sky with his big dreams, fantasies and the way his stories come alive in his hazel eyes.

Terry is comfort and safety. Eddie is fire and passion. With either, she could find a home.

Ignoring the sloshing of the mop on the wooden floor and the little looks and nods that Sandra throws her way from time to time, Rayna hums the melody of a tune the band plays as she works. She knows the words to the song because she has heard it sung by Sarah Vaughan when Terry plays it on his record player from the upstairs flat.

She starts singing the chorus, over and over. Sandra won't be able to probe her if she continues. Each time, her voice rises in volume and she enjoys the sound the echo in the room gives to it. Her voice is light but there is a fullness in tone. Every note is in tune. Her voice flows into and around the furnishings and fixtures in the room, gliding over the table tops and creating a brightness in the saloon bar that the morning's winter sun fails to do. Her mind travels away from the chilly London weather to the sun of Dominica and the times when singing was a treasure she had once shared with a person from her past.

Rayna puts the last ashtray in place. As she stops singing, there is a ripple of applause coming from behind the bar. She turns to see Terry and Eddie Keane. Neither speak. As Eddie continues to clap, shaking his head, Terry rushes over to her.

'I didn't know you were still here,' Rayna says, looking over to Eddie.

'Too drunk to find the station last night,' Terry says as he pulls Rayna to the bar by the shoulder. He sits her down on a stool and takes the one beside her.

'Is something the matter? Why everyone looking at me?' Rayna asks. She looks from Eddie behind the bar to Terry and then to Sandra, who stands holding the mop with her chin on her hand, mouth agape. Eventually she comes over to sit on the other side of Rayna. Eddie leans on his elbows across the bar towards her.

'Why didn't you tell us you could sing?' Sandra finally says.

'And not only sing, I mean you can *sing*,' says Terry.

'Oh yes,' Eddie draws out his response. 'You … can … sing. You so tiny and such a big voice. And that tone. You got colours in your voice, Rayna. It's light but strong, too. Where did you learn to sing like that?'

'Yes, where?' Terry's voice shakes with excitement.

'It's a gift.' Sandra places a hand on Rayna's.

Leaning over closer to take it, Eddie kisses her other hand. 'You have to sing next week. I've got the perfect song.' He strides around the bar over to the stage where he raises the lid on the piano. 'Come on.' Eddie beckons with his head and starts tinkling at the keys. Terry and Sandra each take one of her arms and guide Rayna to the stage.

'Sing for me.' Eddie plays softly while Rayna stands like a lost child on the stage, her hands twisting in front of her. At the chorus, Rayna begins to sing. Stepping up to the piano stool, she sits next to Eddie who does not take his eyes off her. Rayna closes hers and continues. When she stops singing, she opens them again as though coming round from a dream.

'You have to sing it just like that next Friday,' Eddie says.

'Do another one.' Sandra has her hands clasped together at her chest. 'Can't wait until next Friday.'

'No–no. I can't sing on stage. I'm not a singer.' Rayna raises both hands.

'Yes you are, Rayna, you really are,' says Terry.

'No, Terry. I'm a barmaid.' She stands and attempts to step off the stage. Together, Sandra and Terry block her.

'Listen to them.' Eddie's voice behind her is calming. 'You can pour a drink, Rayna, but there's more to you than that.'

She turns slowly to face him, to find him walking towards her. She looks out to the empty tables and chairs. She is used to seeing the place packed with people and used to them staring at her while she stands behind the bar, but she can't imagine singing to them. The noise and chatter they make, she'll look silly. They'd laugh at her. Rayna dodges around Terry and Sandra and jumps down from the stage.

'Terry, if you need a singer, Eddie can find someone.' Rayna looks around for the duster she has left somewhere. She should get back to work.

'How many numbers do you know?' Eddie calls to her.

'Maybe one or two,' she says over her shoulder as she retrieves the duster.

'Rayna, you know you can do this.' Eddie skips over to her and takes both her arms. She trembles at his touch. 'You came here, all the way to London, just you alone. You never knew what you would find. And this is it. This is what you had waiting for you. And you won't be alone up there.'

'You really believe I can do it, Eddie?' She frowns at him.

'So what happen? You don't trust me?' His moustache sweeps up with his smile.

'Ray,' Terry says now. 'You'll feel more like it when you know more songs.'

Eddie releases her arms and nods.

'Come with me,' Terry says, grabbing Rayna's hand and striding back to the bar. 'I'll play my entire collection. You'll learn 'em all.'

With that, Terry barges the door to the flat open, his eyes never leaving Rayna. The door swings closed and very soon music starts up in the living room above. Terry has his record player on full. There are no neighbours to complain and it's hours to opening.

The music is so loud that for a moment the tension in Rayna's stomach slackens and she can imagine herself singing, freely, happy, just like a time before. As Terry talks about the singer on the shiny LP, Rayna's nerves return and she shivers.

'Wait,' she says. 'I have to speak to Eddie before he go.'

She trots back down the stairs, happy to hear Eddie is still in the bar, talking to Sandra. He crosses the saloon in his raincoat, saxophone case in hand.

'Eddie,' she calls and runs from behind the bar to the open door, where he is putting on his hat. She pulls at his arm just as he steps into the street.

'Eddie, I'm scared.'

'Rayna, you have nothing to be scared of. They are the ones who will fear you.' He nods towards the open door of the pub. 'Wait until they hear you.'

'Can't you stay?'

Eddie looks up towards the bridge. Rayna follows his eyes and sees a young man, white, a heavy jacket over his suit, trousers narrow at the ankles, black shoes pointed at the toe. He stands like a monument, unmoving yet unnerving as he looks down at Rayna and Eddie.

'You better go, Eddie. I don't like the look of him. Go quickly.'

'Go in and lock this door, Rayna. I'll see you next Friday.' He bends to kiss her cheek and makes his way to the station. By now, the man has descended the bridge. He passes a hand over his slicked hair as he walks past the pub, all the time looking in at Rayna who bolts the lock. He is walking in the same direction as Eddie.

'Has he gone already?' asks Terry standing impatiently behind the bar, hands fisted in his pockets.

'Yes.' Rayna nods.

Terry waves her over. 'Come on then. We can manage for now and he'll have his say on Friday. Let's get to it then, Ray.' Terry is impatient but still as excited as earlier, holding the door open with his back.

Rayna looks at Sandra who is adding the finishing touches to the saloon.

'Don't worry about me. I'll get rid of the bucket and let myself out the flat entrance.'

Rayna allows Terry to lead her upstairs. Her jazz education begins with Sarah Vaughan and her orchestra playing so loudly the windows in Terry's flat vibrate with sound. The music is like magic around her, but all the while Rayna can't stop thinking about Eddie.

<h1 style="text-align:center">12</h1>

Her Saturday evening shift is a heady mix of words, faces, spilt drinks, voices mingling in a haze of cigarette smoke and women's perfume. All Rayna can think about is the stage on the far side of the saloon where tables and chairs support a throng of heavy drinkers who laugh carelessly as if they don't realise that in less than a week, she will have to stand there and sing to them. Not one of them takes pity on her or notices the turmoil whirling in her head. She wipes glasses dry, looking over at the punters from time to time, expecting a look of support or sympathy.

Maybe she doesn't deserve it. Not after everything that happened from the day she discovered her voice. It hadn't been at The Pelican. It happened a long time ago, back when she was in Dominica and her world was full of love and dreams. She could sing very easily then because she was sure she would have a bright and happy future. She had been so young and naive then. Where was her voice the morning she needed it? It had been trapped in her throat and perhaps she should have left it there this morning. Not singing the way she had and not letting Terry and Eddie, of all people, hear her sing. She thinks of Eddie now, his raincoat over his arm as he walked away earlier, cool and steady, not caring about the threatening way he was being followed. Then there was Terry making her forget about the way she used to sing back home, playing practically every one of his records. She wonders now if he hasn't worn them out, playing them over and over and making her sing. Terry was unapologetic for his praise of her; he saw it as her responsibility to sing for his customers come Friday night: they deserved to hear her. He'd been so kind, so considerate that by the end of the afternoon she'd forgotten that her voice had been lost to her for so long.

Now, as the bar is closing and Sandra is rubbing her calves, Terry invites Rayna back upstairs to the flat to continue listening to more of his record collection.

'Do you want the girl to wear her voice out before next week?' Sandra tuts and dumps a crate of used glasses beside the sink. It sounds as if they've smashed and the noise echoes out notes and chords in Rayna's thoughts.

'If you promise to make me some of that strong tea and walk me home, I'll come and listen for a while.' Rayna sounds weary as she helps Sandra to clear up.

Terry is elated, his ears reddening as he takes the bin from under the bar so that he can go and pick up the debris in the snug.

'You'll give that man ideas,' says Sandra tying up her hair with her headscarf before turning off the tap and immersing the beer and shot glasses into the soapy water.

'Terry is so lovely,' Rayna says, absently wiping down the bar.

'Yes but you should have seen Eddie's face when you two went up to the flat this afternoon. One of these days you'll have to pick one and put the other out of their misery.'

Later, when Terry locks up after Sandra has left, he turns off the lights in the bar and leads Rayna upstairs. He's already got the kettle on and it whistles with a shrill hiss just as they enter the kitchen.

'What a night it's been,' says Terry. 'What a day it was, too.' He starts the pot brewing while Rayna slips off her shoes and pulls at her toes, trying to separate them from within the trap of her stockings.

They sit in the living room under the glare of the overhead light. It has no shade over it and the brightness forces Rayna's eyes closed. The words of the songs are seeping into her, the melodies running through her as naturally as the blood in her veins. Her feet tap minims and crochets onto the carpet and her eyes begin to get heavy. Sunday morning tip-toes in and Rayna yawns.

'Why don't you just stay in the spare room, Ray? You don't have to leave.' Terry is wide awake, his enthusiasm never waning.

'Yes I do. I shouldn't be here in the morning. People will start to talk about us.'

'You mean Sandra?'

'I mean everyone. And I don't feel right staying. Please understand, Terry.' She slips on her shoes and, reluctantly, Terry walks her downstairs and helps her on with her coat.

'I said I'd walk you.'

'Thank you.'

The streets are quiet and Rayna can't shake off the look on Terry's face from earlier when she was learning song lyrics in the afternoon. With each song, he'd look at her as though he was hearing her voice for the first time. Their footsteps are the only ones echoing in Tavistock Crescent, and just before they cross the road, Terry stops and faces her. She turns away so that he won't see the feeling of sadness she has because she won't see him until the following Thursday. Though she would never say it aloud or admit it to herself, she misses him on her days off.

'This as far as you go, Terry?' She giggles and keeps her eyes averted from his. 'I thought the deal was all the way home.'

'No, I … I just want you to know it's more than your singing I like.' She turns to him now. He looks like a little boy, not a grown man in his thirties, the owner of a business.

'Terry, you have a girlfriend. You shouldn't flirt.'

'I'm not … I mean. I am. But me and Mandy. That ain't nothing, Ray. She's a lovely girl but a kiss and a cuddle, that's as far as it goes with her, and it's been a long while since any of that happened. Besides, you seen the way she and Eddie make eyes at each other? He's the Casanova, not me.'

'Well, you can only have one girlfriend at a time.' She laughs and begins to cross the road. Terry follows, and for a fleeting moment, he places a hand on her back. It's gone again by the time they reach the opposite side of the road. Now it's Rayna's turn to stop.

'I think you're more of a gentleman than a Casanova, Terry.'

Neither speaks for the rest of the way. Terry replaces his hand and they keep physical contact until they reach the stone steps of her Basing Street lodgings.

'Have a nice week, Ray. Take care, won't you?' His face is lit by the yellow lamppost a short distance away but Rayna can see his cheeks are flushed. He doesn't blink.

'I will.' She nods. 'I'll have all these lyrics to memorise, won't I? So I won't be going anywhere.'

'Well, night, then.' He turns to go.

Inside, instead of the smell of fish and chips or the stew that Patrick usually cooks for dinner, there are the welcoming aromas of home. They remind her of her mother's kitchen and the days she spent cooking for the dysfunctional family in the big house all those years ago. She was seventeen, immature in many ways, but had left there feeling as if she were a hundred years old. It comforts her to know that Junie is home as she takes the stairs in the dark, not wanting to disturb her downstairs neighbour who must be fast asleep by now.

In her chilly room, Rayna gets ready for bed. Lying back, she looks around at the shadows. Sandra had said Eddie had a look in his eyes when she'd gone up to the flat with Terry, but as her eyes flutter open and closed, all she can see of Eddie is his grin. The one he has for her is the same one he has for Mandy. It's like a dance that the four of them take part in, a game with no rules that she no longer wishes to play. Sandra is right, she has a choice to make between the two men and she should make it soon because somewhere along the line, someone stands to get hurt. As she gives in to fatigue, she sees Terry smiling but she also sees the face of an unwelcome memory and falls into a fitful sleep.

13

The three of them sat waiting for Mr St Jean: Rayna, her mistress and Darius, who watched her intensely from across the table she had set with the best crockery and cutlery at Mrs St Jean's insistence. Her mistress was so happy to have her son back, she really couldn't care less that Daniella, yet again, had refused to eat with them. Rayna knew for a fact that Daniella hated her brother. Her hatred seemed to go further than the fact that Darius was his mother's favourite child. There were depths to the family that Rayna hadn't been able to unravel. She had heard Mr St Jean have stiff words with his son about his sudden arrival home from New York in the middle of the term. Their raised voices carried through from behind the closed doors of the living room and into the hallway where she had been cleaning. Mr St Jean shouted something about commitment and how did Darius expect to have any kind of profession abroad without the right education. Education was everything, social standing was everything and his son should heed his words. Rayna hadn't understood many of the words Mr St Jean had used and he had been doing most of the talking. Eventually, Darius had walked out into the corridor, red-faced, smirking the instant he saw her there kneeling on a thick cloth, washing the floor.

'What a wonderful sight,' Darius had said as he passed her on his way to the front door. 'Do you stay overnight?'

'No,' said Rayna, going back to her work.

'All right. Well, I won't see you later, then.' He smiled at her. His smile was wide and his eyes large like his mother's but with a cheerfulness within them and long dark lashes surrounding them. He hesitated at the door as he studied her and Rayna felt the warmth of his gaze. She liked the way he looked at her and the rare moments they'd been alone or saw each other in passing.

Mrs St Jean had forced the issue of Rayna staying for dinner, saying that Darius would be going back to New York soon and they ought to get to know each other. At first, Rayna couldn't believe that Mrs St Jean had been serious about trying to make her a suitable wife for her son. She thought there were bound to be rich, educated girls he could choose from for himself. And though Rayna welcomed the idea of becoming his wife, she didn't think for one moment that Darius would agree to this arrangement.

They continued to wait for Mr St Jean. Rayna in the borrowed dress that Mrs St Jean had forced upon her, saying that hers was too dirty for dinner. It had belonged to a much younger Amelia St Jean who had kept several of her old dresses though she was not likely to fit into half of them.

Rayna felt ridiculous in the dress. Though it was pretty in light blue cotton with puffed sleeves and a tapered bodice, it had a high collar which made Rayna feel stuffy and not at all like herself. Besides which, Darius had seen Rayna in the tatty dress she had been cleaning in earlier and hadn't seemed to mind it. He'd seen her wearing the small-collared blouse and the brown calf-length skirt she often wore to work, too. He seemed to admire her regardless of her clothes.

'I don't know where that man is.' Mrs St Jean looked at the carriage clock on the shelf and then at the open dining room door. 'I told him six thirty because Rayna has to get home in good time. As it is now, your mother will be worried about you.'

She sighed impatiently and began to fan her face with the large white napkin from her place setting as she looked at the unserved bowls of food. Rayna had prepared the meal in great haste after a day of doing washing by the river and coming back to run a bath for Mrs St Jean and styling her hair.

'For that reason, we should just start.' Darius picked up the platter of roast chicken and handed it to his mother.

'Damn him,' said Mrs St Jean. She pressed the platter back to Darius. 'You carve it as he's not here.' She continued to fan herself as Darius made a terrible job of slicing pieces of chicken. He grinned at his poor attempt and pulled a face at Rayna that made her giggle. Mrs St Jean frowned.

Daniella thumped her way down the stairs, but she walked straight past the dining room and into the kitchen.

'Go and tell that girl we can set a place if she's changed her mind about eating with us,' said Mrs St Jean.

Rayna found Daniella ripping a chunk of bread from the loaf she had baked earlier.

'That won't be enough to fill your belly,' Rayna said, picking up the bread knife and finishing the job.

'I'll have warm milk with it.'

'That's not a proper dinner. I'm eating at the table with your family. Why don't you come? Just for tonight.'

'She can't stand to look at me.' Daniella pushed up her glasses and frowned in much the same way as her mother.

'Not true. She was the one who send me to ask you.'

Daniella looked at the kitchen door. She closed it and turned back to Rayna.

'Don't be fooled by my family,' Daniella said in a near whisper. 'She's dressing you up to sell you to him because no one else will want him. He's not right.' Daniella tapped her temple. 'In here. He's too angry and he probably upset someone and that's why they send him home.'

'He told your mother he wasn't well and needed the Dominican air.'

Daniella snorted a laugh. 'Don't listen to a word they say and watch yourself around...' She did not finish her sentence because the front door opened and Mr St Jean came striding into the house. He called a good evening in his booming voice and immediately Rayna heard Mrs St Jean begin to berate him in patois. She was afraid to go back to the dining room. She wasn't sure Mr St Jean would be pleased to see her sitting at his table.

Mr St Jean was a strange creature to Rayna. He usually looked miserable. His eyebrows crossed so deeply, they shrank the spheres of his already small eyes. She felt uncomfortable around him. He always looked as if he were accusing her of something and she felt guilty in his presence. She was glad he worked long hours and was secretly hoping that he would be too late for dinner and they could have carried on without him. She was nervous enough without him being there.

Eventually, the angry voices in the dining room abated and there was laughter coming from the room.

'Will you come?' Rayna looked imploringly at Daniella.

'If I don't have to be in his company then I won't. I can keep a secret but it doesn't mean I have to eat with him.'

Daniella had filled a glass with milk and piled the rustically cut bread onto a plate and left the kitchen. Rayna watched her walk up the stairs and again felt uncomfortable about this girl living almost in exile from her family in her own house. Daniella was only thirteen but had the demeanour of someone ten years older. On several occasions, Rayna had asked Daniella the reason why she preferred to stay away from her family. Each time, the young girl appeared close to confiding in Rayna but then gave a different reason for keeping her distance: her mother banished her to her room because she had bad table manners, her mother was jealous of her and didn't want her around, Daniella reminded her of someone she didn't like very much, her parents hated her pure and simple. Rayna thought all of these reasons had been exaggerated by the moods and tendencies of a teenage girl. She did something similar herself at that age. Gave her mother hell at times. Daniella would grow tired of it. On the other hand, Rayna's mother helped her through those years and she hoped Mrs St Jean wouldn't ignore her daughter forever.

When Rayna walked back into the dining room, Mr St Jean looked up at her with a knotted brow, his plate piled high with food. Mrs St Jean tapped the chair beside her and Rayna took her place. No one asked about Daniella.

'Good evening, Mr St Jean,' Rayna said. Her mistress began to serve Rayna.

'Remember this dress on me?' Mrs St Jean's face gleamed as she waited for a response from her husband. He slowed the noisy chewing of his food and cast a lingering look over the dress as it fitted over Rayna. Her mistress and Darius continued to eat, but Rayna's hand trembled as she held her fork, waiting for Mr St Jean to take his eyes off every tiny detail of the fabric of the dress. He eventually did so, peeling his gaze away as if it were removing a layer of Rayna's skin at the same time.

How could she have been so stupid to think that she could be a part of this family? Even if Darius had real feelings for her, Mr St Jean would not allow her to marry into the St Jean family. Becoming one of them was a foolish notion. And hadn't Daniella told her not to trust them? Perhaps her mistress and Darius were laughing at her, teasing her. She ate some food so as not to be ungrateful or impolite. Even if she couldn't be a part of their family, she still needed her job there.

After having to sit through a silent meal, which later Mrs St Jean remedied by talking constantly about what a good cook Rayna was and what an excellent asset her skills would be as a wife, Rayna quickly washed the dishes and left the house wearing her old, time-beaten dress.

14

Rayna stands in front of the mirror in Terry's bedroom. The dress she wears belongs to Sandra and, as she looks at herself, it's just too big in every angle. Her body won't fill the bust area and the waistband swims around her middle as if she hasn't eaten in months. She and Junie had been talking about the performance at The Pelican all week. Rayna had told Junie that she was so nervous she thought she would die.

'What's this?' Sophie from upstairs had found the two women talking in the kitchen when she'd come in early from her job at the carpet shop in Kensal Rise.

'Rayna is singing at The Pelican,' Junie had said before Rayna could tell her not to say anything. She knew what would happen if she told Sophie.

'I'm coming to see that!' Sophie had exclaimed. It was exactly what Rayna had feared. More people than necessary would be at the pub, more eyes than she needed staring at her on stage. Too many people to judge her. What was she thinking?

Junie could see her discomfort and told her she could make her look like a professional singer if she straightened Rayna's hair and that would be half the battle won.

'You straighten hair before?' Rayna had asked, tentatively.

'Of course. Many times. It's how all the coloured women wearing it for big occasions.'

She had straightened Rayna's hair with a hot metal comb heated on the stove, pulling it through Rayna's hair until the curls and coils were smoothed out and it shone with the grease she'd coated the strands with. Then she'd combed and combed it and rolled small sections with sponge hair rollers and told Rayna to keep them in until just before she left so that she could style her. Rayna had been shocked when she saw the results. It would take some getting used to, but Junie had said she looked like any one of those American stars.

'Will you come?' Rayna had asked Junie, holding both of her tiny hands.

'I really don't like places where men drink a lot. If I can summon the courage, then maybe. But if you don't see me, good luck, you hear? Remember. You are a brave girl.'

Out of everyone, Rayna wished Junie could be there.

'It's not altogether a great fit, Ray.' Sandra comes into the room now, recreating the heightened energy Sophie and Junie had sent her out of the house with, fussing over the headscarf Rayna had tied loosely over her new hair, saying to just tease it out when she arrives. 'But it's a beautiful colour on you.'

The dress is tan-coloured with a scooped neck and short sleeves.

'Try this with it.' Sandra hands Rayna the patent leather belt she has on around her skirt. 'Pull it in tight so you look sexy.'

'I don't want to look sexy. I'm not sure I even want to sing.'

Sandra takes her hand and leads her down to the bar. No one notices her appear. No one knows Rayna is going to sing. Terry planned it this way.

'Doesn't she look wonderful, Terry?' Sandra presents Rayna to a flustered Terry whom she'd left to tend the bar on his own and look after the musicians.

'Absolutely stunning.' Terry barely looks at her until he dries his hands on a tea towel and turns around. 'Your hair, Rayna. What did you do to your hair?'

Rayna raises her hands to her head and stares at the mirror behind the bar. 'You don't like it?' She faces him.

'Well, it's a bit – different,' Terry says.

'Don't listen to him,' Sandra says. 'You look like a proper singer. Like her.' She points to the poster of Ella Fitzgerald.

'Okay. Never mind that,' Terry interrupts. 'It's the voice I'm concerned about. Look, the boys are setting you up a microphone.'

'Terry, wait.' Rayna holds his arm before he can head for the stage. 'I never use a microphone before … and where is Eddie?' She hasn't failed to notice that the stage of musicians is missing its band leader.

'I've no idea. But what I want is for you to come on in the second set. I'll introduce you, and you don't let on to anyone. It'll be a shock surprise – a real show business moment. Can't wait.' Terry briefly places his hands on her cheeks before darting over to the band to help set up.

Each time the door opens, a wave of cooled air breezes through the room and the band members sing the chorus from a Calypso, rubbing their hands together and laughing.

'You look worried, Ray. Don't be.' Sandra hugs her shoulder. 'And don't get your dress messed up. We'll have another pair of hands back here in a minute, so don't go round collecting glasses for someone to spill a drink all over you.'

'But where is Eddie?' Rayna stares at the door. 'How could he be late? I don't even know what I'm singing. I don't know anything. Maybe this is a bad idea. Let me go and tell Terry.'

'No you don't.' Sandra pulls her back by the arm. 'Go for a walk, do something. He'll be here before you know.'

Rayna slips on her coat and lets herself out of the flat door. She stands looking up and down what is a dark and deserted street for several minutes before realising it's a ridiculous thing to do, standing in the cold like that. She could make herself useful behind the bar. She turns to push the door to the flat open only to find she has locked herself out and she'll have to go round to the saloon door to get back into the pub. She thinks of Eddie, his room in Leyton High Road. He'd described it in detail. The table he writes his scores at which is always covered in the plate, cutlery and glass of his previous meal. The butter dish is always uncovered and a knife, leaning against it, smeared with butter. There are crumbs on the table but he brushes them off when he lays out his score sheets. He practises in the afternoons when the house is empty, his music stand by his unmade bed, the window open just a little. Sometimes a neighbour calls for him to shut that noise up, but all he does is close the window and carry on playing. Eddie says music is his life, the blood in his veins, and it's all he knows and ever wants to know. She thinks of the way his eyes dance when he talks about a time when he will be playing on big and important stages around the world, of cutting a record. She smiles when she thinks about this and knows that someday that may come true and she doesn't know what she will do if Eddie is not in her life. For now, he composes songs and keeps his sheet music in a brown leather case, waiting for the day he can share his music to an audience far greater than the one at The Pelican. Was he so engrossed in his writing he forgot the time?

At the corner, just before Rayna turns to go back into The Pelican, she hears voices. They are loud. They are swearing and they are saying the word 'Nigger' more times than she has ever heard in one breath. There is movement, too, a huddle of bodies in the road leading to the pub. They have someone trapped beneath them, crouching on the stone cold ground. They kick. They punch. They swear. The body cannot move away from its aggressors and she hears groans of agony.

Rayna's fear of the stage has gone, leaving only a sick feeling in her stomach, her body icy though beads of perspiration appear above her lip. Her lips are dry and her throat clenches shut. The heels of her shoes make a two-time beat on the pavement as they run to the pub. She pulls open the door; eyes wide, she screams to the whole room.

'Help me. They're killing a man in the street!'

A group of men by the door rise at once and head outside. The pub starts to empty and Rayna is pushed aside, back into the frosty night. The cold impacts her skin again. She trembles. There are arms around her shoulder.

'Get in there and pour yourself a whisky.' Sandra shoves her to the open door, and just before she enters the pub and its starkly quiet saloon bar, she turns her eyes to the street and sees the crowd returning to the pub. They have Eddie propped between them, each of his arms being supported by a couple of the punters, his feet scraping the paving stones as the crowd progresses towards her.

'Get him in.' Rayna hears Sandra take command of the rescue party; she is seeing the whole thing play out as if it's a dream.

'That's it, in the snug. Don't worry, Eddie, you're all right now. The rest of you, get in the saloon.'

They sit Eddie down. He rubs his face and looks at his hand: blood leaks from his nose and lips. He has a large gash across his forehead and someone hands him a large white handkerchief. Despite Sandra's order for everyone to go back into the main bar, several fill the snug, and Rayna is jostled around and can't make her way to Eddie. She sees Sandra and members of the band, and all of a sudden, her legs have no strength, and all she can do is stare at the unfolding scene and can't wake from her trance. She closes her eyes and pictures Eddie on the street, his saxophone, his music scores, quavers and semi-breves like litter to be stamped into the ground.

'You think 'e'll need stitches?' Someone dusts off Eddie's fedora.

'No, I'll fix him up,' says Sandra. 'Keep that hankie on your head. Stop the blood running in your eye. I'll go and get some antiseptic.' She moves bodies out of the way, including Rayna's, so that she can fetch supplies.

'My horn.' Eddie's voice is a rasp. He looks at the faces crowding him.

'Here's your horn, Mr Keane.'

'Eddie!' Terry comes running in from the street into the snug bar. 'We've seen the buggers off, mate. You gonna be able to play tonight?'

'Is that all you can think about?' Sandra brushes past the people gathering around Eddie. 'Here, let me take a look.' She puts down a bowl of water and tilts Eddie's face up. 'Jesus, those little beggars. You can't play tonight, Eddie. Not with this swollen lip, love.'

'No, I can do it,' he says. 'Where is Rayna?'

'I'm here.'

The crowd separates for Rayna to draw closer. Sandra begins her task of cleaning Eddie's wounds. He squints at Rayna and smiles.

'You look…' Eddie flinches at the antiseptic stinging his lip. 'That's fine now, Sandra.' He holds Sandra's hand so she stops dabbing his wounds with a bloody cloth. 'Let's play some music.'

The dream continues as the band starts up. It's like none of the violence ever happened. It's as if Eddie is completely healed because he plays his best notes even though the effort makes him grimace and his body sag forward. The band members watch him all the time and so does Rayna. With Sandra stroking her arm, they stand by the wall opposite the stage, the relief barman taking all the drinks orders.

'He's a fighter that one,' Sandra keeps saying.

Then Terry leaps onto the stage and Rayna hears her name. She wakes from the dream when Sandra guides her, half pulling, half encouraging to the stage. She pushes the punters aside and delivers Rayna to Terry who holds out his hand so she can step onto the raised platform. She positions herself in front of the microphone and looks just over her shoulder at Eddie standing there with a smile, holding his saxophone. His eye has swollen and there is a bulky bandage around his head, but he winks and leans in.

'Don't get up too close to the mic,' Eddie whispers to her. 'And breathe. Everything fine.' Only then does she relax a little, a half smile for Eddie and then one for Terry.

She opens her mouth and hears the first notes pass her lips. Her voice echoes in a strange way from a speaker on the stage and she has to adjust her ear to make it resemble the voice she heard when she sang in Terry's living room or at the piano when she practised with Eddie. Her voice seems little to her, distant, even though it is being amplified. Then she hears someone whoop and the crowd start to clap, they're encouraging her, and she glances at Eddie as he moves his body to the music. She moves, too, just a little sway and a hand touching the cool microphone stand.

Rayna closes her eyes and absorbs the vibrations of the stage. The music wraps around her and each musician embraces her as if she has sung with them for a lifetime. She feels their enthusiasm: she feels the wink Truck gives her from the piano stool; she feels the nodding heads of Cedric and Hinton and the grinning cheeks of Pearson as he plucks the strings of his guitar. They are all supporting her, and that sense of being home she always feels with Eddie lifts her and makes her voice soar.

Far away on an island in the Caribbean is the place she used to call home. She has not seen the mother she loves or received one of her letters in over a year. She has given up hope of ever seeing her again. The home that haunts her is exactly where it should be. Far away, and it can't touch her here: the words, the actions, the acts of kindness and those of brutality. None of it can touch her now. But she knows, as she stands there on the stage, that the island she left behind is never going to leave her thoughts completely. For now, at least, she allows the past to melt away. Her eyes ease open at the closing bars of her last number. She sees Terry standing close to the stage, blocking the view of the people sitting behind him. The start of the evening was not the 'show business moment' he was looking for, but in his face, with a smile that shines through his eyes, she knows he is proud of her and that is all she needs from him.

The round of applause breaks the bubble she is hovering in. A damp kiss on her cheek from Pearson makes her grin.

She turns to the crowd to bow her head just a little before accepting Terry's hand as he helps her step off the stage.

'You are a one in a million, you know that? Hear that applause? That's all you, Rayna. The band never get that on their own.'

She turns to see Eddie and the rest of the band shaking hands with each other and receiving pats on the back from the punters. Lively banter always follows each set but now everyone talks about Rayna's performance.

'You were marvellous tonight, Rayna,' one person says.

'Couldn't believe that was you,' says another.

Rayna has no words so simply nods to convey her thanks. Someone pulls her and hugs her. It's Sophie.

'Jesus Christ,' she utters, shaking her head and raising her glass to Rayna. Turning she reveals Junie who stands just behind her, clad in a red coat that's fastened tight to her neck. She has no glass in her hand but she blows a kiss just as Sandra whisks Rayna away to the bar.

'Here you go, Rayna girl,' says Sandra, handing her a whisky. 'Get that down you – you wonder, you.'

'We got to work on next week's repertoire,' Terry practically shouts into her ear. Rayna notices that Mandy is behind him but he is oblivious.

As Rayna sips her whisky with a nervous hold on her glass, she watches Mandy make her way to the stage and throw her arms around Eddie. She appears to be kissing his bruises and Eddie appears to be enjoying it.

15

Rayna sat with Daniella on the beach. They wore loose-fitting cotton dresses. The caramel hues of their feet covered by white sand. The sand was warm and they were hot from laughing so heartily about the man who had just strolled by. The legs of his shorts were different lengths. They'd looked at each other and had started to giggle, becoming more giddy with laughter the further the man walked away. Rayna used to laugh at things like this when she was Daniella's age and it was wonderful to see the girl being more of the child she should be having thrown off the characteristics of a bitter and cynical middle-aged woman. It was nice to see her out in the fresh air, to be delving deep into the bowl of cured meat and egg-filled rolls that Rayna had prepared for their picnic.

It was Rayna's day off. She worked for the St Jeans for six days in the week. Her day off varied, depending on her mistress' whims. If she wasn't careful and lost track, Rayna could easily find herself working for seven days instead of six. Mrs St Jean was keen to make sure she kept Rayna busy, as if to keep her away from Daniella. Rayna was enjoying the young girl's company and seeing her happy. She taught Rayna how to play tunes with one finger on the piano. Sometimes Daniella played the piano and Rayna sang.

'That's a very fine voice you have, Rayna,' Mrs St Jean said from the doorway to the living room one day. She crooked a finger for Rayna to follow her to the kitchen. 'You should save that lovely voice to sing songs to your children.'

'Did you sing songs to Daniella as a baby? Is that why she have the music in her?'

Mrs St Jean turned and slapped Rayna swiftly around the face.

'I don't need anyone telling me how to bring up my children.' Mrs St Jean was seething and looked on the verge of tears. Rayna was sorry to have upset her, she hadn't intended to.

'I'm sorry, ma'am,' she'd said as Mrs St Jean called for her to wash the kitchen floor over her shoulder after leaving the kitchen flustered.

The girls held hands and walked to the sea. The water lapped at their ankles. It was cool and welcoming on a hot day. Daniella looked at Rayna with an expression that suggested they should go in further.

'In your nice dress?' asked Rayna.

'Why not? I'm hot, aren't you?'

'Yes, but we only just eat our lunch.' Daniella giggled and danced into the sea. Rayna called after her. 'Don't wet your head.'

It was too late, Daniella had plunged into the water. She came up and allowed the salty waves to keep her afloat as she lay on her back, the sky dazzling so brightly she had to keep blinking.

'What are you doing?' Rayna was bobbing beside her, curling her legs and arms to stay close to Daniella. 'What will your mother say when she sees you?'

Daniella rolled to face Rayna, still smiling as they floated. 'She doesn't. She never sees what happens to me. Or she says she doesn't.'

'What you mean? What happen to you?'

Daniella didn't answer. She splashed a handful of water in Rayna's direction and began swimming back to shore. Turning now, Rayna followed and saw the outline of a tall man walking towards the edge of the water. Darius. He sat down and crossed his legs watching as the girls waded out of the water, their dresses sopping and clinging, their hair drenched as if they had just washed up from a wreck.

'I thought you go back to New York.' Rayna waited for Darius to answer. She saw Daniella standing a little way off from him, trembling and crossing her arms over her newly forming breasts. The water showed the outline of them and Rayna realised she must look the same. Darius had not taken his eyes from her wet clothes. She crossed her arms now.

'No need to hide from me. I know what they look like. I am twenty, you know? Besides, if you don't want to give me a show, then wear something under that dress.'

'I wearing something,' Rayna said, dropping to her knees on the towel she had brought from home. She signalled to Daniella. 'Come. Let me dry your hair.'

Daniella kept her gaze on her brother's back and shook her head repeatedly.

'What do you want to do, then?' Rayna asked her. 'We have some sorrel left. You thirsty?'

'I'm cold. I'm going home.' Daniella turned and bolted towards the palm trees lining the beach.

Rayna got to her feet. 'Daniella!' she called but the girl did not turn back.

'Leave her,' said Darius as he leant back on his elbows. 'She's always so nervous all the time.'

Rayna knelt down again and wrapped the towel around her chest.

'Why is she so nervous?' Rayna asked. 'Anything happen to her?'

Darius was quiet a long time, looking deep into Rayna's eyes as if he were probing for something within her. Did he wonder if he could trust her with a family secret? God knows that family had a few.

'Something happened. Some time. I only know that whenever she looks at me she looks like she wants to kill me. I don't know what I ever did. Nothing so wrong. Nothing that terrible, I don't think.'

Rayna looked at him curiously. He looked genuinely worried, but in an instant, that sly grin returned to his face.

'I didn't go,' he said. 'Back to college, I mean. For one thing, I don't like doing what my father says and for another, I wanted to get to know you better.'

'Me?'

'Come now, Rayna. You must know I like you.'

'No. Your mother like me for you. And I know that's ridiculous.'

'Is it?'

'Well, look at you. With your fancy ways, your American voice and your clothes. Look at me.' She looked down at the towel, tight around her. So tight she could hardly breath, but she felt safe with the barrier between his eyes and her wet skin.

'I am looking and I don't see anything wrong.'

'Don't play a game with me. Daniella is a child but I'm not.'

'Are you a grown woman?'

'I work for my living.'

'That's not what I mean.'

'I don't know what you mean and I should go.'

'Wait, Rayna. I'm sorry. I say stupid things sometimes. As though I'm the child.' He approached her, knelt beside her as she gathered the picnic debris and packed it into the large basket she'd carried from home.

'Do you need help?' he asked.

'No thank you. This is my work.'

'You know, if we were to get married, you'd have someone to clear up after you.'

She stopped and looked at him. The idea wasn't a terrible one for a young girl whose hands became red raw when she was scrubbing floors or bone dry after a day of washing and a back that became as sore as her mother's did.

'Darius. Don't let your mother confuse you. I'm not the person you will marry.'

'And if we got a chance to really get to know each other? What if you came to New York?'

She grinned like a school girl. 'Really? You mean that?'

'Of course. Look.' They both stood now. Rayna clutched the handles of her basket with two hands, the towel still around her. 'Forget about my mother. Forget about this family. I like you, Rayna. You are a good girl and I need some goodness in my life.'

She looked down and smiled.

'It's not to flatter you.' His face, his voice were both very serious. 'I mean it, Rayna. Look, I have to go back to New York. I'll finish my studies and we can talk again. See each other again.'

'And your mother will have a chance to make me into a lady for you.' She looked earnestly at him.

He shook his head. 'Forget my mother. What she says. I believe she is half mad, anyway.'

'Darius! Don't speak of your mother like that.'

'It's true. But forget that now. Can I see you? When I come back in the summer?'

'I'll be here but I really don't expect anything.'

Rayna walked home gripping the wicker handles so tightly she didn't notice the weaving imprinting itself into her hands. She thought of the possibilities. Without Mrs St Jean buzzing around creating a scenario in which Rayna could transform into a lady fit enough for her son, she could see Darius in a way her mistresses couldn't. The light she'd first seen him under when she looked at his framed photograph on the piano. She had liked him then, liked his smile. So what if he'd come across as undesirable when he first came home with his silky looks and grinning lips. He'd softened not long after and she'd started to see the boy from the photograph through his eyes. At the beach, he was more like she'd imagined him to be: kind, nice, a gentleman.

She remembered Daniella talking about his bad temper and that it must have got him suspended from college, but she had not witnessed a temper. He had been nothing but charming, and she completely welcomed the idea of a future with Darius in it. *Why not?* she thought to herself. Rayna hurried home. She couldn't wait to tell her mother that one day, she might be someone.

16

Another Friday evening performance and Rayna's confidence grows just that little bit more. Outside, in the streets that wind and spread around The Pelican, there is less talk of Eddie's assault by the Teddy Boys on her début night. This may be because assaults on other black men are on the increase and there is always some poor soul afraid to step into the shadows of night or who decides it's safer to stay in a group of three or more. Then there are those who end up in casualty at St Charles Hospital. The only black women in the streets at night are the prostitutes near the Bayswater end. Terry insists on walking Rayna home every time she's on a shift.

Rayna grips and excites the pubgoers, and on this Friday night, the outside world is non-existent. Her delicate fingers weave a tiny pattern in the air in time to the music as she sings, her slim wrist flowing in rhythm and the gold bangle she bought from Portobello Market is reflecting the red and blue of the spotlights. She is developing a style of her own and she is, in the eyes of the audience, outshining the already outstanding musicians in the band.

'You were great again tonight, Ray,' says Terry.

Across the room when the drinkers have all gone home, Eddie shows Mandy how to dance calypso.

'Can you do this, Terry?' Mandy calls as she throws back her fair hair. Terry and Rayna are stacking chairs on top of tables, ready for the sweep up of lost property and Friday night detritus.

'Not with my back,' Terry jokes.

Eddie waves a hand to Rayna. 'Come, Rayna,' he calls. 'Come and show me your motion. You remember how to dance, right?'

'I remember.' Rayna joins the two by the stage and Eddie takes both her hands. Mandy steps aside and crosses her arms to watch the pair dance. The other musicians clap. Pearson begins to sing and clicks his fingers to create a tune for them.

Rayna hasn't forgotten how she used to dance back home. How could she? Everything that happened there is always only moments from spilling into a conversation, but always, she restrains herself. Singing in church and at school concerts were some of the memories she cherished the most from those days. They were the happier times and the only ones she'd dared to talk about to anyone. She never dared talk about singing with Daniella at the piano. Not after the way things were left with her.

Eddie draws her close. Gently holding the fingers of her left hand, he spins her in front of him. They laugh.

'My feet are sore, Eddie. I tired,' Rayna says, pulling away now.

'You need to rest,' Eddie agrees and gives a slight bow of thanks for the dance.

'Get your coat on, Ray,' Terry shouts from the bar. 'I'll walk you.'

'And what about me, Terry?' Mandy also raises her voice. The song, the finger clicking stops. 'Am I just supposed to wait for you to come back?'

Rayna turns to him, but his face has turned red and he has nothing to say, only to stare back at Rayna, his lips pulled into an odd angle.

'The boys are going to a party in Shepherd's Bush,' Mandy continues. 'It's on me way home, anyway. Thought I'd go.'

'Please yourself,' Terry says with a kindly enough smile but he barely looks at her. Mandy has been showing up less often at the pub and, as far as Rayna knows, Terry has not taken her out anywhere in months.

Rayna walks behind the bar to fetch her coat. 'You still have to lock up, Terry. I'll walk myself.'

'No, you're all right. I want to.' He turns to Mandy. 'Sorry, Mandy love. You know what it's like around here, late at night. She's a woman on her own. Look, if you want to go with Eddie to the party, just go. Have a good time. Ray, take a seat, I'll walk you once I've finished.'

She watches the pace at which Terry helps carry the musician's instruments and equipment from the pub. She sits in her coat, nodding and saying goodbye to the musicians as they leave. She gets no response from Mandy who links Eddie's arm on their way out.

Outside, Rayna shivers while Terry locks the pub door behind them.

'Why do you treat Mandy like that, Terry?' she asks.

'I'm being as nice as I can. I told her ages ago it was over between us. What am I supposed to do? You want me to tell her she's barred?' He puts his arm around Rayna's waist as they turn into Tavistock Crescent.

'You mean you finish with Mandy?'

'Yes, and she knows it. Besides, I thought she was coming here for Eddie, anyway.'

'Eddie like her like that?'

'Probably. Yes. No. How should I know? Does it bother you?'

'Eddie is a man, he can do as he please.'

'Exactly, Ray. We're all grown ups, we do as we please. That includes you.'

Rayna doesn't say anything. She has been hesitant to commit to a relationship with either Eddie or Terry. She was only seventeen when she first fell in love, only to have her heart shattered into fragments, her spirit broken. It had been hard to trust a soul after that. Her mother had warned her about Darius, not to give her heart away to her employers' son. He was from a different class and his words couldn't be trusted. Her mother had been right. She'd had to leave the island after her soul had almost been destroyed. That was six months after the rape. And she hadn't loved another since.

'And that means,' Terry is saying as they are only doors away from Rayna's lodgings, 'that it's up to you, Ray. You're free to decide who it is you want to be with. I only hope it's me.'

She doesn't answer because in the semi-darkness, she hears footsteps, slow ones, and the sniffing sound of a child crying. But it is not a child Rayna realises as she turns to the two figures getting closer to her. She sees Junie. Her arm is around another woman and the woman is hobbling. She is wearing a cardigan, too thin for this cold night, and as they approach, Rayna notices her bare legs and the rip at the hem of her dress.

'Junie?' she says.

Junie looks at Rayna and shakes her head. She shares a glance that begs for her not to ask the question and gives Rayna a mirthless smile in appreciation. Rayna and Terry step out of the way for the two women who progress slowly to Rayna's front door.

'Looks like she's taken a bit of a hiding,' Terry says. He stands shaking his head until the women disappear into the house.

'That's my neighbour.'

'What? The poor girl who's had her face knocked for six?'

'No, the one helping.' The light goes on in Junie's room. 'I don't know much about her. She keep herself to herself. I don't always see her. She's Dominican, too, and we can speak our language together. Reminds me of having conversations with my mum.'

'You miss your mum?'

'Of course. But I lose touch with all of them back home. I'm on my own now.'

'Not anymore you're not, Ray. I'm here. I can look after you.'

'Terry, I can look after myself.'

'I know. I don't mean like that. I just mean, you and me. We could be something, you know? What about giving it a chance?'

Rayna looks into his eyes. It could be worse. She could spend the rest of her days all alone, coming home to a cold room and not leaving the house unless it's for shopping or to go to work. The singing is one thing. Singing has the power to transport her away from the rumblings of the rail tracks, the drunks after hours, the racism on the street and the longing to see her mother again, beg for her forgiveness for the lies she got her involved in. But singing can't wrap its arms around her through a cold night and tell her that everything will be all right. She sings for an hour on stage, but with Terry, she could have all her day filled with his enthusiasm, his kindness and perhaps, one day, his love. Her mother's love was the only true love she'd known. Could he love her? Could he be honest?

Rayna looks up at Terry with a tentative smile. She nods softly.

'You mean it, Ray? You'll be my girl? And we can tell everyone? Including Eddie?'

She laughs, lightly and as wearily as her body feels, but she thinks she is making the right decision.

'Yes, yes, yes,' she softly says and Terry hugs her.

'Come on,' he says. 'You need your rest and I need to get off in case you take one more look and change your mind.'

At the front door which Junie has left slightly ajar, Rayna turns to Terry. 'I haven't change my mind but could we just keep it between us? Just for now?'

Terry nods, kisses her smiling lips and skips down the stairs, landing on the pavement with a soft thud.

She waits a few moments as she hears Terry heading back to Tavistock Crescent, whistling a song she recognises from the Horace Silver record he loves to play.

17

It's early on Saturday, crisp and dreary like any other February morning. The sun eludes the grey expanse of sky, clouds promising rain for later barely move in the sky. Rayna's slumber is deep and heavy and she dreams a dream she wishes she can wake from. But she can't. She is a teenage girl again.

She is aware of her duties: making the beds, washing clothes, cooking the next meal. Her mistress doesn't bother her, except to ask if she will sing her a song while she rocks in a chair on the veranda. Now she senses danger and a man's breath is on her neck and a man's hands are on her body. Her mistress doesn't seem to care because she encourages the man to dance with Rayna who by now knows full well that this is more than just a dance. She shifts in the bed, the blanket entwines her waist, her head is damp on the pillow and there is a knocking sound coming from somewhere. The man's arms seem to have multiplied as they surround every part of her, and Rayna looks over her shoulder at her mistress but her eyes are closed. Rayna can't sing anymore, it hurts her throat, and when she realises that the hands are around her neck, she starts to beat her fists at the man. He's strong, though. Stronger than he looks even though she can't see his face. Not properly. She screws her eyes shut in the dream as if this will make the man disappear, leave her alone. *No, I don't want a kiss. I will tell her about this. She would never believe you*. The man still wants to dance and

94

her mistress wants to hear her sing, but Rayna refuses to utter another word. So someone puts on music.

Rayna wonders if the music she can hear is a memory of the pub and last night's live music session. The faces of figures whirl in and out of view. She is on Mrs St Jean's veranda in one moment and back on the stage at The Pelican in the next. There is laughter and someone calling her name. 'Rayna, Rayna, Rayna.' The knocking persists, so does the pulse of the drums on stage. When her name is called again, she sits up and shouts, 'No!'

'Everything all right, Rayna?' Junie's voice sounds anxious from the other side of her door. Rayna clears her throat, looks quickly at the closed curtains then back to her locked door.

'Yes. I coming just now.' She has to de-tangle the blankets from her waist before she can get out of the warm bed. Lunging at the door, she catches her reflection in the small mirror on the wall, the sight of her hair sticking up and the scruffy nightdress she's owned for ages. The hair around her temples is frizzy with perspiration and the ring of lipstick on the edges of her lips is still there because she hadn't washed the pub out of her pores the night before. Perhaps her clothes, flung onto the upright chair in the corner, smell of beer and nicotine.

'Junie, hello. I'm sorry, I was asleep and…'

'And I thought someone was up here with you and something was wrong. That white man you were with last night.'

Rayna steps back and Junie's eyes sweep the entirety of the small room in one second.

'Who? Terry?' says Rayna running her hands back over her hair. 'Terry is a saint. And I wouldn't have had him stay.'

'But I did hear voices,' insisted Junie. 'After I let my friend out.'

'I had a dream. Well, a nightmare really.'

Junie looks even more concerned but Rayna laughs it off. She doesn't want anyone to know how much the weight of the past smothers her so much. How visceral the attack still feels and how hard it is to act as if everything is fine when it isn't.

'I'm making breakfast just now,' Junie says. 'Come downstairs and we can talk.'

'Your friend wasn't hungry?'

'She has children. They by her mam so she had to go.'

'What happen?'

'Another poor woman who come in the casualty last night. She thought her jaw was broke but it wasn't, luckily.'

'So she's not your friend exactly?'

'None of them are, to start with. But they become friends in a way. I do what I can and I listen to them and I watch them go back to the same bad man who put them in the hospital.'

'But why is you who have to do that? They don't have family?'

'Not all. And not all want to tell family nothing.'

'That's horrible. But how often this happen?'

'You would be surprise. And they don't always come in the hospital and they not always poor like her. And some have family who couldn't care less.'

Rayna knows that Junie has a job cleaning at the hospital. She cleans at a hotel in Lancaster Gate and one at Sloane Street. She must see them all, these ill-treated women, the rich, the poor, the black, the white. So why is it Junie is the one they turn to?

In her pink dressing gown, Rayna makes her way to the kitchen. Junie wears a black sweater and slacks. She has such lovely skin and thick dark hair but she doesn't care for it, and Rayna has never seen her in make-up or known her to bring a man home. Mostly, these two have been ships that pass in the night as both women work shifts. Sometimes Rayna can go days without seeing Junie or the neighbours across the way. She only hears them, either on their way up or down stairs, coming and going from the bathroom or kitchen. She smells Sophie's bubble bath, Junie's cooking or Patrick's cannabis.

'Sit,' Junie says as she pushes a cup of steaming tea across the table to Rayna. Settling down across from her, she looks into Rayna's eyes. Junie's are large, clear, serious wells of dark brown, her lashes curling up. She sighs gently before she speaks. 'I came here on my own, like you. I have secrets, like you.'

'But I never–'

'You didn't have to say anything, Rayna, but I know a person who carries her past on her back. They wear their secrets like a coat. They can take them off and they can put them down, but comes a time when you have to pick that coat up and carry it around again.'

'I can't…'

'You never have to say a thing to me. I don't need to know what you don't want to tell me. One day, maybe you will but it's a guarantee that you'll never come to know what I have done. I learnt to place that coat I used to wear in a very deep place, far away. If I didn't, I would go mad.' She exhales slowly and picks up her teacup. She purses her thin lips to blow into it and takes a short sip. It's hot and she puts the cup back down before continuing. 'Those women. They can't hide what happened to them. You can't hide blood, cuts or bruises, even if you don't want to say how you got them. I know because I was like them. A man who beat me so bad I think I might die one day. In a way, I did. But I'm fighting back to being me again. I want to fight for these women. I can't punish the men but I want their wives to know that someone is in their corner. They have a shoulder to cry on and a place to stay, even if it's only one night I can keep them here.'

'I don't understand why they come to you. How do they know to come to you? You said they don't all end up in the hospital.' Rayna has both hands around her cup and leans closer to Junie.

'It helps them to know they are not the only one. The first time, when I met the first woman I help, I was in the hospital. I was disinfecting the floors and I saw her. Black and blue. Waiting for stitches for her eye, and they just leave her sit there with a cloth on her head, and the tears were hurting the cut on her face, and she just looked at me and she told me everything, what he do, who looking after the children, that it's her mother who keep sending her back to him and she scared to go home. I tell her my shift is nearly finish and if she need a place for the night, she can come by me.

'And, this happen more than once. I see the same woman come back with a dislocated shoulder one afternoon. Then there was another and another. Sometimes it's the boyfriend, other times the husband. If it's a prostitute, the police not interested. There have plenty around the All Saint's Road. You see them? Both black and white. They get beat up from the men who own them, the men who say they are the boyfriend and the ones who pay for them.'

'I had no idea.'

'And women like us, sometimes younger. We are the ones who cannot look out for ourselves.'

'You look out for them, Junie. You're a brave girl.'

'I'm just as scared. Been scared for years. Scared before I even come here. But I help because I can't stand to see another woman suffer. I suppose the word about me offering tea and a bed has spread. Twice already, the door knock and a broken woman come looking for me. I wish I could keep them here for good but I can't.'

Rayna looks down at her tea. It is stagnant: an inner circle a shade lighter than the rest of the tea is forming. She hadn't taken her eyes off Junie for the whole conversation. Now Junie is quiet and the air in the room brushes cold strokes over Rayna's face and arms. Goose pimples raise on her skin and she shivers. She can see a long and dark story in Junie's eyes and she wonders if it's anything like the one Junie can see in hers. It's comforting to know that neither has to tell the other the real story of their pasts but she knows that one day they will.

'I said I would cook something,' says Junie, sitting up as if she has been roused from a trance. 'Those two will come down soon. I will make some eggs. You butter bread. I think Patrick had some black pudding in the fridge when last I look.'

'And who looks after you, Junie?' Rayna asks as she unwraps the loaf of bread she finds on the counter. The butter is hers and so is the milk, but all food is common property on a Saturday morning and she likes that it is.

'I look after me.' Junie beats eggs into a metal bowl.

'Like I look after me.'

'And your boyfriend? The man from last night?'

'I don't know our future.'

'I think I know your future, Rayna.'

'How you mean?'

'I think your future is a good one. But I think you need to watch out.'

'Watch out?' Rayna is about to insist on an answer but Sophie comes into the room wearing a baggy T-shirt over a long skirt. She has black make-up rings under her eyes and a cigarette between her fingers.

'I was going to do it,' she says and puts down two mugs that are stained brown. One has a cigarette butt in it that she drops into the bin. 'Well, Paddy and I will do the dishes.'

'But won't you be late for work?' asks Junie.

'Oh. Maybe.'

She sits down with a sigh and yawns without inhibition. Junie looks at Rayna and winks.

'You make it next week,' Junie says just as Patrick turns the radio on loudly upstairs.

18

Rayna watched her mother returning home from the river with a pail of wet clothes on her head. It was Sunday, the Lord's day, but her mother, Urma, worked every day and usually started before light. Rayna knew that it pained Urma to work on Sunday but she'd established a number of jobs that brought in a fair wage to enable the family to keep a roof over its head and their bellies full. Rayna's wage helped a great deal, but considering what the St Jeans were worth, she felt sure she should be making more money.

It had been a year since Rayna began working for the St Jeans and she had established Sunday as her official day off. That Sunday she had planned to help her mother with the washing but only came home at first light, having stayed all through the night helping the St Jean's who were having a party that went on far longer than her mistress expected. Mrs St Jean had agreed to pay Rayna a little extra for staying late on the Saturday evening to serve drinks and clear up after the party, but when Mr St Jean kept reaching for more and more bottles of rum and filling the ever expectant glasses, the party continued and no one wanted to go home. When Rayna was able to leave, she saw some of the guests in the front garden sitting and lying like ornaments on the front lawn with empty glasses beside them. Not one of them stirred as Rayna left, but she hurried out of the gate in case Mrs St Jean came out and asked her to collect the discarded glasses to wash and pack away.

She had landed face first onto her bed, her shoes still on and the sleeve of her cardigan only off the one arm. When she woke with a stiff neck and back, she thought she must not have moved all night. She wiped her mouth, rubbed the corners of her eyes and got up to ask what time her mother wanted to go to the river. There had been no sign of Urma when Rayna went looking and her father was not home, either. He stayed away from the house a lot lately and Urma never questioned why.

'I'm sorry I slept so late.' Rayna took the heavy pail down from her mother's head who immediately began to rub her neck. Rayna hadn't the heart to tell her how sore she felt herself. Instead, they went to the back of the house to hang out the sheets and towels. Urma would fold and deliver them to their owner the following morning.

'You look tired, Rayna,' her mother said as they helped each other lift a heavy towel over the washing line. 'You should have just stay in bed.'

'I was supposed to be helping you today, Mum. But that party…'

'Was it good?'

Rayna giggled. 'Very good. They drank so much. Mr St Jean gave me two glasses of rum for doing a good job. But he didn't want Mrs St Jean to see.'

Her mother tutted and shook her head.

'It's all right. I wasn't drunk. Not like some of them. I sneaked a whole side of chicken up to Daniella because she refused to come down, no matter how much her mother coax her.'

'The girl still acting funny? Staying in her room?'

'She's unhappy. That's all.'

'How a person could be so unhappy with so much money?'

'Money doesn't mean happiness. I will have so much money one day but I will still look for happiness.'

'Happiness is clothes on your back and a nice hat to wear in church. Happy is going to church because you don't have to work on the Lord's day. Unhappy is watching your husband give most of the money you make to another woman.'

Rayna stopped what she was doing, a soaking sheet in her hands wetting the front of her dress.

'True?' she said to her mother. 'That's what he do?'

'Rayna, you are not a child anymore, you must see these thing for yourself.'

They finished the work and Rayna followed her mother into the shade at the side of the house. Under the hot February sky, the washing wouldn't take long to dry. Rayna and Urma sat on the stone wall watching the sheets blowing up like sails on one of the lines. On the other, the towels were so weighty, they almost touched the grass.

'And why don't you just send him to her for good?' Rayna crossed her arms. 'If he keeping another family then he might as well go and stay there. We don't need him.'

'I know I don't go to church as often as I should but marriage is a holy sacrament, Ray. If he would just go, nothing I can do about that. That's his sin, but I promised to love and obey.'

'When I marry Darius, I'm not going to promise to obey.'

Her mother kissed her teeth and raised her eyes to the blue swirling sky.

Rayna looked at her damp dress. 'I know you think he won't marry me, but he says he loves me and I love him. Mrs St Jean is very happy. She says she coming and talk to you.'

'Rayna, please. Don't tell me you serious about this boy.'

'I love him. I wasn't sure at first, but when he come home in the summer break, he was very kind, very good to me and he make me laugh.'

'And his family have plenty money.'

'It's not the money, Mum. And so what if he have money. It don't make him a bad person.'

'That family, Rayna. They are not … they not normal. The way they treat the girl. Mr St Jean is a monster to work for. None of his workers in Roseau or Portsmouth have anything good to say about him. He have a bad reputation. You must have heard.'

'You tell me I mustn't tell tales and don't listen to anyone who do.'

Her mother sighed and shook her head. 'Rayna, open your eyes. And what about the mother? You see her everyday. She don't have funny ways?'

'People should mind their own business.'

'That woman mind turn after the second child and she talk to herself.'

'That's not true. It's just a bad rumour people spread.'

'But she do drink. And she do drink a lot.'

Rayna was quiet.

'And that Darius,' Urma went on. 'He have fair skin, he handsome all right but he have an evil streak in him. You have to be careful.' Her mother stepped down from the wall and turned to Rayna. She rested both hands on Rayna's folded arms. 'Be careful of that whole family. Rayna, you are a good girl. Don't let them turn you … don't think if you marry into that family you can make them into good people. They are not good people and they will turn you bad. She chose you for her son because you innocent, you young and you don't know enough about them. No one would marry into that family who have sense.'

Rayna lifted her arms and her mother's hands away. 'And why you send me to work for them?'

'Only for the money, Rayna. Only for the money. But there are other jobs.'

'But that's the one you send me to. Why you changing your mind? Because of Darius?'

Her mother paced and folded her arms. Her shoulders slumped forward as Rayna waited for an answer.

'Rayna. Please. I'm sorry. You hear? I had no idea you would become so attach on them. It is just a job. Plain and simple. They are not your future. All the things you're saying about wanting to be with Darius, that his mother is keen for you to marry him, I never wanted all this for you. I want more for your life than I have. That is every mother's dream. I never thought … I just never thought.' Her mother's eyes grew dim, lines appeared at the sides of her face, sorrow in her eyes.

'And so now you regret it,' said Rayna. 'You want me to just leave?'

Her mother nodded, the tears building in her eyes making her blink, but she looked intently at Rayna. 'For your own sake. For mine. Please leave them, Rayna. You'll find another job.'

'I can't just go like that. I mean, apart from Darius, there's Daniella. I promise I will never leave her. She's a frightened child.'

Rayna's mother caught hold of her daughter's hand.

'And you should find out why she frightened before you decide to marry into a family where a child stay in her room and doesn't want to come out.'

19

The thick summer air is tight around the chest. It loves to stifle and squeeze and draw perspiration to the brow. But the English don't seem to mind it. They strip down to shirt sleeves and sit in the park. The coloured men wear their jackets and fan themselves with newspapers and flat caps. August in London W11 holds more than stifling heat. It bears tension on the verge of boiling over, as if the tattered streets are not hot enough.

Rayna sits on cushions in the window seat in her room, her forehead against the glass. The window is raised a few inches for air. It is Monday evening. She looks out onto the grey pavements and fading paintwork of Basing Street. Children laugh and tussle outside, running fast and carelessly towards Tavistock Road and back again as many times as they can before their mothers call them in. On the record player Terry bought for her, Rayna plays a Coleman Hawkins 33. A gift from Eddie. Outside, a tubby black man walks by, his hands wedged into the pockets of his neatly pressed trousers. He wears a yellow shirt and a pair of RayBan sunglasses, even though the brightest part of the day ended hours ago. The children gather in the road and start singing a song as he passes them: *Nigger, nigger, pull the trigger, bang, bang, bang*. Over and over, they sing the song and don't stop until the man disappears from view. Rayna would turn up the music but she can't stop watching, can't stop listening to the children and their ugly song. Who would teach this song to a child? Their chanting voices continue though the man is long gone. Close by her window now as they skip, she hears them, louder than the saxophone blowing low in her room.

Soon the children are out of sight but Rayna hears footsteps, fast feet, pounding past the house. A group of men – one with a chain in his hand, one with silver shining from his knuckles – follow in the same direction as the man in Ray-Bans. She hears a scream, not from a child but a grown man. Her body stiffens. The weakness behind her knees doesn't stop her standing and slamming the window shut.

'What's all that?' Terry wakes up and lifts his naked torso onto his elbows. He squints towards the window where Rayna stands with her arms wrapped around her body. 'I fell asleep. I'm sorry.' He sits up now. 'What's wrong, Ray?'

'I see them chase another man.'

'Who? What man?'

'How should I know? Doesn't matter who. It's still wrong. We're living with animals.' She sits hard on the bed with her back to Terry. He rubs her arms in silence, drawing her close.

'What can we do about it, love?' he says.

'Someone have to do something. A man was killed the other night. He's someone's son, brother, husband.' Her eyes close and tears fall from them. She brushes Terry's hand away when he tries to dry her face.

'I wish there was some magic spell I could weave,' he says. 'If I could, I would. I'll put another record on.'

'Don't. Get something from the off-licence.' She looks down. 'Stay with me tonight.'

'Of course, Ray.'

Rayna has the window open again when Terry returns. She leans far out, this time into the dusk. The children must have had their tea and are getting ready for bed.

'What can you see?' Terry asks, placing snacks and drinks onto the side table.

'Nothing. I don't hear nothing, neither.'

'That's good, isn't it?'

'No. It make me more worried.'

'Rayna. I don't want you here on your own. Come live with me.'

She steps away from the window. 'Because of this?' Rayna points over her shoulder.

'Because of this. Because I want you with me. All the time.' He puts his arms around her. 'Look, better than that, Ray. Let's get married.' Rayna backs away from Terry. His eyes search hers.

'Married, Terry?'

'Yes.' He laughs weakly and blushes.

'To keep me safe?'

'To keep you safe. To show that I love you.' He circles her waist with his arms again.

'I don't know what to say. It seem like a rush to me.'

'Not for me it don't. I knew I wanted to marry you the first day I heard you sing. I saw you for the first time.'

'You saw me? You don't even know me.'

'I want to. Tell me everything there is to know.' He opens the shandy and pours two glasses, handing one to Rayna. 'Tell me everything,' he says.

'There's no everything. Just me.' She raises her glass and drinks fast.

'Well then, tell me the other thing.'

'What other thing?'

'That you love me and that you want to marry me.'

'Yes, Terry. I love you. I'll move in with you.'

'Marry me?'

'We'll see.'

'That's good enough for now. Let's go over The Pelican. Make a big announcement.' He puts down his glass and starts looking around for his jacket.

'Terry, it's almost nine o'clock on Monday. The place will be deserted by now.'

'Quarter past eight,' he says, looking at his watch. 'But you've got a point. 'Sides, they all know we're together, we'll say something Friday about us being engaged.'

'Engaged.' She looks at the finger where a ring used to be. She looks at the wrist where there was once a gold and emerald bracelet.

'I'll buy you a ring,' says Terry. 'Nothing dodgy off the market stall. Something nice from a North London jewellers or something.'

Everything changes from this moment and Rayna is swept into an agreement that she hopes she can live up to. One she wishes will last but worries that, as before, all wishes, hopes and dreams are going to be swept away by a rushing tide, just like the one she couldn't control back in her life on the island.

Come Friday, she gets kisses from Junie, Sandra and even Mandy when Terry declares his love on the microphone just before she sings with the band. Eddie seems to lose the abil-ity to move from his spot on the stage but she can't make herself look his way. It's impossible to. She takes a breath and smiles into the crowd of people who congratulate her and Terry and pat Terry on the back, telling him he's a lucky bastard. The band are happy for her; she'd be sure Eddie is, too, if she could only bring herself to look at him. He does not come to congratulate her. But Rayna is convinced that this is the right decision. Terry is a good man. She has met his parents who live in Kent now that his father has given the pub over to Terry. They were not cruel like some of the white people who see them together. Terry's parents were so meek, humble and friendly. Just like Terry. They were in no way capable of harbouring the kind of lies and secrets her previous future in-laws had. She believed Terry's parents trusted their son to keep her safe, love her and marry her. She only wishes he could make her an honest woman. But he can't.

Rayna touches the small diamond on her ring so often during the evening that Sandra pinches her cheek and says, 'It's not a dream. You are getting married, love.'

The days slip by, so do the weeks and eventually August comes to an end. The ring becomes more comfortable, but life outside the pub is not.

*

It's Friday 1st September 1958 and it still feels like summer. At nine p.m. the walls in The Pelican drip with condensation. The crowd whoops as another tune is announced and they try to rid themselves of the tensions of the last week: the rioting, the bloody faces. The whites say the blacks are at fault; the blacks accuse the whites. Some say the tension is down to the slum landlords and the growing number of pimps and whores, but everyone blames the police.

The tables in The Pelican are pushed back and dancing without inhibition is the only kind of dancing acceptable. Rayna is up on stage for the first set ready to start singing an up-tempo swing. Eddie had said to her earlier when the band were setting up, 'Come in with a bang, not a whimper. Let them know you're here.'

Tonight Eddie wears a short-sleeved shirt and a large white handkerchief tied into a neat cravat around his neck. His thin moustache looks like a black line painted with a shiny pen against the glow of his skin, and soon there is a line of sweat beads on his brow. The band is tight; they don't even have to signal to each other for solos, and Eddie just calls number after number and the music flows endlessly from each member combining into a wave of sound that swirls around the pub.

Rayna's dress is new. It zips at the back and she'd give anything in this sweltering heat to just undo the whole garment, toss it aside and sing. The louder the applause grows the more she puts into her performance. She can feel the sweat in the creases of her elbows under her three-quarter sleeves. She can feel it dripping from her temples and making her armpits clammy. When she sings her final song, the audience yell for an encore, but by now, Rayna needs a break. She has given everything she has and she'll collapse if she sings one more bar. Eddie winks at her, and just as she prepares to jump off the stage, she sees Terry appear and falls into his arms. They are warm and wrap around her. Their bodies are locked in close and they sway, rocking from one foot to the other until the enthusiasm of the crowd almost causes them to lose balance.

'Come on, I'll get you a drink,' Terry says just as Eddie counts his band into another number. Terry and Rayna weave their way to the bar. Sandra beams a smile from behind it, ready with a glass of shandy for Rayna and a whisky for Terry.

On stage, the brown faces of the musicians gleam. They smile through the warmth and keep on playing. Truck Harrison, his back to his fellow musicians, sits at the piano facing the window. The curtains are closed and he grins as he plays. His whisky glass bounces on top of the old upright. Cuthbert Goode, the Dominican trombonist, hands the solo to trumpet player, Hinton Beckles from Barbados. His cheeks puff and his eyes squeeze shut. The floor is his for as long as he wants to blow. Minutes into Hinton's solo, their guitarist, Pearson Gladstone, stands up from his stool and walks over to Hinton. He wants the floor. Eddie laughs and forces Hinton into a sudden halt by playing a loud and off-key riff.

'Okay, Pearson, boy,' Hinton shouts. 'Show me what you got.' He doubles over as he laughs, his trumpet at his knees.

Pearson would love to hold the audience captive, but after only a few licks on his guitar strings, there is a loud crash. A brick flies through the window above Truck and hits Pearson to the side of his head. He is immediately stunned and collapses forward off the low stage directly into the line of people in front of him. The music stops dead. A wave of movement ripples through the saloon when the audience impulsively steps back from the stage. Eddie and Hinton leap down to tend to Pearson.

'Jesus Christ!' Truck stands with his chubby fingers outstretched above the piano keys. He is covered in shattered glass. In seconds, a woman comes in screaming from the snug into the saloon. She shouts 'Fire' at the already stunned crowd, and at first, no one can move.

'Quick!' Terry calls to Sandra as he pushes towards the snug. 'Call 999!'

Rayna barges her way to the front of the stage where Pearson is beginning to come around. She leans over and shouts into Eddie's ear.

'You have him?'

'Yes,' Eddie shouts back. There is more noise now than when the music was playing. People are shouting, calling, crying while Sandra yells for everyone to get out.

Rayna looks up at the faces, the looks of fear, confusion and disbelief. This is their Friday night haven. What's happening? Rayna sees a clear line through the crowd as they begin to bundle their way out onto the street and she runs to the snug.

Smoke fills the tiny room. Flames have caught hold of the furniture and the carpet near the exit. Terry ushers the last few drinkers into the saloon. He attempts to pull down a curtain to throw over the fire.

'It's too late, Terry,' Rayna says from the door. Her voice is thin and he isn't likely to hear her.

'Get the hell out of here, Terry!' Sandra yells from behind Rayna. 'The fire brigade's here. And the police.'

Terry runs a hand over his head, his cheeks hot and wet with tears. Rayna's eyes smart as she watches him drag his feet towards her, the flames engulfing the curtains on the floor behind him. Rayna reaches her arms out.

'I'm here, Terry,' she says. They embrace, his face buried in her neck, his shoulders heave up and down and the tears fall.

'Pearson will be fine,' she whispers into his ear. 'Everything will be fine.'

They walk heavily into the saloon where a few people have already started to return, undeterred by the protests of the firemen.

A police sergeant who towers over both Rayna and Terry approaches them.

'You the guv'nor?'

Terry sniffs and wipes his face with the back of his arm.

'Yeah, this is my place, what's left of it.'

In a state of numbness, Terry answers the Police questions, the sergeant taking notes as Rayna goes to console a sobbing Sandra.

'How could they do that, Ray? The bastards,' she says. 'If I hear who it was, I swear I'll kill them myself.'

'You'll never find out,' Rayna tells her. 'Cowards – that's what they are. Stupid, dirty cowards.'

'Look at this place,' Sandra says. 'What are we to do?'

In less than ten minutes, the police, fire brigade and the ambulance service have left the street and Pearson is on his way to the hospital. Voices whisper about seeing a van and men climbing into the back of it, just after the brick came through the window and the fire bomb was thrown into the snug. People claimed they'd overheard talk of an attack on the pub, though no one provided a statement to the police.

At least twenty people, including some members of the band, help Terry to clean up the crumbling ruins of the snug and the mess caused by the chaos of the evacuation. Chairs are upturned, glasses and bottles smashed. It's as if a tornado has blown through The Pelican. At the bar, Terry stands with open arms.

'Everyone. Everyone.' The conversations in the saloon die down. 'I just want to say thank you for doing this. You don't know what this means to me. Those people ... well.' His eyes are watery and he swallows hard. 'They've done it, haven't they? They've been threatening a long time but now they've done it. Got us scared, got us beaten.' A rumble of half-hearted agreement fills the room, heads shake in disbelief. 'However you want to dress this, it's hatred, pure hatred, and I can't put you at risk. I think it might be best if we stopped the music for now.'

'Terry.' Eddie walks over to him. 'This is your place and what you say goes. If you want to cancel, go ahead but only if you really want to. But don't let people like that stop you. You see me running? I'm not running. I got a right to be here. I'm a musician, pure and simple. I'm not causing anyone any harm. Who wants to hear me play, then hear me play. Who wants me to stop, I'll stop. But don't threaten me – because I'm not scared.' He turns to point at the window, holding his arm in place while staring at Terry. 'And if I stop playing, then I'm telling them I am scared, and you'll never hear me say it, no matter how much they try to hurt me.' He lowers his hand. 'I'm not giving those people the satisfaction of driving me away. I'm supposed to be here.' A cheer goes round, followed by some faint applause and everyone then looks at Terry.

'You'll play next week?' Terry asks.

'I'll play next week, I'll play the week after. I'll play until they run out of bricks.'

'Or until Terry sacks you because you played out of tune.' Truck still has a bloody handkerchief in his hand and swishes it in Eddie's direction. Laughter returns. Everyone laughs, whether it's heartfelt or nervous laughter or to dry the tears they've shed. Terry walks slowly towards Eddie and holds out his hand. Eddie extends his and Terry covers it with both of his for a strong handshake. Their expressions are serious as they look, unblinking, into the eyes of the other. Slowly, a smile spreads over Terry's face and Eddie surrounds him in an embrace.

'We're not beaten, man,' Eddie says.

'That means the world to me,' Terry whispers back.

Next week there are boards on the broken window. The curtains in the snug are new and the carpets taken up. For the next few weeks, the band line up is the same and there is music at The Pelican.

20

Daniella sat in front of her mirror, Rayna behind her combing her hair. It looked a lot prettier since Rayna took charge.
If it had been up to Daniella, or her mother come to that, her
thick head of hair would have been dry and knotted and continuing to break. As it was, Rayna could very easily pull it
into a cute bunch at the back of her head and tie a ribbon
around it.

'That's better,' Rayna said even though she still fussed over
the direction the ribbon fell. 'Don't you like yellow?'

'I do.'

'So why you looking so serious?' Rayna asked the girl.

'I want to know if it's true.'

For the whole week, Daniella had been playing popular
songs on the piano from sheet music her father had bought in
town, and though Rayna couldn't read the sheets, she knew a
lot of the songs by heart from listening to them on the St
Jeans' radio. She had encouraged Daniella to sing as well as
play and had discovered what a pretty voice the girl had.
They had played and sung for an hour one afternoon before
Mrs St Jean came to complain of a headache. She asked
Rayna if there wasn't something more important for her to
do around the house. The girls giggled and slipped out of the
room, Mrs St Jean eyeing her daughter. She must have seen
the changes in her, Rayna had been convinced, though she
made no comment.

'You want to know if what is true?' asked Rayna as she sat on the edge of Daniella's bed.

'I was in the kitchen and I heard them in the hallway. My mother and father.'

'Doing what?'

'Talking about you. You and Darius.'

'Oh?' Rayna looked down. She hadn't mentioned to Daniella that she and Darius had become close, that they'd been writing to each other and how much she'd been looking forward to him coming home now that he was in his last year of college. She knew Daniella despised her brother and he had little or no patience with his sister and her so-called silly ways.

'Are you really interested in marrying my brother? He's not a good person, you know?'

'I know you said he has a bad temper…'

'A wild temper. Like an animal. Especially when I was very little and troubled his things. I was only a girl.'

Rayna smiled softly. 'You're still a girl. And you don't know how it feels to like a boy yet.'

'So you really like him?' Daniella screwed her face in contempt and shook her head. 'My father is not happy. He has been putting up with Mother's foolishness, he said, and that he won't let his son marry an uneducated, country girl whose father is a drunk.'

Rayna went to stand by the window. She was too angry to look at Daniella. 'I'm not my father.'

Daniella got up and put a hand on Rayna's shoulder. 'If you marry him, you'll go and leave me here, won't you?'

Rayna turned to her. 'If I marry, of course we won't live here but you'll be welcome all the time.'

'It's not safe here without you.'

'What do you mean? Not safe from who?'

'Him.' She looked quickly at her bed and back at Rayna. 'I told my mother, I need a lock on my door to stop him getting in. But she doesn't listen and he comes in here anyway.'

'Who does? Not Darius?'

'Rayna, please don't marry him.' Daniella's plain-talking voice grew soft, her fourteen years didn't show in her face or demeanour. She was like a scared five-year-old and Rayna couldn't understand what she was hearing.

'Promise me, Rayna.'

'What do you mean? Did Darius hurt you?'

'He said if I told anyone anything, he would come in here and slice out my tongue and he'd do what he does anyway.'

'But, Daniella, when? When did this happen?'

'More than once. When everyone is asleep.'

Rayna's stomach leapt into her throat. Swallowing hard to mask the need to throw up, she cast her mind back to Darius' last mid-term break. They had spent a lot of secret time together. He'd bought her a ring. Though he'd put it on her finger, he'd told her to hide it for now. They'd met on a Sunday. Prior to meeting Darius, Rayna had been on a rare visit to church with her mother. She had fidgeted throughout the service, excited to be seeing him yet guilty about not having told her mother. She ran all the way to the beach after church and saw him on the sand, his trousers rolled up to his calves as he threw a small stick into the water. He'd filled out, his arms and shoulders more muscular.

'What are you doing?' she'd asked, making him jump before he spun around.

'Is that your best dress?' he asked, dropping the sticks he'd gathered. 'You look very pretty.'

They'd kissed, and not for the first time. She pressed her lips into his and sighed at the feeling of his tongue gliding down her neck and along the collar of her dress. She had wished the neckline was lower when her breasts cried out for the touch of his tongue on them. She'd pulled away and gig-gled.

'It's the Lord's day. We shouldn't.'

Darius had taken her by the hand and walked with her along the beach. Her stomach rumbled because she'd rushed away before her mother had lit the stove to make breakfast. She'd lied when her mother had asked why she wasn't eating and lied again when she said it was Daniella she was meet-ing and that she would bring breakfast from home. She hated to lie to Urma but it wasn't time to announce her and Darius' intention to marry. What had started as a fantasy in Mrs St Jean's mind had become Rayna's reality, and she had lived to receive Darius' letters and the postcard he sent her with pictures of America and no message apart from the letter D. She had collected them from the post office in secret only praying that the busybody man at the counter would say nothing to her mother. Luckily Urma had little business there: no one ever wrote to her.

They'd been sitting on the beach when Darius reached for her hand and placed the thin gold band with the onyx stone onto her finger.

'There'll be more,' he'd said. 'As soon as my father re-leases more money to me.' He'd kissed her ring finger and smiled, both so warm and blissful in their secret. How could she now find out this devastating news from Daniella? The Darius Daniella described was at odds with the man she was in love with.

'Daniella,' she said and gripped the girls folded arms. 'You wouldn't make this up, would you?'

Daniella shook her head, her gaze piercing Rayna's anxious eyes. 'And you mustn't say anything because he'll do it. He'll cut my tongue out.'

Rayna threw her arms around Daniella and pulled her into her chest. She pressed her cheek onto Daniella's head and inhaled the bergamot oil.

'He won't do it again,' Rayna whispered.

'How can you stop him?'

'I'll talk to him.'

Daniella pulled away, shaking her head frantically as she looked to the door. She put her hand over Rayna's mouth. 'Can't you just stay in the night? Stay in my room? If you talk to him, he'll know I told.'

'Daniella, this shouldn't be happening.' She embraced the girl again. 'And don't worry, I won't be marrying Darius.' She felt Daniella's body soften into hers and her chubby arms circle her waist.

'I need to run from here. Can't you take me away?' There were tears in Daniella's voice, reducing itself again to that of a five-year-old child.

'It will be hard, Daniella.'

'Please. Promise me. Promise to never go away and leave me with them.'

'How can I–'

'Because you're all I have.'

'I'll do what I can. I promise you, Daniella.'

She knew she'd have to seek her mother's advice. She had no idea how best to handle this. She had no money and no future. And now that her prospect of marrying Darius had been snatched away, she'd have to find another plan. With each second of standing by the window and holding the frightened girl in her arms, her heart splintered just that bit more. Sorrow for the girl and for herself, too, as she had no idea how she could block out the feelings she had for Darius. Her whole future had burned away and in the ashes was a young girl she had sworn to protect.

21

'Rayna, love, there's a man sitting in the snug wants to have a word with you,' Sandra says just as Rayna finishes singing and makes her way behind the bar for a drink.

'Which man is that?' Rayna feels a pricking sensation all over her skin and opens her eyes wide as she holds a glass of water to her lips. Quickly, she turns to see where Terry is. He and the band are busy saying farewell to Cuthbert, the trombonist, who is off on a tour of Europe with a big band.

'I don't know who it is,' Sandra says. 'He was in all night, sitting at the back, staring at you while you were singing.'

'Well, what does he look like?'

'Big. Smart suit. Tie. I don't know. Don't keep him waiting, it might be important.'

'I have to help clearing up.'

'Get in there this minute.' Sandra waves a tea towel towards the snug.

Rayna puts her head around the door and looks into the smaller bar. All the people there are white, no one from home. She lets out a long, silent sigh. Before she can speak, a thickset man comes bouncing towards her carrying a tumbler of melting ice.

'Rayna Laurence,' he says, as if she doesn't know her own name. 'Nice to meet you. My name is Michael Solomon. You can call me Sol.' He holds his hand out, the hand previously carrying his glass so it is damp when Rayna reciprocates. Though his skin is soft, his hand swallows Rayna's delicate one like a boxing mitt. 'That was a great set. Your voice just gets better, my dear. Better and better. Can we sit?' He walks backwards towards the banquette he occupies. Rayna hesitates before sitting on the stool on the opposite side of the table.

'You been here before?' she asks.

'Oh, a few times but I didn't get time to stop. Been busy travelling around securing dates and contracts for some of my other acts.'

'Other acts?'

'Yes, I'm a music agent. I've got a business card.' He sucks back what is left of the gin in amongst the melting ice in his glass and grimaces before bringing it down to the table. 'Here, you see? Michael Solomon, Solomon Entertainments. Thing is, one of my female singers has taken off to America. I got her the leads and she won't be looking back any time soon.' He nods with excitement. 'You'll be listening to her on the radio. She'll be cutting a record soon.'

'That's nice.'

'Nice? She'll be bigger than Peggy Lee, she will. See if she isn't. And remember who got her started.' He jabs a thick thumb several times into a large chest.

'So, why you wanted to see me?' Rayna says, looking back towards the door adjoining the saloon.

'To shoot you to the top, Rayna Laurence. You shouldn't have to change your name – has a great ring to it for cabaret.'

'But I'm a jazz singer.'

'Jazz.' He shakes his head from side to side. 'Well, you know, jazz has had its day. Next year we'll be in a new decade and I really can't see its popularity lasting. All the female jazz singers have made their mark. Anyone new will just be an imitation. A pale one at that.'

'I don't believe–'

'Believe you me, my dear. Believe you me. Who have we got in this country that's better than Ella? Better than Sarah? Better than Billie? Just imitations.'

'You saying I'm a copycat?'

'Not at all. Your voice is special. But it's not a jazz voice. Cabaret. Variety singing in night clubs, that's where the money is. You'll cut records, get on television. Jazz is just for the coffee shops. No glamour in that. Yes, I can see you: long gowns, bows, sequins. That's where the music business is headed for women into the sixties. Once the rock-n-rollers take over the charts, no one will want to know about jazz. The mums and dads, uncles and aunties, they just want to hear a good pure voice singing a good old song. And that's where I see you, Rayna. Believe me. I know.'

'Mr…'

'Call me Sol.'

'Sol, I think you've got me wrong. Cutting records, television. That's not for me. That's for somebody like Eartha Kitt.'

'And your voice is one hundred percent better than hers.'

'Oh come on, Mr Sol.' Rayna laughs. The snug bar and its handful of drinkers are silent, listening to the verbose Mr Solomon, seemingly very convinced by his announcements.

Rayna gets to her feet. 'Look, I'm very flattered but I'm not that person. I'm happy doing what I'm doing.' As she turns to leave, he catches her arm.

'Take my card anyway, Rayna. In this smoky pub, your voice will be shot by the time you're thirty. How old are you, anyway?'

'Twenty-four.'

'We'll tell them you're eighteen. Here. Put this in your pocket. Don't forget me. I'm sure one day you'll be in my office. Wells Street, look. The West End. You'll be in my office and we'll be talking tours and percentages. Tours and percentages.' He follows her through to the saloon where the cigarette smoke is thick and voices are still animated, even though it's after closing.

Rayna shakes his hand and bows slightly. She puts the card into her pocket and makes her way back behind the bar as Mr Solomon leaves.

'Who was that, love?' Terry asks, calling over to her as he wipes down the bar.

'Oh, no one.' She waves her meeting with Sol away.

'No one? Sandra said he asked for you special.'

'Just some agent from the West End who thinks he can turn me into a star.' She frames her face with her hands and smiles a large and dramatic smile at him.

'So what did you say?' He stops wiping up.

'That I'm not interested.' She picks up an empty tray and begins to collect glasses, telling everyone she brushes past that time has been called a long time ago. She is aware that at least two sets of eyes follow her around the pub as she chats to and ushers out the drinkers.

*

Another cold winter comes around; a draft of cold air follows Eddie into The Pelican as Rayna lets him into the saloon bar early on Saturday morning. Rayna shivers beneath her thick sweater. She crosses her arms as she scuttles towards the bar, hitching up onto a stool where two cups of coffee steam on the polished surface.

'England is too damned cold,' Eddie says, blowing into his hands and joining her at the bar. She pushes a fresh cup of coffee towards him.

'And you are a real Englishman,' she says. 'Always talking about the weather.' He snorts a laugh. 'Drink this, it will warm you up.'

They rehearse new songs together at the pub most Saturday mornings, now, spending two hours together before Terry comes down to start setting up for the afternoon session. By now, Rayna understands jazz and how the songs are structured. She has been working a long time on her scat singing and is developing a distinctive style of her own, despite what the music agent, Michael Solomon, had said about poor imitations and that jazz music would not last.

'You were at Mandy's place last night?' she asks Eddie without looking at him, both hands on her hot cup.

Eddie hesitates. 'How do you know?'

'You have the same shirt on you play in last night. And you, Eddie, are too stylish to wear the same shirt twice.'

'I don't have clothes at Mandy's yet.' He sips his drink. 'You don't mind?'

'Mind? Why should I mind? I know you two been seeing each other.'

'Well, it isn't supposed to be a secret.'

'You're a man, you please yourself.'

'So why you sound angry?'

She doesn't answer.

'I would ask if you were jealous,' Eddie says, 'but you and Terry are–'

'Very happy together,' she snaps, taking her coffee over to the piano. Eddie follows behind. He opens the piano lid. Rayna pulls up a chair. She used to share the piano stool with Eddie but Terry said she needed to have space to breathe when she sang.

'You know, I would be flattered if you said it was jealousy, Rayna.' His hands move across the keys as he plays a familiar chord progression. 'I took too long to tell you how much I liked you when we first met. Then, when I see how you were with Terry, I kept my mouth shut.'

'And now you have Mandy. I'm sure you both happy.'

'Oh we're happy. Everyone is happy.'

Rayna notes his raised shoulders, the sharpness in his voice. 'You must tell Mandy to come more often if you two are not a secret,' she says.

'Like I said, it was never a secret. Mandy and I get on well. I'm lucky to meet a girl like her.'

'I'm glad.'

'Talking of secrets. What you going to tell that music agent?'

'Him? Nothing. I already tell Terry I'm not interested.'

'You could be making a mistake. This business isn't easy. Any help you can get would be good, Rayna.'

'I know but he was talking about a cabaret act. I sing jazz.'

'A lot of girls sang jazz and changed to something else.'

'What would you think of me if I did?'

He stops tinkling the keys. 'So you considering it, then?'

She lowers her head.

'I'm not judging you, Ray. It's up to you.'

'But Eddie, imagine if what he saying is true. Imagine I make it big. I would have money, a house, a car. I could travel. Go back home to see what happened to–'

'To who?'

'Everyone,' she says in a soft voice after a moment of hesitation.

'And Terry?'

'And Terry will support me. He would.' She shuffles through the scores Eddie has brought with him and chooses a song. 'I come from a poor family, Eddie. Is there anything wrong with having dreams?'

'There's nothing wrong with it. I dream, too. I take the work when I can get it and I look for opportunities along the way. Next week, I'm in Paris again, recording for a big name. Anything could happen at any time, and when the time comes, decisions have to be made.'

'And you'll leave?'

He turns completely to face her. 'Rayna, I would take you anywhere and everywhere with me. I would stand and watch you sing, just like we do now. What I can't stand is to watch you walk into the bed of another man.' He lowers his voice. 'I know that for certain. I wish things could have been … I wish you knew…'

She leans forward in her chair. 'You are my best friend, Eddie.'

'And that's all there is for us?'

She nods, chin sinking deep into her chest.

'Then,' he says, 'as a friend, I'll always be here for you, Rayna.' He edges towards her. Specks of brown dance in his hazel eyes. His eyes always seem to smile whenever he looks at her and she wonders if hers do the same.

'Promise you'll always be there for me, Eddie.'

He nods with his entire body.

There are footsteps coming down from the flat and the door behind the bar swings open.

''ello, Eddie!' Terry pokes his head round the door. 'Just getting the paper. Don't let me interrupt.'

'Morning boss,' Eddie calls back. Terry disappears and Rayna stands up.

'I suppose we should start.'

'I would start from the beginning with you if I could, Rayna. I don't understand how we got here.'

'The important thing is where we end up. If something happens for you, Eddie, a great opportunity and you have to go away, remember me.'

'Always.'

*

Michael Solomon's Entertainments in Wells Street in the West End has less glamour than Rayna expected. The agency is nothing more than an upstairs room in an office building, most of which is unoccupied. It looks out onto howling traffic and busy pedestrians. Though the building is old and weathered, the room at least is light and airy, spacious with a high ceiling and two large windows decorated with off-white nets and red curtains that once belonged in a living room. The patterned linoleum on the floor makes Rayna's shoes squeak as she walks across it to take a seat on the dining room chair facing Solomon's desk. The desk gives him the appearance of an oversized child in a classroom.

The telephone rings as soon as she takes a seat and Rayna gazes around the room while Sol makes small talk to a club owner. Apart from the desk and two chairs, there is a tall filing cabinet between the two windows and six framed photos of various variety acts on the wall.

'I was so glad to hear from you, young Rayna. Kept wondering when you'd do the right thing by yourself – give me a call.' His voice echoes in the room. Rayna puts her handbag on the floor beside her and takes her headscarf off.

'Well, things have been changing. With the band and everything,' she says.

'I haven't been up that way for a bit. Busy with my acts.' He leans back in his chair and folds his hands together on the desk. 'Can I get you a tea, coffee, glass of water?'

'Oh no, I'm fine. Thank you. Well, I suppose you know why I'm here. You haven't been to see the band but it's down to a trio. They call it The Pelican Trio and Eddie does guest appearances when he's in town.'

'I heard he's been playing with some big fellas on the jazz scene. Got quite a name for himself, eh?'

'Yes, everyone going off and doing new things. Exciting things like tours, cutting records, radio. So much has happened.'

'And you want something to happen for you?'

'Well.' Her head dips with a shallow nod. 'You once said you thought I was good.'

'I can't be the only one who says that.' His wide smile brims with warmth.

'Well, it gets said a lot and I just, well, I don't know what I'll do if Eddie takes off and doesn't come back.'

'Bloody talented musician that man. Pardon my French. Really don't know why he even goes back to that old joint to play, can't be the money. Don't get me wrong, your pub's got a very good reputation in West London, but a singer like you and a player like Eddie Keane, well, let's just say you two were meant for better things.'

'You really think so?'

'Why are you here, Rayna?'

'Because I love to sing. I mean, really love it. More than anything I've ever done in my life. I would miss it all if… '

'If Eddie gets snatched up or the pub closes down?'

'Only one of those things is likely to happen but I want to be ready. I was just hoping you knew of any opportunities, places where they might need a singer.'

'At least a million places, my dear. And not just West London. All over the country. I could pick up the phone now and book you a two-week residency at a club in Manchester.'

'Manchester! But…'

'Look, Rayna, if you really want my help, you've got to take it seriously. This is my business and I'm not here for the fun of it. There are very few decent places to work in West London, if at all.' He raises an eyebrow.

'I am serious,' she says in a quiet voice.

'Don't be afraid to say you love to sing, Rayna. I've seen how alive you are up there. That natural style and that little thing you do with your hands and fingers. So charming, such individuality, and that's what we're looking for.'

'We are?'

'Absolutely.' He is out of his chair. He walks around to Rayna's side of the desk and props himself onto it. 'I have to ask you, Rayna my dear. What does your old man think of the idea?'

'Terry?'

Solomon nods.

'Terry knows how much I love it.'

'Does he know you're here today?'

'He thinks I'm shopping.' She blinks several times and looks towards a window.

'Well, I've had problems in the past with spouses. God knows mine is a royal pain in the you-know-what. So I need to have a commitment from you, Rayna. If you tell me you're serious and I book you to sing anywhere and then you can't make it because Terry needs his shirts ironing or the dinner made… Am I making myself clear?'

Rayna nods, her lips drawn into a line.

'We have to keep it professional, so we don't want any skeletons in cupboards and we don't want angry spouses saying you can't wear this or that. We'll have a contract and everything.'

'I understand. Terry knows I love to sing and he will never try to stop me. He says himself I should have a record or be on television.'

'Brilliant.' Sol jumps from his perch and bounces back to his chair, rubbing his hands as though they are cold. Rayna laughs.

'Nice to see that smile,' he says. 'Only ever seen it when you're on stage. Remember always to smile. You give me a week. I'll have a contract drawn up and I'll have a string of dates for you. Don't worry, we'll start you off with a few in London. I'll need to think about your wardrobe. I've got ideas. What you need to do first off, though, is let Terry know. Then have a talk with Eddie Keane and have him do you some sheet music. All the popular stuff, you know like on the radio. Just to get you started. But you've got to stay originally you. That's our secret weapon. That lovely little flower with the Caribbean lilt and the voice as pure as honey. Rayna Laurence. But as far as anyone's concerned, you're nineteen years old. Got that?'

'Yes, Mr Solomon.'

'Call me Sol.' This time he stands to shake Rayna's hand. 'You and I will be in business a long time so let's drop the formalities now. I'll be honest and up front with you if you are with me. Honesty is the best policy.'

As Rayna travels back across London, Sol's last words play in a continuous loop in her mind. Being honest is something she can't be, not completely, not with anyone. Not with Terry and not with Eddie.

At The Pelican, Eddie is at the piano working on one of his compositions when she pushes open the door.

'Rayna!' He stops playing. 'You're looking very thoughtful.'

'No one here? Terry?' She removes her headscarf and places it onto her handbag on a table.

Eddie shrugs his shoulders. 'Popped out. For an hour or two, he said. Come.' Eddie gestures with his hand. 'Sit with me until he gets back. Come and sing.'

She slots herself on the corner edge of the piano stool and draws in a breath.

'You going to tell me what's up?' Eddie says, facing down at the keys, shaping a chord with his long fingers.

'You really know me well, don't you?' says Rayna.

'I should do. We're friends, aren't we?'

'Yes, Eddie. And I need a friend right now.'

'What's troubling you? Let me help.'

'I went to see the music agent. Michael Solomon.'

'Without Terry?'

She looks, briefly, from Eddie's profile back to the piano keys. 'He doesn't know.' She shrugs.

'Well – what did he say? Solomon. What did he have to offer?'

'Some work. Singing. Places other than here.'

'I see.'

'Do you? I'm just so … I just love it, Eddie. I don't want it to stop.'

'I can see that. And the people love you.'

'But there's more to it than Friday night at The Pelican. You know that. I need your help, though. Getting some scores together. Can you help me?'

'You've got lots of songs in your repertoire now.'

'I need something more popular. Not from the jazz repertoire.'

'So you decided to turn your back on your first love.'

'Don't be disappointed. Sol says I need to branch out.'

'I understand, and I will help you.' He turns towards her and rubs her arms, slowly, up and down. The thin cardigan she wears crackles with the friction. She sighs with relief to have Eddie on her side. His eyes are already smiling. The smile spreads to the rest of his face. A door, somewhere, in the back of her mind, creaks open. She is only concentrating on Eddie's face and in the intense way he studies hers.

'Thank you, Eddie.' Rayna says. The door closes, and when she looks over her shoulder, Rayna sees Mandy approaching the stage.

'What you two in cahoots about?' Mandy crosses her arms, her hip cocked as she waits for an answer. Eddie steps off the stage.

'Just helping Rayna with some songs.'

'Well, don't let me interrupt. I've only come in to do my evening shift.' She storms to the bar but turns back to Rayna, still on the stage, adjusting her cardigan and looking blindly at her hands.

'Evening all.' Terry sweeps into the saloon from behind the bar. He smiles to each in turn. 'Blimey, who died?'

'No one, Terry.' Rayna skips her way from the stage to his side and hooks his arm. 'Everyone is just getting ready for tonight.' She follows him upstairs and into the living room where he places a new record next to the player.

'I'm not an idiot, Rayna.' He doesn't turn round. 'You could cut the atmosphere with a knife.'

When he swings around, Rayna is hovering between sitting in or standing next to an armchair.

'Well?' He approaches her.

'Well, what?' she says.

Terry does not answer. He only looks at Rayna who knows it is time to tell Terry the truth.

'I – I went to see Michael Solomon. You remember the music agent?'

'I thought you threw his number away.'

'I kept it just in case. You know? If one day I … I wanted to hear more about what he could do to help my career.'

Terry nods, sagely. 'I see.'

'You don't see, Terry.' She holds his arms. 'You don't see what my future could be. Sol does. He can get me engage-ments, singing engagements, all up and down England.'

'You never told me that's what you want.'

'You are the one who said I had a voice and could cut a record.'

'I know, but…'

'But now you change your mind? You don't think I can do it?'

'It's not that, Rayna.' He pulls away, takes out a cigarette and taps it on the packet. 'You never said you wanted to sing other places. Is this something you talked about with Eddie?'

'No, Terry. I want it. I been thinking about it a lot.'

'And you didn't think to talk about it with me?' He lights the cigarette and takes a long pull. 'But of course not. Why would you talk to me about anything? I ask you about yourself and you shut me down. Does everything have to be so hush-hush with you, Rayna? I tell you everything. There's nothing you don't know about me.'

'You saying you don't trust me?' Her tone changes from pleading to stern.

'I'm not saying that. What I'm saying is why don't you trust *me* enough to talk things out with me? You think I would stand in your way? Because I wouldn't. I want you to succeed, Rayna. Don't you think I do?' He allows his body to flop onto the sofa.

'So why you angry?' Rayna asks.

'Because I … because you … because I don't want you taking me for a fool, Rayna. That's all I'll ever ask of you.' He stubs out the unfinished cigarette into a full ashtray on the coffee table and runs his hands over his hair. Rayna joins him on the sofa.

'And I would never do that. You're no fool, Terry. But I love to sing and the band is changing.'

'I can get another band for you, Ray.' He rests a hand on her lap.

'Sol can get me so much more.'

'I know that.' They sit quietly for a few moments. 'I'm sorry I got angry. I just love you so much, I don't want there to be secrets. Always talk to me first.' He looks deep into her eyes, unblinking.

'I will, Terry. From now on, I promise.'

Terry takes a long breath in and slowly releases it.

22

By the time Darius returned from New York, Rayna had shown Daniella how to drag the chest of drawers at the side of her bed to the door. She'd told Daniella to keep it pressed against it because it wouldn't budge if someone came in the night. All she needed to do was pull the three deep drawers out, move the frame to the door and put the drawers back in. She could also pile heavy books on the top, so if anyone managed to make the chest budge, then the books would topple and make a lot of noise and anyone else was bound to hear.

Rayna's feelings for Darius had been fading in the months that followed Daniella's confession and she'd tried desperately to get Daniella to tell Mrs St Jean about the nighttime visits.

'She won't listen, and what makes you think she doesn't know?'

'She's a mother. She can't...'

'You're talking about my family, Rayna. You have no idea how my parents are with me and they are both as bad as each other. This family is not like yours.'

Rayna thought about her own family. A father who drank so heavily she hardly saw him sober or even awake. A brother who had joined the British army and gone away in 1943, never to return from the Second World War, presumed dead. She herself had been forced to leave school early so she could work. And her mother. Oh, her mother. Working all hours of the day in several jobs, travelling far from the house, carrying a broken heart in her battered chest and a drunk for a husband on her weary back. Rayna had nothing but love from her mother, Urma. She wasn't abused like Daniella, but there was nothing normal about Rayna's family, either.

'I wish you and I could run away from here,' Daniella said. 'When Darius comes back, you and me could go to America.'

Rayna laughed but she could see the earnest look in the young girl's eyes.

'Daniella, what could we do there? Two girls. Playing piano and singing isn't enough to keep a person. And that's all we can do.'

'It's not impossible.'

'Your dreams are big. Too big.'

'You shouldn't give up before you try.'

Daniella was taller now. At fifteen, she looked awkward, her hairstyles juvenile because she still liked to wear ribbons in her bunches. She had put on so much weight that her mother, though complaining continually, had to buy her new clothes. Rayna had gone to town with them and she'd noticed how quiet the usually animated girl became under the gaze of her mother, how shy and unassuming she was. Too shy to pick up a dress from the rail in the shop. Her mother lifted a few dresses, waved them in front of Daniella's body as she looked her up and down and told the shop assistant, 'We'll take this.' Daniella pushed her glasses up her sweaty nose and walked to the shop door, waiting for her mother to pay.

'Do you like what she chose?' Rayna had whispered. Daniella disregarded the question.

Daniella continued to raise the idea of her and Rayna having a future playing music together. Rayna knew it would be impossible. Daniella was too shy around everyone. Only Rayna could bring her out of her shell. Besides, Rayna had always seen Darius as her means for improving her life and helping her mother. Now that that dream was shattered, Daniella's talk of performing in music halls and night clubs was nearing on ridiculous.

Mrs St Jean had heard them perform and had told Rayna what a beautiful voice she had. For her own daughter, the praise was not forthcoming, but Rayna knew that Daniella could play the piano much better than she herself could sing and she knew that Daniella had a remarkable singing voice. She'd witnessed it only once but it was enough to know that the young girl was exceptional.

'I think we need another plan,' said Rayna. 'And I need to go and prepare dinner for you all before I go home.'

'I wish you lived here.'

'I would miss my mother too much.'

'I miss you when you're not here. And Rayna, if you do go away. Leave Dominica, ever. Take me with you.'

'I'm not going anywhere. I may not marry Darius but he will marry someone and I will be here, making the meals and cleaning the floors.'

'But you want more.'

If only Daniella could see her dreams. Yes, she wanted more, but without any real prospects, all she could do was dream.

23

It is in a quiet pub in a back street off Holborn that Rayna meets Eddie. It's easy to get away to see him because Terry is used to her not being at The Pelican, no longer pulling pints and no longer singing on his stage. It's important that she sees Eddie today, though, and she has to pretend to Terry that she has a rehearsal that lasts until the evening. She has a train to Liverpool to catch first thing in the morning. She'd told Terry that Sol booked her a hotel for after the rehearsal so that she is close to the station. Rayna hasn't seen Eddie for the best part of a year. Their lives have taken such different turns. Sometimes she doesn't know if she's happy or not. For the first time, she has her financial independence. The money isn't great – not yet, Sol says – but she doesn't have to ask Terry for money and she has been able to save some here and there. The money won't get her far, but she thinks that one day she can buy back her life, that she can pay back Mrs St Jean's money. Without which she would never have been able to plan her escape. She can send money to her mother because she must need it desperately. Rayna has still had no word from home.

'You look beautiful, Rayna.' Eddie sits by the fireplace whose flames light the dark corner of the pub with a warm amber glow. Everyone stares at Rayna as she enters and she cannot get used to the fact that people have started to recognise her. Just last week, she had made another television appearance on a variety show. Eddie rises from his seat with a broad smile on his face, his moustache looking as if it has been outlined with a thin brush previously dipped in shiny black paint.

'And you look very handsome, Eddie. The Parisian air is doing wonders for you, or maybe this is because of a certain Parisienne.'

His bashful smile isn't accompanied by his usual humorous response, and she knows that after all this time abroad there must have been a few women in Eddie's life. He is handsome, intelligent and talented. All the things she would look for in a man if it wasn't for Terry. Terry allows her to do anything she pleases and that suits her fine. He will never treat her the way she has been treated by men in the past, but yet something in her life with Terry is missing. She wishes she could mix some of Eddie's flame with Terry's calm, but she knows she has to love the whole and she can't realistically fashion the ideal partner out of the two men. Terry has asked her to marry him on so many occasions and Eddie has offered to show her the world. No stability. No wedding ring on offer. Even though she can't trust anyone with her story, she has to know that she can trust any man she might consider marrying.

'You don't have to tell me her name, Eddie, but I hope she's being good to you.'

'Rayna, I don't have to tell you how many hangers-on you get in this business. Right now, I'm just holding on to the work while I have it, to this life while I have it and I take each day as it comes.'

'And that's it? You'll never get married and settle down?'

'Who do you see me with, Rayna? Because you know better than anyone that there can only be one person for me.'

She looks at the glass of whisky in front of Eddie. 'Aren't you going to buy me a drink?'

'Of course.' He stands abruptly and goes to the bar, not asking what she'd like. He already knows and she likes that about him. He returns shortly with her half of shandy.

He leans unapologetically across the table, gripping the circumference of the glass as if it might escape him. 'What did I do wrong, Rayna? I was only ever good to you. Wasn't I? I didn't have a pub to offer you or a job to give you, but God knows you are welcome to everything I have.'

Rayna is quiet, contemplating the hours that they can spend together and wishing that they didn't have to have this conversation. With Eddie, their talk – when they've had the opportunity – has been light, undemanding. That's how it's supposed to be. Music, shows, their cultural background. He laughs at her accent and she imitates his. They joke together, they laugh together and neither gets hurt because they share a comfortable distance. Up until now.

'I never lied to you, Eddie.'

'And you never told me the truth, either. But listen, I put my past behind me a long time ago and all I do is look forward.' He motions with his hand as he says twice more, 'Look forward, look forward.'

'That's what I want to do,' Rayna says with a sigh and then sips her drink.

'But not with me.'

'Things are already in motion. There's my career. There's Terry.'

'You are a wonderful singer, Rayna, but you are a jazz singer. Come with me to Paris. For once, you should do something that is true to you.'

'You think I'm a fake? I'm not authentic like you?'

'I think you are running to a future that isn't yours and you could run into trouble.'

'I know what I'm doing, Eddie.' She drinks fast. Her head is tilted and she senses the pull of the muscles in her throat with every swallow and she hopes they won't choke her. All she wants to do is run out of there. This is not how tonight was supposed to go. Before she can reach for her coat, Eddie stops her.

'Rayna, wait. I wasn't trying to chase you away. Let's have this evening. Let's have this night, like we planned, and I'll never talk to you about the future again. We take things as they come.' He has both hands up trying to conjure peace back to their space in the dimly lit pub, the table speckled with cigarette ash and the chairs tucked under it so tightly, their knees touch. Being so close to his body is sending sensations through her. Their bodies close together is what tonight is supposed to be about, but afterwards, they are supposed to remain friends. She wonders if Eddie can leave it at that. She wonders if she can.

'I could eat,' she says. 'I'd like to go and eat. What do you think?'

'This is our night, Rayna. Yours and mine. Let's do it.'

Before checking into the hotel, they eat at a small Greek restaurant that also has fish and chips on the menu. Their conversation returns to the usual topics, only now it is Rayna who has stories of her shows, the people she has met and the plans she has for taking her career further. She sees Eddie smile and nod and she anticipates the moment, the opportunity that they have carved for themselves, to finally be together for the night. In the morning, she will be on a train to Liverpool and he will be on a flight to Paris.

The double bed dominates the rectangular room. On it, two crisp white pillows sit regally at the headboard. The puce bedspread, which has an embossed leaf pattern running its way up the middle, is tucked tightly under the edges of the mattress so that the wooden legs of the bed are visible.

The walls are painted a fine shade of yellow with an oval-shaped mirror on the wall beside the door. A picture of a countryside scene with rolling hills of green and yellow and frothy clouds in a pale blue sky hangs on the wall over the bed. There is a tallboy in one corner and a very upright arm-chair in another. On each side of the bed is a side table where a lacy doily supports a sturdy lampshade on one and a beaten-up book of psalms on the other.

The curtains, also puce, are of a heavy fabric and tied back on each side of the narrow sash windows by black velvet bows. The carpet, old but clean, is patterned by indistin-guishable flowers in deep red. The scent in the air is sweet but artificial.

'Shall I open the window a little?' Eddie asks.

'Yes please.' She sits on the bed in her coat and runs her hand over the bed cover. The candlewick is thinning and she wonders how many people have slept in this bed before her. All her life, she has slept in beds where several bodies have lain before. Even her bed in the cluttered room back home had belonged to her older brother and had been given to her family before that. She is tired of rented rooms and apart-ments, being put up on couches and, at one time, a floor. She wants, one day, to be led by the hand to a bed she owns or owns with a man she loves. It seems petty, but it would mean the world to her to be the owner of the bed, the sheets, the covers, the room the bed sits in and the house the room belongs to.

The air from the window is cool and the cadence of street traffic lightens the atmosphere, but only a little.

'Is that okay?' Eddie's voice brings her back to the room. The bed. The reason they are there. Several stolen moments, whispers and letters from Paris have led them to this point, but all of a sudden, she doesn't know why she agreed to come. They'd consented to being together and sharing one night. No more secret calls and meetings because it was clear to both that something physical was bound to happen, that there was a sensuality in quiet cups of coffee, in phone calls late at night. This union, the first and last, would be a way of punctuating the end to their lust and anticipation. Their dreams would end and the longing would, too, with this one final act. Now the idea doesn't sit well with her. For one thing, she would be being dishonest to Terry. For another, the quaking of her body is telling her that once will not be an end but a start to something more. New sensations, a new direction to take their relationship. Out of friendship and into something else.

Eddie sits on the armchair and then gets up to take his jacket off. She can't bring herself to look at him when she feels him sit beside her on the bed, his body strong and warm against hers.

'If you're cold, I'll close the window.' He rubs her arm and she is aware her coat is still on and she's gripping the handles of her handbag as if she's afraid of losing it.

'No, I'm not cold, Eddie. It's just…'

'Look, I understand. We said there would be no pressure. That we could change our minds, even at the last moment.'

She turns and leans into him and he brushes a finger over her lips. Her eyes close and he touches a kiss to each eyelid.

A faint touch and a whisper of breath on her skin. She looks up.

'I shouldn't have come.'

He kneels in front of her, gliding to the floor in one smooth gesture. His fingers tug at each button of her coat and she lets go of her handbag when he pulls her coat off. He sits beside her, his lips nestled to her cheek. She doesn't pull away and he doesn't stop kissing her face. Their bodies recline onto the bed and he feels heavy above her and her back arches up and her legs clasp around themselves behind him. She looks into his eyes.

'I'm sorry, Eddie.' Her body slackens and her toes skim the floor. She lets go of her embrace and touches a finger to his chin.

'It's okay. It's fine,' he whispers. 'I'll go for a cigarette outside, you can get into bed.' He gets up quickly tucking his shirt into his trousers. On the other side of the room, he searches his jacket pocket before putting it on and walking swiftly to the door.

'You'll come back?' she says.

'Of course I will. This is our night. I don't know when I'll see you again. I don't know where we will be in a month. Of course I'll come back.'

Rayna dresses for bed. She pulls at the bedspread and struggles to rescue its tightly secured edge. Her nightdress is probably too scant to wear in front of Eddie and she doesn't want him to think she has changed her mind, so she stays hidden under the cover. She turns to face the window. The overhead light is harsh but she can't get out of the bed in case Eddie walks in and sees how she is dressed. So she closes her eyes and waits for him.

Eddie turns off the light and locks the door on his return. She hears each item of his clothing land on the floor and feels him slip between the sheets. He curls his body into her back and places an arm around her waist.

'How do you feel?' His voice is warm against her neck. She looks out at the timid light a lamppost casts on the dark sky.

'You have to understand, Eddie. I have to make something of my life or else what is the point of me? Why am I here?'

'Rayna...'

'I can make people happy when I sing and that makes me happy. People care I exist.'

'You don't have to sing to me to make me care about you. I care.'

'I need more than that.'

They stay in this position until early the next morning when Eddie accompanies her to Kings Cross Station.

She waves to Eddie who walks alongside the train as it pulls out of the platform, heading north. She lifts her hand to wave but holds it in mid-air as she watches Eddie mouthing something she thinks is, 'Come home safely.' But she can't be sure.

Rayna takes off her raincoat and settles back into the seat. She ignores everyone inside the carriage and watches the stone greys and browns of the city sneaking up from behind her and rolling into the distance. She doses on and off, blinking heavy eyelids at the trees and grassy hills that tell her she is miles from London. Just hours later, the countryside becomes the hard surfaces of glass and bricks of Liverpool. Sol is there to meet her at the station.

He waits for her again in the night outside her dressing room which she shares with two other acts. She opens the door two minutes before she is due on stage.

'Beautiful, Rayna,' Sol says. 'You look the absolute business.'

Her dress is bottle green lace over a beige-coloured lining. The bodice is fitted with moulded cups that shape her bosom, her shoulders and arms are bare. The dress is tight at the waist and hugs her hips and thighs. Her stockings are black and silky and her stiletto shoes form neat points at her toes. On her lips, a matte dark red lipstick, her eyebrows defined by a black pencil and finely drawn black liner around her eyes make her look dramatic. Over the lids, silver eye shadow. Her pressed hair is set with neat waves that circle her slender face, and on her ears, a pair of clasp earrings in white. She smooths down the skirt and follows Sol.

The presenter introduces her, holding out his arm as she walks on stage to the welcoming applause of the crowd. She nods to the conductor and stands open armed as she moves to the microphone. The band plays the introduction to her first song. Rayna feels the butterflies fluttering in her stomach.

She sings with her eyes closed a popular love song that she cannot connect with. She knows Sol will want her to smile, so she does, forcing emotion into her voice so she won't lose her audience. After each of her four songs, the applause becomes louder than the last and the cry for more is overwhelming. She looks off-stage and the announcer winds his finger in a circle so she will continue on. A second of conferring with the conductor and she is into another song; this time she is lost in the melody, the joy of the audience lifting her far away from the confusion in her mind and the fact she can never forgive herself for what she has done to Terry, to Eddie, and somewhere, further away, is the reminder of what she has done to her mother and the St Jeans. She forces the memories from her mind, pushes their faces away and sees only the bright lights ahead of her.

On the drive back to London, Rayna sits staring at the road ahead. Sol drives fast, drumming his thumbs on the steering wheel and speaking out of the side of his mouth as ash creeps up the cigarette balancing on his lip.

'You know how many bookings I can get you now? You're on your way, Ray my girl. Definitely on your way.'

When the taxi pulls up, Rayna wonders if Sandra is right, if she should become the mistress of her own house and let Terry be the master in his. How can she be blamed for her success? She was lucky it came to her but she's had to work hard. It hasn't been an easy journey, from being the fifteen-year-old Rayna who gave up school just as she was about to turn sixteen and who kissed goodbye to her girlhood at age seventeen. What had become of that island girl who dreamt of marrying the rich man she loved? Who dreamt of saving a young girl who was being traumatised by her family and whom she'd promised to take with her? The Rayna who is about to turn thirty would have so much to offer Daniella now. Much more than she ever had when she fled the island in shame, disappointing her mother and doing what she did to her employer. She can't go back, she can't take it back and she can't help Daniella.

'Taxi's here.' Terry states the obvious when the three loud toots from outside peel into the quiet hallway where Terry stands, head down, fists buried in his pockets and where Rayna waits, agitatedly, in leather pumps and a red wool three-quarter length coat in the style of a fifties movie star. Her luscious red lipstick finishes off the look. She picks up her handbag.

'I should get going, then. Paris calls.' She gives him a joyless grin as Terry opens the door, keeps his back to her and carries the suitcase to the black cab with its rattling engine. The driver jumps out quickly when he sees who is with Terry.

'Is that really you?' he asks Rayna.

'Yes, it's her,' Terry replies as both he and the driver try to get the suitcase into the back of the taxi, their hands and fingers crisscrossing the other man's.

'Airport is it?'

Rayna nods and looks at Terry. The taxi driver is ecstatic and rushes to the driver's seat, smirking to himself, and Rayna can tell she'll have to talk about her music and hear again how everyone in the taxi driver's family loves Rayna Laurence.

'I'll see you then,' she says to Terry.

'Yeah, see you. Hope it all, you know, goes off well and that.'

'Well, Sol will make sure it does.' She steps closer to the open taxi door, and before she steps aboard, Terry taps her arm and she turns to face him. He pecks a sharp kiss on her cheek that reeks of Benson & Hedges. The smell of cigarettes and Terry's sad blue eyes stay with her all the way to the airport.

Darius returned to Dominica on a Saturday morning. Rayna had just walked through the gate carrying some limes from home. She was going to use them when she made fresh fish for lunch. The grand lunch which Mrs St Jean had planned to celebrate her son's graduation and his return home. She had invited her sister, Iris, up from Scott's Head along with Iris' husband who had decided, at the last minute, that he was too ill to travel all the way past Roseau just for lunch. Rayna knew her mistress was very excited about her son's graduation: she'd wanted to have a celebration party to show off her educated son to all their friends. Mr St Jean had convinced her of doing something more low key. He'd decided that spending all that money to travel to New York for the graduation ceremony was enough.

Mrs St Jean had returned exhausted from the trip to New York the previous weekend and had slept for three days straight. With the couple away, Rayna and Daniella had free rein of the house. Mrs St Jean had given Rayna serious instructions to make sure the house was spotless before their return and to make sure Darius' room was pristine.

Rayna could feel Daniella pinching her waist as Mrs St Jean delivered the instructions while dabbing her brow with a silk handkerchief. Mrs St Jean ran down the list of things to do at least three times because she kept forgetting what she'd said. Rayna had struggled to keep a straight face and the two girls collapsed on the hallway mat in fits of laughter the second Mr St Jean closed the front door and the wagon drove them to the port.

Leaving the front door wide open after they'd had a breakfast of cornmeal porridge with jam mixed into it, the girls ran into the bright sunshine. They held hands like little children and danced on the front lawn before their excitement spilled over into a game of chase. They were both so excited. Rayna felt liberated from thoughts of Darius, the regret and anger becoming a bitter memory she could stop herself visiting as often as she had been. They chased around the garden and, in her excitement, Daniella tripped on a bump in the grass and fell head first into the thorny yellow roses along the white wooden fence. Rayna froze, panicking because it looked like a serious fall. Daniella made no sound at all. She didn't even move. Slowly, Rayna approached her and knelt beside the girl whose face was buried in the clumpy soil, fallen petals outlining the place her head lay.

'Daniella?' Rayna's voice was tentative and laden with tears. She pulled Daniella gently by the shoulder and rolled her onto her back. 'Daniella? You all right?'

A white smile slowly spread on the young girl's face beneath the coating of dark earth. Just as slowly, she opened one eye. A laugh burst from her throat and she covered her lips with a chubby hand.

'If only you could see your face.' She could hardly speak through her laughter.

Rayna gently slapped her arm and pulled back onto her heels. 'How could you worry me like that?' She leant back to Daniella and gasped. 'Your head is bleeding, you have a really bad graze. Get up.'

As Daniella sat, a pool of deep red blood began to ooze from her hairline. Daniella touched her hand to it and her fingers coloured with silky crimson. She blinked and the blood dripped off her eyelashes and onto her round cheek.

'Get up,' said Rayna pulling Daniella's arms. 'This is bad. Your mother is going to kill me.'

Daniella grunted as she helped herself up. 'My mother won't even notice. You're the only one who cares.'

'All the same. We have to clean this, dress it. I wish my mother was here. She would know what to do.'

'Then let's go.'

'To my mother's house?' said Rayna squinting at the wound. 'She'll be at work. Come on. Inside.'

Rayna pulled Daniella by a bloody hand, the wound continuing to seep.

In the kitchen, Rayna did her best to clean and bandage the gash. There was too much flesh showing and the blood didn't want to stop. It soaked through the white bandage and Rayna began to cry.

'It doesn't even hurt,' said Daniella, looking apologetically at Rayna. 'They will be gone all week. It'll heal by then and my mother will never have to know.'

'I'm so sorry.'

'It's okay, it wasn't your fault.'

Daniella's glasses were broken and Rayna began to panic again. Daniella tried to reassure her, telling her constantly not to worry and not to cry. To be on the safe side, Rayna brought the girl home for her mother to take a look. Urma cleaned and dressed the cut again and told Daniella she would always have a scar but there was nothing that could be done about it. Rayna walked Daniella all the way back in the dark to the big house and vowed she wouldn't let anything else happen to Daniella for the whole week she stayed with her.

The fall was just a slight upset to the week that they went on to spend together. Rayna was thorough with her cleaning tasks but they didn't take long. For the most part, the girls sang and made music together. Daniella wanted to teach Rayna how to play the piano but Rayna thought it would be too difficult. She had done her best to keep Daniella from bringing up the idea of the two of them running away to America to become famous performers on a stage in New York. Neither had known what the country would actually be like but their imaginations were big and the time they had alone was vast.

They ate so much food at meal times they made themselves feel nauseous. They spent so long at the beach, their skin was red hot and tender. Daniella's shoulders peeled the only time Rayna could convince her that no one was around and she could afford to strip down to her slip. But they laughed at the ups and downs of the week, and when Saturday came around, Daniella cried all morning while Rayna swept the porch one last time before her mistress crossed it, Darius and her husband following solemnly behind.

*

Darius barely ate at his celebration lunch; in fact, he left the table early and went to find Rayna who was busy tidying the mess of cleaning and gutting fish in preparation for the meal. She had had to learn so many household skills along the way. After two years with the family, she had become quite an expert at keeping house and being a guardian to an adolescent girl, though she was only seventeen herself.

Darius was quiet as he sneaked up on her in the kitchen. He wrapped both arms around her waist and dragged her away from the bloody water she was using to clean away the fish guts. Her hands were wet and stained pink.

'What are you doing?' Too afraid to shout at him so as not to upset Mrs St Jean, Rayna pulled away, angry at the intrusion.

'Hey,' said Darius. 'I was only playing.' His voice had changed with each of his three-year stay in New York. He sounded like an announcer that Rayna had heard on the radio on the station she and Daniella listened to when they played the music hall songs that they loved to dance to. Rayna waving her arms and Daniella shifting her thickset hips from side to side.

'You stopped writing to me at college.' Darius' smile faltered. 'I was beginning to think you had gone off me.'

She stared hard at him, wondering how this tall, handsome and intelligent boy, who must have slept with so many girls in New York, would want to interfere with his own sister. She was not able to talk about the subject with Daniella again, so disgusted by Darius it made her stomach turn to think about him sneaking into the bedroom. Daniella was so shaken by it she had been sleeping with the door wedged shut even when Darius was away at college. But it was making Daniella feel safe and Rayna saw that the girl was gaining confidence. All it had taken was the chest of drawers as her new nighttime companion.

'What is going on with you, Rayna?' Darius was serious. 'When I've come back on my breaks, you don't even talk to me. You run away from me.'

'Your mother keeps me busy. I can't stop what I'm doing.'

'But we have an understanding, me, you and mother. It's you and me, Rayna. It's all been planned and last year you told me you loved me.'

'I did.'

'*Did*?'

'I think I was young and stupid. What do I know about love?' Her chest constricted, her already broken heart twisting into a tight red knot that failed to beat in time and which made her feel breathless. Yes, she had been young. But not stupid. She knew what she'd felt for Darius was love. She knew how much she had battled to drive those feelings for him aside and close her heart, keeping him out. He would tire of her. He would find another girl. If she stalled enough, Mrs St Jean would get bored of the wedding plans she kept on suggesting only to have Rayna bat them away. Her plan was to wait it out as long as she could, and if Darius and his mother didn't desist from the idea of marriage, then she would leave and take Daniella with her.

*

In the back room next to the kitchen, Rayna lay on the narrow bed, her ear cocked so that she could listen for any sound that Daniella might make from upstairs. A doctor had been called because Daniella had a fever. He had told Mrs St Jean to keep Daniella cool with a damp cloth and to make sure she drank lots of water. If her condition got worse, if she grew too hot, if she passed out rather than slept, then she should send for him straight away. He wasn't far.

Mrs St Jean had asked Rayna to stay overnight to attend Daniella because she was already suffering a disappointment of her own, and how was she expected to lie awake to listen to her daughter snore?

Mrs St Jean's so-called disappointment had been because of Darius' departure from the house. It was final. He'd said as much after the enormous fight he had had with his father which came to blows. Mr St Jean had called his son into the living room on Saturday afternoon. Rayna was dusting in the hallway and heard Mr St Jean ask Darius about his future. She hadn't meant to listen but she was curious to know what Darius would say and whether he would tell his father that there was no future between them and hoped he would eventually leave the house. She thought of Daniella and of keeping her safe. With him gone permanently, she could stop worrying.

Mr St Jean wanted his son to come into the retail sector like him but Darius was adamant that he wanted to travel and make up his mind later.

'You can't waste that education,' said Mr St Jean. 'It cost us an arm and a leg.'

'You can afford it.'

'Son, I have been very patient with you. I didn't say anything when you were going along with the ridiculous idea of marrying a servant girl. Indulging your mother's romantic whims of moulding the perfect girl for her son.'

'It was a ridiculous idea. I was just humouring her but I fell in love with Rayna.'

On hearing her name, Rayna stepped closer to the door. It wasn't shut tight and she angled her body to the wall so that she would not cast a shadow on the slight gap.

'And I told you that was out of the question.' The words peeled loudly from an angry Mr St Jean.

'You don't have to worry. She turned me down anyway.'

'Good. There was no chance in hell I would let my son marry a gold digger.'

'That girl has more grace than this whole family could muster. And my decision is to go to Europe and not come back.'

'Then I'll cut you off.'

'My mother will have something to say about that. You didn't have a penny until you met her. This was her house before you married her. She owns everything in it. Don't think she will allow you to cut me off.'

Rayna heard a crack like a meaty weight colliding with bone. Darius' jaw perhaps. Then she'd heard a grunt closely followed by tussling and someone falling onto the floor.

'If you raise your hand on me again, I'll kill you.' She had never heard Darius sound so menacing. In that very moment, a crash of lightning streaked the sky and an almighty storm darkened the afternoon below it. Rain began to pour. Darius yelled that he was leaving and never coming back.

'I'm glad,' his father yelled back. Rayna could hear him picking himself up from the floor. 'You're a worthless fool. Go and take the bad genes you carry from the man my damned wife spread her legs for before trapping me into thinking you were mine.'

Rayna stumbled backwards into the dining room when she heard footsteps approaching the door. The front door slammed shut. Darius had marched out into the storm and Mrs St Jean had found her way downstairs. She began to shout at her husband, begging for him to go and apologise to Darius. Rayna didn't dare to move when an almighty argument erupted between the couple. She heard Daniella bundle down the stairs imploring her parents to stop, to have more sense, to let Darius go. To let her go.

'This is not your prison, child.' Her mother rounded on her and Rayna peeked very tentatively around the door. She witnessed Mrs St Jean grow several inches taller as she shouted at Daniella.

'You! You're just like your father. Between the two of you I am ruined, and if I lose my son because of you, I'll put you out, too.' She turned to her husband. 'Both of you!' She looked unsteady on her feet and reached for the bannister. It bore her weight as she made slow progress up the stairs, Daniella and her father watching her. Once she was at the top of the stairs, Mr St Jean reached for Daniella's wrist. She pulled it away, aggressively, and then she, too, ran out into the storm, leaving the main door wide open.

Rayna stepped into the hallway, intending to run after Daniella. She stopped dead when Mr St Jean cast her a look that felt like a knife piercing her chest, slicing its way to her abdomen. She swallowed hard as he crossed the hallway to his small study where the large cabinet containing spirits was kept. He did not emerge for hours.

The rain eased somewhat before Rayna had to go home. She hovered in the doorway, securing her headscarf, tying and untying it with fidgeting fingers. The silk square slipped out of her hands and blew onto the cold and wet stone doorstep. Darius had since been back and had already packed a case and left. He'd told his mother he'd stay with friends for a while before he came for the rest of his things. The house was quiet, Mr St Jean in a dead sleep and Mrs St Jean in her bedroom sobbing between the covers, a candle lighting the bedside cabinet.

Still, there was no sign of Daniella and Rayna didn't know where on earth she could be. She had no friends and Rayna was worried sick. With a knot in her stomach, she ran home, half hoping Daniella might be there, but there was no sign of her.

'You look like you just meet a ghost,' her mother said when she stumbled through the door. 'Why you come so late?'

'I waited for the rain to stop.' Tears gathered in her eyes.

'Rayna?' Her mother reached out a hand. At the soft touch of Urma's hand on hers, Rayna collapsed into her arms and poured her heart out about the day's events.

*

It was almost daylight and Rayna had barely slept, still listening for Daniella from downstairs in the back room by the kitchen. A local man and his young son had carried a bedraggled and trembling Daniella home on the Sunday afternoon. They'd spotted her bright dress by a line of trees on the outskirts of a forest where she'd lain, cold and wet, too afraid to go further into the forest for shelter from the rain. Instead, she had been soaked to the skin, cold freezing her bones and she was near enough delirious when the doctor came. That's when Mrs St Jean sent for Rayna. Despite it being a Sunday, Rayna was happy to go to the house. It was a miracle Rayna had got her to settle. She'd tiptoed up to Daniella's room twice more, and each time, she'd been fast asleep.

Still exhausted, Rayna heard a noise from the kitchen. Mr St Jean was up, about to make his coffee and leave for work before anyone was out of bed. Rayna knew his morning routine because of the times she'd had to stay overnight. She wrapped a shawl around her and went out to see if she could make coffee for her employer.

164

'You,' he whispered in the cool, shadowy kitchen. He still appeared drunk. He'd been boozing since Saturday afternoon when Darius left and it was now Monday morning.

'I was going to make you coffee.' Rayna went for the coffee pot but Mr St Jean held her in place with his glare. His eyes were red, his lips dry and cracked and he reeked of whisky and cigarettes.

'There is only one thing I want from you and that is for you to be gone.'

'I...'

'You have caused nothing but trouble since you came here. You added to my wife's fanciful disposition. You know what they say about her is true. She *is* mad. And she was lucky that I married her because no one else would. The money was a good incentive mind you. Because I can have what I want.'

Rayna said nothing and filled a pan with water which she set to boil. Perhaps she should have left the kitchen but she was there now, and the quicker she made his damned coffee, the quicker she could excuse herself. He followed her around the table, leaning close behind her as she lit the stove.

'Because of you, I can't have everything I want,' he said in a low growl. 'I used to be able to have the girl late at night and sometimes in the early mornings if she didn't call out.'

Rayna turned slowly.

'What do you mean?' Her eyes narrowed.

'Because of you, that big old chest behind the door has stopped me and I have to put up with the sluts in town.'

'You?' Rayna's throat clenched shut. She couldn't move or breathe. Hadn't Daniella told her that it was Darius who came into her room? Mr St Jean looked at the shawl that had loosened from Rayna's shoulders and he pulled her close to him with the ends of it. She made to run but he threw her onto the kitchen table, her stomach crashing into it. Before she could right herself he'd slammed her face into the wood panels and was raising her night dress. Her body was trapped. He'd sealed her against the table and he was too heavy for her to battle him away. She tried to struggle, she did all she could but in no time she felt him enter her, a hard tight rip between her legs that made her want to wail. She wanted to but there was no sound. She couldn't cry, and she couldn't get up from the table. She heard the pan on the stove hissing and bubbling, she felt pounding in her ear as it ground into the wooden table. It was over as quickly as it had started. His weight, his body, gone from her. He staggered away and Rayna ran into the back room. There was no lock on the door so she stood behind it and put on her clothes. No one would notice if she'd left the room in a mess, didn't make the bed. But why should she care now?

Rayna wrenched at the kitchen door, forgetting it was locked and almost dislocated her shoulder in the process. Once she was free, she ran, her arms holding her cardigan closed, all the way to the sea near her home. The day before, the storm had turned the sky grey but today it was bright, the sun just risen. The sea was cold and hurt her skin, but not as much as he had.

*

When Rayna woke up, her mother was sitting by her bed looking tired.

'Mum,' Rayna whispered. 'You have work.'

'How I could go and leave you?' Her voice was small, shaky.

They sat in silence as they had done when her mother put her to bed three hours ago.

'Was that the first time?' her mother asked.

'And the last. I'll kill him.'

'No. You will go and tell her you leaving and get what money she owe you and come back.'

'Not tell her? Not tell anyone?'

'It won't do you any good and you can survive this.'

'I don't want to go back.' Then Rayna thought of Daniella. The promise she'd made not to leave her. But what could she do with her? She had no way of looking after a teenage girl. Though, she should at least tell her goodbye.

There was no one downstairs when Rayna found herself back at the big house. Climbing the stairs, she found Daniella in her bedroom doorway gesturing for Rayna to come in.

'You weren't here when I woke up,' said the girl, screwing her brow.

Rayna lowered her head. 'Why did you tell me it was Darius?'

'What was Darius?'

'The one who came into your room at night. Did those things to you.'

'I didn't.'

'Yes, you did.' Rayna raised her voice. Daniella shook her head.

'I only said Darius was a bad man, you just thought I meant him. I didn't want you to go off with him.'

'So you made me believe it was him. So that's why you kept the chest by the door even when he wasn't here.'

Now Daniella looked down. 'He said he would kill me. Take me by the bay and drown me.'

'It was a threat,' said Rayna. 'Like he said he would cut out your tongue. He wouldn't have done it.'

'I was a child. I believed it.'

Rayna shook her head and crossed her arms. 'And so he did it to me. He raped me.'

Both girls turned to see Mrs St Jean emerging slowly from her bedroom.

'She's making you lie, too?' Her mistress was shaking, holding onto the wall for balance.

'It wasn't a lie.' Rayna flew at her, making Mrs St Jean stumble backwards. 'How could you let him do that to your own daughter all this time. She is your child, your girl. How could you?'

Mrs St Jean shook her head from side to side, her hand pressed against her cheek and then both hands at her ears as she fled, back to her own bedroom. Rayna chased after her.

'My mother says I can't tell the police but I want what you owe me. Two weeks' wages.'

'Rayna, you know I have no money here. He has to bring it on Friday.'

'I'm not coming back. I want it today and then I'm gone.'

Daniella rushed up to her and wrapped her arms around Rayna's waist from behind. 'No. You can't leave me here. You have to take me.'

'Rayna,' said Mrs St Jean. 'Take these.' She pulled open a small drawer in her dressing table and pulled out a handful of expensive looking rings, a bracelet and a necklace Rayna had once admired. 'Take these to sell in town. Come back with the money so I can give you your wages. But you have to promise me you will not breathe a word of this to a soul.'

Rayna looked down at the treasure Mrs St Jean placed into her palm and wrapped her fingers around it. 'It's a lot,' said Rayna, feeling Daniella's arms tighten around her.

'It is,' said Mrs St Jean, beginning to regain her composure. 'But I can keep the rest of the cash you bring back. It might come in handy one day.'

Rayna unravelled the girl and looked at her. 'I have to do this one thing and then I'll come back.'

'And take me, too?' Fear rose from the girl. Rayna could see it in her eyes, feel it in her trembling hands, clammy over the ones she held the jewels in.

'Daniella.' Rayna put the jewellery into her skirt pocket. 'Listen. You can't really believe that I can take you from here. You can't.'

'I can work,' the girl implored. Hands in prayer at her chest. 'I can do anything. Just don't leave me.'

'Let her go to town, silly girl,' hissed her mother. 'We'll talk when she comes back. Hurry Rayna.'

Rayna ran down the stairs, a small bleat coming from Daniella as she descended, and Rayna didn't have the heart to look back at her.

She left the house with every intention to sell the jewels, give Mrs St Jean the balance of the money and say a proper goodbye to Daniella, with a promise that someday she would make it possible for them to get away somewhere, together. But after just two steps along the path, she hesitated and felt her pocket for the shining jewellery. Was it enough to get her away completely? The escape she wanted so badly, away from poverty and her broken-down home. But what about her mother? She would take her, too, of course, though it would be difficult to persuade her to leave. She took another slow step away from the house and heard an upstairs window open. Daniella's cry tore into the air.

'Rayna! Rayna, please. Please, Rayna. No!'

Rayna walked away, not stopping once to look back.

Part Two

The Truth

<h1 style="text-align:center">26</h1>

The rain hits the skylight in the bathroom in rhythmic pulses. The tiny bath tub stands on carved legs a few inches above the wooden floorboards. There is no rug, no linoleum, just the look of a place well used and needing care. With no light bulb in the bathroom, either, Rayna cannot see the crack in the ceiling, the peeling white paint that flakes so badly it could fall away at any moment and land like crisp autumn leaves.

The door to the bathroom is open and a table lamp with a psychedelic shade casts a burnt orange tint into the bathroom. Rayna rests her head back and looks up to the sky. It is about three in the morning, not light yet. All she can see is the square window and raindrops, like tiny beads bouncing onto the pane.

She closes her eyes and lets the calm sound of Coltrane seep through the open door as the water gently laps at her chest. The water has been slowly cooling; she'll have to get out soon and wrap up warm.

Rayna and Eddie had walked the short distance from *Le Chat* to the main road and caught a taxi. It was chilly in the street and is equally so in Eddie's flat. The bath and his arms are the warmest things in the place.

Her show had been pretty ordinary. L'Olympia in the 9th arrondissement in Paris was sold out. The crowd was welcoming and the orchestra probably the biggest that Rayna had ever sung with before. She couldn't believe the size of the stage as she stood in her drainpipe slacks and ballerina pumps, surrounded by the enormous faux fur coat she hugged to her body. Sol had outdone himself again. But the European audience loved Rayna. As Sol said, they could not get enough of her, but after touring the world for ten years, living in hotels, jumping on planes and performing in cities she'd forgotten the names of, she had grown weary. She wasn't ungrateful. Not in the slightest; she felt blessed for every second of those years. She still enjoyed the moment the curtains opened on stage, lights focusing in on her, their warmth and brightness and the people. They did love her and she loved to sing for them. They had given her a life she never thought possible. As a seventeen-year-old, she had dreamt of having more. She'd had love and money in her grasp then but it had been pulled away only seconds after being dangled in front of her. But something, deep inside her, hoped that one day she would escape what life had dealt her back then. She just didn't realise that singing would be her escape. She had once scoffed at the idea of making a living by singing on stage. And even now, she looks at the silk fabrics, the elegance, the landscapes and her decadent lifestyle for several moments before she realises it's all true. She has achieved more than she ever dreamt of.

She had slipped on her fur coat and escaped via a side exit to avoid the fans at the stage door. She looked like any other woman going for a walk on a cool Paris evening, except it's spring and a fur coat is excessive but that hadn't occurred to her when she ran off after the show. She had walked quite some distance from L'Olympia before noticing a taxi which she hailed and asked the driver to take her to The Latin Quarter. That's when she saw the narrow white building, the black door and the black awning with a drawing of a white cat in a bow tie on it. She'd spotted the A-board and the words, Eddie Keane Quartet, and asked the driver to stop. Jumping out, she handed him a bundle of francs and ran back to *Le Chat* where people were smoking and talking outside with tall beer glasses. So engaged in conversation they hadn't spotted the singer enter the premises and follow the sound of the music into the cellar bar.

It had been hot and airless. The room was thick with perfume, sweat and nicotine, but the band was tight and the musicians played with their eyes closed for the most part. Rayna sat by a clammy brick wall painted sky blue and listened and watched Eddie's smooth movements and realised that she had made the biggest mistake of her life letting him go.

On the other side of the main room in his apartment, Eddie wears nothing but a shirt. He mixes a whisky and Coke into the only clean tumblers left in the small kitchenette and walks into the bathroom with the drinks.

'I should come out,' Rayna says. 'The water is getting cold. Do you have a towel?'

'Here.' Eddie places the glasses on the shelf above the sink. Pulling a large white towel from the hook on the door, he holds it up. Rayna steps out of the bath, her body shinning as she looks up at Eddie.

'Thank you for running it for me, but you must be tired after your gig.'

'Not too tired to make you comfortable.'

Rayna dabs her body with the towel and wraps it around her shoulders. She shivers as if the faster pace of the rain outside falls on her through the skylight.

'You're cold. Here, let me.' Eddie rubs Rayna dry. She looks down at her body. She is still in good shape at thirty-four, but she wishes Eddie could have seen her naked years ago. But years ago, she was in love with Terry. She shakes images from her mind that don't belong in this moment.

With the towel tight around her chest, Rayna follows Eddie into the living room.

'This place,' Rayna says, stopping to look about her for the first time since they arrived. 'Why are you here and not in a hotel?'

'I bought this place. It's where I stay when I'm in Paris.'

'Why would you keep such a rundown apartment?'

'Oh, I don't know. Something about the cracks takes me back. I bought it for me and you all those years ago. A fantasy I had that we could write music here, live here. Just us two. Decorate it together.'

'So you keep it like this as a memento? One you never told me about.'

'How could I? There was Terry, your career. That all happened so fast. One minute I thought … and then you were gone. Like I said. A fantasy. A friend was renting it for years. It is a shame I didn't fix it up because it had potential.'

Just outside the tall windows is a balcony. Rayna imagines Eddie stepping out onto it and playing his saxophone to the rooftops. The sound carrying across La Seine to Montmartre; it would stop the busy traffic by day and lull lovers to sleep by night.

'We could have lived here happily together,' Rayna says. She sits on the sunken sofa and tucks her legs underneath her, still shivering. Eddie lifts an old blanket from over the back of the sofa and wraps it around her shoulders. An aroma of fifty strong French cigarettes a day for several years wafts from it, the scent of a history they hadn't shared in this apartment. With his arm around her, she rests her head on his chest.

'I left our drinks in the bathroom,' he says and tuts.

'It's not exactly a room. Just a partition. I'm surprised the place doesn't fall down.'

'Okay, so it's no palace.' He chuckles. 'But it always feels like home to me.'

'Eddie?' Rayna shifts so that she can see his face. Read it. His thin moustache always moves upwards when he smiles and curves downwards when he plays his saxophone. There is no movement as he waits. 'Is there someone in your life now?' she asks.

'You could say that.'

'Well, is it serious? Is she likely to walk in that door?'

'It's a bit late to ask me that now.'

'Will she?'

'No. She's in London.'

'Waiting for you?'

'Like Terry is waiting for you.'

'He shouldn't be. We've been miserable for so long. I should put us both out of our misery and end it.'

'Those words are music to my ears, Rayna. If you mean them.'

'It's so strange. When I'm away, he moves back into the pub, leaving a perfectly good house standing in Notting Hill Gate, cobwebs and dust everywhere and I have to get some-one to clean it before I come home.'

Eddie takes her hand in his and kisses her fingers as he looks up at her, his large hazel eyes, looking sad now.

'You have to decide, Rayna. I feel as if my whole life I've been waiting for you to see me.'

'And I do. I won't be back in London for another month or so. I'll end it with him then.' She looks deep into his eyes; they are joyful in an instant. 'And your ... who ever she is in London?'

'Gone. I'm back next week. I'll tell her goodbye and I'll wait for you to come to me.' He pulls her to her feet and walks Rayna to the large bed in the corner of the room. 'The Dominican mystery woman,' he says and laughs. Rayna puts her arms around his neck and the blanket on her shoulders slips away. 'Will I ever discover what's behind those eyes, that smile?'

'If you knew, you wouldn't love me and you wouldn't wait for me, Eddie. I am what you see right here in front of you. If you look for anything else, it won't match up to the person you've been waiting for. There's just me now. Is it enough?'

He nods and holds her waist tighter, giving a weak laugh. 'Look Rayna, I don't need to know your past. I just want your future.'

'And tonight we have that, right?' She smiles as Eddie picks her up in his arms and lifts her onto the unmade bed. The ceiling slopes above it. Strips of wallpaper hang like flags on the wall above the headboard. The sheets are worn and smell of their love-making, her perfume, his cologne. He lays her gently on her back and removes his shirt. She reaches out her hands to hold him and he gently releases the damp barrier the towel makes between their skin and lowers his body to hers.

'I'm a mystery to myself sometimes,' she says in a whisper. 'I wish I knew who I was.'

Their lips meet. There are no more words, just two bodies, entwined on the bed until light, until the birds sing outside.

The sun shines onto the psychedelic lamp and steals its electric light, drowning it in a white haze. Eddie phones for the taxi that whisks Rayna away.

27

Terry is fascinated by the young black woman who walks into the bar. She is new to the area, he can tell. By the way she dresses, she doesn't appear to be doing half bad for herself, and he wonders what brings her here, to his place, and if, perhaps, she's lost. She has a round face, cute, no make-up and a small afro. Her large silver hooped earrings cause a glint as she looks around. It's early evening. The late spring afternoon has faded to a soft hue of greyish dusk that is the backdrop of her slim figure as she stands, taking in her surroundings. Her slacks are narrow at the thighs and flare out at the knee – typical sixties fashion – and someone as young as she looks can pull it off. But you wouldn't catch him in a pair of those things. He admires her style, from the high-healed boots to the shaggy bomber jacket and the gypsy style blouse with the drawstring neckline. Her large eyes skim across the punters as if searching for one in particular. Sipping their beers and spirits, they keep one eye on their drinks, the other on her. Terry cannot take his eyes off her and finally the young woman rests her gaze on him. He feels the muscles in his stomach tense. He straightens up, relaxing his shoulders when, at last, she smiles.

The door creaks shut behind her as she saunters in like a regular who has entered the pub a million times before. At the central point of the long bar, she props a leather patchwork shoulder bag and eases herself onto a stool. Without re-alising what the other is doing, both Terry and Sandra head straight for her from opposite ends of the bar.

'Can I help you?'

'What you having, love?'

Terry and Sandra speak at the same time and the young woman looks bemused and smiles at them both. Her teeth are white against her plum-coloured lips.

'Well, I only want one drink.' It's an American accent she has. Terry was right about her not being local. He knew there was something different about her, but at the same time, there is also something very familiar.

She turns from one to the other, her eyes dwelling for a few moments longer on Terry.

'I'll let the boss serve you as you're new in town.' Sandra, who has been eyeing the woman with as much intensity as Terry, steps away and calls over the counter to another of their customers.

'All right, Dave, keep your 'air on. What you having, then?'

The young American keeps her eyes on Terry.

'So – what will it be?' Terry stutters.

'Um, let me have a whisky.' She casts a quick glance at the row of drinks behind Terry. He leans towards her on his el-bow across the bar and looks at the bottles of spirits, too, the ceiling lights reflecting on them all.

'Tell you what,' he says. 'I'll let you have some of my spe-cial reserve.' He smiles at her though she says nothing. 'It's what I drink all the time. Try some?'

She nods.

Terry looks at her in the mirror behind the bottles as he pours the whisky. He watches as she looks around the pub.

As if she is taking in every aspect of the interior. Her eyes hover on the door leading out to the flat, and when they land on the piano, they stay for a long moment until she grins to herself and looks away. There is a sort of haughtiness in her manner that he can't understand or thinks he misunderstands. She must just be curious. They can't have pubs like The Pelican in America. No wonder she's eyeing everything up.

Terry places the glass in front of her and she stares at it before taking a sip.

'I'm no expert,' she says, 'but this is good.'

He has to go now, serve another customer, but Terry returns throughout the evening to chat with her. Her name is Nell, she's from Michigan but was last in New York. She has no other family.

'So why London? Why here?' Terry asks. It's close to him calling time and he wishes he didn't have to. He turns to Sandra. 'It's been a quiet night, why don't you go home?'

Sandra looks at the young woman. 'You sure? Can you clear up on your own?'

He nods as the last few punters, bar one, heaves their coats and jackets on. Nell stays put as she watches Sandra and the others leave, running a finger around her empty glass on the counter.

'Sorry, did you want another?' Terry reaches for the bottle that he has also been topping up his own tumbler with.

'I think I might be at my limit. But go on. I can call a cab from here to my hotel.'

'What hotel you staying at?'

'Somewhere near Knightsbridge. I forget the name.'

'So how will you get back?'

'I'm sure it'll come to me. But I better make this my last or I'll never remember.'

The last customer gets up and leaves. A regular who salutes Terry and gently nods.

'I guess I should be going,' says Nell. 'I wanted a bit of British hospitality and I think I've had my fill.' Nell's jacket is thrown across the stool beside her, her bag beneath it. So far, she hasn't paid for a single drink. Terry has refused her each time.

'I hope we meet your approval,' says Terry. 'It can be a bit of a rough old place. The people can be. I did renovate the whole pub recently.' Terry walks around to Nell's side of the bar, hands in his pockets. He looks up and around, proud of how his pub is looking. The local area has been decaying and new plans for knocking down houses and putting in high rises are on the cards for the houses down Tavistock Crescent and beyond. It'll be unrecognisable, he thinks, but people will always want drinks, so he doesn't think he'll go out of business.

'It's a nice place you have here...'

'Terry. It's Terry. I did tell you but maybe you've had one too many of those.' There is a drizzle of whisky left at the bottom of her glass. He reaches out a hand to shake hers. Maybe he can delay her a bit more. There is something about this woman that he finds familiar but is also so very new to him. He hopes he can persuade her to come back. Her fingers are not long but her hands are graceful. There are several silver rings on her right hand. No wedding ring on the left. Just a silver charm bracelet, the cheap kind that she could have picked up from the Portobello Road. Her expensive clothes, cheap jewellery, the very fact she is an American in an English pub in North Kensington is a bag of contradictions and she fascinates him further. She's young, though. A bigger age gap than the one between him and Rayna probably, and look how that turned out. She grew up and grew away from him. Though she is coming home soon and she says they need to talk. He can't think about that now.

'We did use to have music playing in here once upon a time.' He nods to the piano with a big dust cover draped over it and the dirty ashtray that sits on top of it. 'Great jazz band every Friday night for a good five years or more.'

'The same band every Friday?'

'I love my jazz and they were a great band. Got too good for in here, mind. All took off to do bigger, better gigs. Eddie Keane. He was the band leader.'

'My God. *The* Eddie Keane?'

'The very one. I discovered him at some dive in the West End. Begged him to come and play here. He was just this lanky nobody. A boy really but bloody talented. Excuse my French.'

She waves this off. 'I saw him play in New York. He's a jazz master. I often wonder how he didn't team up with Miles Davis. Seen him a few times, too.'

'So you're a jazz lover.'

'It's my music, Terry. I grew up on it.'

Terry's cheeks blaze and he straightens his posture. Nell has swung her legs around to face the piano and looks as if she is picturing the scene on a Friday night. He perches himself on the stool beside her and leans towards her.

'I've got a massive collection of jazz music upstairs,' he says. 'Not being funny, like, but you wanna see it. It dates way back, back to before you were born, probably.'

'I'm not as young as I look.' She grins at him and sinks the last of her whisky. She picks up her jacket and plumps it on her thighs but she isn't getting up to go.

'So you go and see lots of jazz bands in New York?' Terry asks quickly.

'As often as I can, if I'm not working.'

'You never did tell me what you do?'

'You never asked.'

'Well then?'

'I'm a performer. Of jazz.'

Terry thinks his chest might explode. It lifts so high it almost transcends his collared shirt and the knitted vest top that fits tightly to him.

'You have got to be joking me.' He takes a quick glance at the stage. 'And so are you performing in London? Is that why you're here?'

She giggles like a child, puts a hand over her lips and hides her smile. 'So many questions at once. I feel like I'm being interrogated.'

'Oh, I am sorry. I get like that. It's just, I find it all so special. To have the talent to be able to perform music to people. Music is like life to me. I live every note, every pattern, every riff the guitarist plays, every lick of the bass and beat of the drum. I just go off into like a trance or something. I don't know. I just know I love it.'

'Do you play?'

'Never learnt. But I wish I could. Never had the opportunity. It wasn't the done thing in our house. Working-class family from Bromley. Only thing that got played was an old gramophone. Even that packed up in the end. I didn't even ask what you do. Sing?'

'I sing and I play piano. I'm touring right now. I'm support act for The Arthur Simpson Band. They've got a few nights and my agent managed to get me on their bill.'

'You've got an agent and everything. You must be quite big over there.' Terry slaps his hand to his forehead and stands up. He swings around to face Nell. 'I kept wondering why I thought I knew you.'

'You thought you knew me? How?'

'I seen you on the television. You were in a band, a trio. You weren't singing but you were playing the piano. You were on that American show we get here. The Stevie Allen Show.'

'Guilty. I was filling in for someone who got in a car accident. They didn't want a girl. Didn't think I could learn the rep so fast. But I showed them.'

'You bloody well did. I remember how you played because it stood out.' Terry looks quickly at the piano. 'How long you in London for?'

'The show runs to Saturday and then I'm on a plane.' Nell stands and puts on her jacket. She shrugs it closed and zips it to her neck then reaches for her bag.

'And what if I asked if you could stay on in London for a bit?' Terry raises his hands in supplication. 'Of course, I'll pay for the hotel and a return ticket. That is, of course, if you could honour us and play at this place.'

'You want me to play at your pub?'

'It sounds mad but I promise I ain't lost the plot. It's been such a long, long time since there was live music. The only music pub nearby has all those hippie types come in and the music is so depressing you'd slit your wrist. Not that anyone'd notice with all that cannabis they smoke. Bloody creepy lot.'

Nell laughs like a teenage girl, giggly and loud, as she crosses the strap of her shoulder bag across her body.

'Could you call me a cab, Terry?'

'Um, yes. So does that mean it's a no?'

'It's a why not.' She grins up at him. 'I was hoping I could stick around. I don't have anything to rush back for. I've got some dates in a nightclub back home, but not until the fall. I have a whole summer to kick back. I've never been to London before but I know people who have, and from what I can tell, they fair pretty well. I could use some of that. Know what I mean?'

Terry looks quizzically at her and shrugs. 'All I know is that if we can come to some sort of arrangement, then I'd have you perform here every night until you decide to go home.'

'My, that's ambitious. You sure I won't get turned away by your wife? She might think it's a bit fishy you getting a young girl in here *every* night.'

'I don't have a wife.'

'Oh?'

'Well, I sort of live with someone.'

'Now who's the hippie? Free love. Isn't that what they're all about?'

'I wanted to marry her. Kept on asking but she turned me down.'

'But you live together.'

'Well – yeah. If you can call it that. She's out of the country a lot.'

'You must miss her.'

'God's honest?'

She nods.

'I never knew love could damage a bloke.'

'But you love her all the same.'

Terry waves his hands and rubs them over his face as if he is washing his memories of love away.

'Forget all that,' he says. 'If you're up for it, I can call you and arrange the gigs with you. Fair warning, though. I'm not made of money, probably can't pay you much, like, but I'll do my best.'

'Just for the sake of having music in here again?'

'I want to come back to life, Nell. Music does that for me. And if you sing as good as you played on that show, well…' He raises both hands. 'I'll be reborn.'

Nell gives Terry the name of her hotel and he writes it down. He scribbles the number of The Pelican on the bottom half of the sheet, tears it off and Nell pops it into the back pocket of her jeans. He telephones the black cab company and they have another whisky while they wait. Terry spends the whole time trying to persuade Nell to play a tune but she refuses every time, saying she's had too much to drink and he'll change his mind and cancel the whole thing if she messes up.

He walks out onto the street when the taxi comes and rocks back and forth on his heels as he watches the taxi pull away with Nell waving from the back window. He goes in and locks up, leaving the clearing up of the stark pub until morn-ing. Rayna will be back soon. He'll have a few more nights sleeping here and then he'll go to the house before she's back in London again.

28

Terry might be waiting for her but Rayna doesn't go straight home. She has a few places she has to be first. Seeing Terry, talking to him, is the thing she wants to put to the back of her mind. She doesn't know how it will end but she's afraid. She hopes to find refuge on stage for a few hours: a gig in London Terry has no idea she'll be performing at. No one does, not even her agent, Sol. Just her, Eddie and his band, and very soon, the waiting audience. For now, she lets nostalgia lead her way.

On this late spring evening at Ronnie Scott's, Rayna steps up to her microphone. Her eyes are turned downwards, her step soft across the familiar stage. In the low lighting, a mist of cigarette smoke moves across the room, invisible and odourless to those who frequent the club. These jazz lovers only notice the music. They listen with respect, they listen with intelligence to the complicated sounds.

Rayna, dressed in a simple shift dress of navy silk, wears high heels and deep red lipstick. Her hair is swept away from her face into an elegant up-do with small flowers threaded through her straightened hair.

She is not sure how she will be received by this jazz audience that sits in quiet anticipation. She had turned her back on the jazz standards in favour of the popular music that had a much wider appeal. Not one fan who'd bought her records and contributed to her fame would be in this audience. Rayna knows full well that the choice she'd made to become a cabaret singer led to the stardom, the wealth, the ability to travel the world and to live in a large and fashionably decorated house in West London. But at the back of her mind, she always wonders what would have become of her had she stayed rooted in jazz. Would she have come so far? Eddie is famous and well known but doesn't earn as much as she does, neither do his records sell as well. The jazz market is a niche market and she wonders if the crowd at Ronnie's wants her to fail because she ran away from them.

Then it happens, as with every one of her performances; the second she opens her mouth and tilts back her head, just a little, she is transported. Eddie Keane's Jazz Quartet plays, their unexpected guest singer is centre stage. She allows the band's vibrancy to feed her; her passion for the music exudes through her eyes, her movements and her voice. She raises her left hand as she usually does and traces the melody in tiny circles with her delicate fingers. She has won the crowd over. She can feel it, the rapture, and it makes her voice soar.

'I told you, Rayna. Jazz music, that's where your home is.' Eddie's hand is on her bare arm when they are backstage after the performance.

'I loved it,' she says.

Eddie looks disappointed by this simple reply. For years he has been trying to persuade her to take to the stage with him. As precarious as their relationship has been, whenever he had the opportunity to speak to her, he would talk about jazz music and try to coax her back. Even if she didn't sing with his band. Their set was as alive as the days on the tiny stage at The Pelican. It brought back the atmosphere and vibrations of those times: the faces in the audience, the young, the old, the mix of cultures, the good times, the bad times and the sense of community.

'This is your world, Rayna,' Eddie insists as he dries out his saxophone. 'I have so many songs I wrote for you to sing. We must record them. We have to.'

'I never knew.'

'How could you? I have said nothing in all these years. Except now.' He draws closer but she steps away because the band members are in the room and it's not fair on Terry to have this closeness between them discussed or broadcast before she can explain herself to him.

'Things might have been different if I hadn't been an eager young thing, so desperate for fame I would have sung the Lord's prayer if it got me out of poverty.' She grins and searches for her coat. The band has one more set to perform, late into the night. 'But Sol convinced me that jazz was dying.'

'Jazz will never die. Jazz is in your soul and that doesn't die. Even after your last breath, the soul will travel on. That's not what I call dying.'

'Your music will live forever, Eddie, and maybe one day, we will record something.' She puts her coat over her shoulders and he watches her sadly. 'But I have to go.'

'Stay for a drink, watch the next set.'

'Before I go home, I need to stop off somewhere and it's already late.'

She slips out of the back room, out of the club and onto Frith Street. It's a mild night and there are lots of people around. Soho buzzes with energy and fashionable people who are loud and don't notice Rayna Laurence walking by them. When she slams the taxi door, the buzz is blotted out in seconds.

'Basing Street,' she tells the cabbie. 'Near Portobello Road.'

'I know the one.'

Very shortly, he pulls up outside the tall Victorian house. Tatty but familiar, she looks up at the first floor window, the room she used to occupy all those years ago. There's a light on up there and a memory of a skinny, sad and lost girl flits across her mind for a brief second and is gone. She tiptoes up the cemented steps at the front of the house and thanks the air above her head that the light is on and Junie is home. The curtain of the bay window twitches and then opens wide. Junie's smile is enormous, her large lamp on the table by the window is like a spotlight and Rayna winces.

'Can I come in?' Before she finishes the sentence, she hears Junie's door unlock and she stands at the front door in men's pyjamas, her hair wrapped in a scarf and her smile as bright as Rayna remembers. They haven't seen each other in almost nine years and their letters to each other have dwindled. Mostly because of Rayna's schedule and she knows Junie is not a keen writer. She writes with large, childlike writing but her words have always provided Rayna with comfort, much the same way as Junie made Rayna feel so safe and wanted in those days. She spoke the same patois, they were close in age and could have been the best of friends if they'd only met back home.

They hug for a long moment and Junie pulls Rayna inside by her hand.

'You look so beautiful, Rayna. I get so excited when I see you on the television.'

'You have a television now?' She looks around the cluttered room where notebooks and boxes fill the space around the bed, the sofa and the coffee table. There is a table by the window covered in more pieces of paper, some pens and a huge box with odds and ends that Rayna can see are clothes and children's toys. Rayna has always offered to buy presents for Junie, including a television, but Junie would never hear of it, claiming she'd send everything straight back if Rayna dared.

'I don't have a TV but my boyfriend has.' Junie's cheeks are hot.

'Ooh, Junie, you never told me you had a boyfriend.'

'It's new. A white man. John is his name. He's so good to me and he works at the hospital pushing beds and things.'

'Nice.'

'Well, not compared to being a superstar.'

'If anyone is a superstar, Junie, it has to be you.'

'Don't be silly. Let me get you some tea.'

'It's all right, I won't stay long but I needed to speak to you.'

The women sit on the sofa, side by side, and Rayna looks around the room.

'I'm sorry it's a mess,' says Junie, following Rayna's eyes. 'But I have to keep track of everyone, remember where they go so I can forward letters to and from the right people.' She looks at the boxes and the open one with clothes and toys in it. 'It's tough when your writing is not so good but I'm getting better and better.'

'You work miracles with those poor women and their children, Junie, and I want to help you.'

Junie chuckles. 'And when would you ever find time, Rayna?'

Back before Rayna was famous, before she moved out of Basing Street, Junie had been supplying refuge to women

who had been physically and mentally abused by their part-
ners. It had started with just one woman, Junie had said.
Rayna had seen a procession of the ones that Junie helped,
coming and going from the Basing Street lodgings, Junie
supplying a bed and sometimes trying to put the women in
touch with places that could provide a few more nights,
maybe look after their children. One of the hardest things
that Junie had ever done was to reveal to Rayna just how
badly she had suffered at the hands of an abusive husband.
She had been lucky, she'd told her. She got away. Rayna
hadn't forgotten those words because she, too, had been
lucky: she got away and she found wealth. She had more
money now than she needed and it was still coming in. For
all of her sins, the things she still hasn't revealed to another
living person in London, she wants to make amends.

'I want to buy you a house, Junie. A shelter for the women
you help. I have the money and I can help you. You need this
and so do these women.'

Junie stares at her, tears filling her eyes. She will not accept expensive gifts for herself, Rayna knows this, but she
can see that Junie will accept this on behalf of the women
and their children.

'You really mean it, don't you?' Junie doesn't wait for an
answer, she throws herself at Rayna and wraps her arms
around her, tears like a waterfall as she chokes her thanks.
'I'll name it after you.'

'No, never. I don't want that. I just want to give back
somehow.' She raises her eyes upwards. 'Show I'm thankful
for what I have now, considering where I came from.'

'You don't believe in God.'

'You're right, I don't. But my heart is pulling me to do this.
I haven't stopped thinking about it. Every letter you ever

wrote me, when you weren't asking after me, you were telling me about the women, wishing you could do more. And now you can, Junie. What you do, it's bigger than just these four walls.'

'So much bigger. Just like me. Just like you. The two Dominican nobodies who became somebody. This work helps me make amends for my past. I can't ever escape it but with every woman I help, I feel as if I'm being forgiven.'

Rayna holds Junie's hands. Neither has told the other the whole truth. Sometimes the past should just remain there. Sometimes there is just no room for some truths in your present.

29

Terry waits patiently for Nell in the narrow road at the side of the theatre. The door keeps opening and he expects her to appear, but each time the door makes a low sweep of the thick mat just inside, the wrong face emerges. A man comes out carrying two full sacks of rubbish. He walks to the end of the road and dumps them down with a sigh. He lights up a cigarette before he goes back inside and shoves the brick that holds the door open with his foot so that the door closes and locks behind him. A man and a woman in formal grey clothes exit next. The door shuts behind them as they hurry past Terry, sounding important and talking about dates and flight times. Still no sign of Nell and he wonders if he got the details correct. *Straight after the main act, I'll be at the exit at the side of the building, in the alleyway. Or you can wait for me on the sidewalk in front of the theatre if you prefer.* He'd told Nell that he'd prefer to wait at the side. He didn't know why he'd said that. It wasn't as if anyone would spot him waiting to take some young girl out for a drink. It wasn't as if it would get back to Rayna. And if it did, would she care? But he'd care. In the ten years they'd been together, he'd never once been unfaithful. He thought she'd been the same. True to him. Yes, there had been the times when he knew she'd been in touch with Eddie, but they were old friends; all three of them went back a long way. They wouldn't do that to him and he wouldn't do that to Rayna. Whatever went missing from their relationship would come back. He just needed to be patient. Even in the times when he'd been so angry with her, so sick of missing her because the last tour was too long and the next tour was coming around too quickly. When Rayna was away, that big house somehow got twice as big and he went back to stay at The Pelican. It had never felt like his house but God how he missed her when she wasn't in it.

How he would explain Nell to her, he wasn't sure. This compulsion he'd had to call Nell the next day, to see her again so quickly was strong. But she was someone who shared his love of music, that was all. He told himself that on the tube train into town. That he needed someone who could understand him. This person was no longer Rayna. Her world was no longer the jazz world. Her world was designer dresses, parties, toffee-nosed types who sat in their living room at the big house and drank all of Rayna's expensive champagne. Hangers-on, he called them. She didn't really like them much herself, yet there they were, laughing and clinking glasses when he came home after closing, exhausted and tired of chatter, the sound of drinks being poured and drunk people lolling around as if they might fall out of their seats at any moment. All he wanted was to put his feet up, cuddle up with Ray. Talk to her. So, when he knew the hangers-on were there, he'd stay at the pub. Rayna would understand.

'You're here!' Nell is wearing a maxi-length coat with tassels down the front. She has high-heeled boots on with a square heel, maybe a short skirt because he can see a stockinged leg with each stride she makes towards him.

''Course I am. Said I would be.' Terry stubs out a cigarette and goes to light another. He remembers his manners and offers one to Nell.

'Actually, I'll pass. It'll do nothing for my singing voice.'

'And my God, what a voice it is.' Terry had been enchanted by her musicianship and had been aching to see her after the show. 'I mean, your piano playing is excellent, don't get me wrong, but it's a rare talent to do two instruments at once. Because it is an instrument. A voice. Right?'

She smiles broadly at him. 'So where are we going, Terry?'

'I didn't think that through. I suppose the pubs will be closing now.'

'I'm hungry, there'll be something open in Soho, for sure, even if it's a food truck.'

'Food truck.' He chuckles. 'You'll get me all American soon. Sidewalks, food trucks. Ha! That's funny.'

She links his arm as they cross a busy street. He feels a warm, or is it a hot feeling, sweeping from his arm and round to his chest. He begins to perspire.

'You all right? You've gone quiet.' She looks up at him.

Terry pulls at his tie to loosen it. 'Fine. I'm fine.' But something warns him about how he is feeling. It isn't fine. It's what he accuses Rayna of feeling when he knows she's met up with *him*. Eddie. He's not so sure this is a good idea any more. Is there such a thing as an innocent drink with a lovely young woman when yours is out of town?

'Are you sure?' she asks.

'Absolutely. We'll find somewhere to eat.'

They are walking quickly down Piccadilly and she is still linking his arm. She looks up and grins at him.

'I suppose we could order room service from my room,' she says, as if he had just put the thought into her head. 'Or, we could go back to your pub. It'll be empty and you could show me that record collection you were bragging about.'

He stops. 'Well, I weren't bragging, like. I mean, it's a big collection but I just thought you might like to see it.'

'And I would.' She giggles, hand over her mouth.

'What? You mean now?' he says. 'Won't they miss you at the hotel?'

'The band? No, they're at another hotel, anyway. My agent booked this one for me. But if we're going to the pub, should we jump in a cab?'

Before he can respond, she sticks out a hand, but the black cab she tries to hail goes whizzing by.

'There's a knack,' Terry says, but before he can show her what he means, she steps around him and whistles through her fingers, bringing a taxi to a halt just inches from where they stand.

'Is that what you meant?' she asks, jumping in and winking at Terry.

'That's it exactly.'

*

The Pelican is as deathly as a morgue. It's surprising how the life drains from the inner walls when there is no one inside. Terry and Nell stand at the door behind the bar looking into the gloom, seeing nothing more than the silhouette of chairs and stools stacked upside down on the tables like the statues of dancers caught in a strange and drunken dance. Cigarette and cigar smoke laces the air and alcohol entwines with it as if the glasses were seconds from being drained and cigarette butts were only recently stubbed out. But there is something else about The Pelican that is missing. It's the history of the place. Booze and smoke you'd expect but the pub's heart has been ripped from it. The changing times have brought new

drinkers, a different type of punter. The atmosphere they create is not the same as it used to be. Terry's rough old crowd
and the idiosyncrasies of some of his regulars are missing
now. It happened slowly, over time. People stopped coming,
moved on. The jazz music pulsing through the evening, albeit for just one night of the week, had pumped life into the
heart of The Pelican. The pub feels like an empty shell.

The idea of Nell filling the void excites Terry. She excites
him, too, if he were to admit it. Standing in such close proximity, looking into the darkness and hearing the light sound
of her breath, inhaling the sweet scent of her perfume, he can
feel himself awakening.

'So, what should we grab a bottle of?' Terry clicks a switch
and the lights over the bar flicker on. 'My special reserve?'

'Yes, please. But I won't drink as much as last time. It
made my head hurt the next morning.'

Terry pours two generous tumblers of whisky. 'Look, if
you're going to sing in a pub, you have to get used to people
buying you drinks. They always did when the band played
here.'

'And did everyone in the band get drunk?'

'Only on excitement.' He hands a glass to her.

'And who was your special favourite in the band?' She
looks away as she asks, over to the piano.

'Um, no special favourite. I don't think so.'

'Oh come on, Terry. You've gone all red, so I guess there
must have been someone. Another female pianist.'

'Singer. Rayna Laurence was with the band for a while.'

Nell shakes her head, a crease forming between her brows.

'Come on,' says Terry. 'You must know Rayna Laurence.
She's a huge star. Not in jazz but she's on the telly, tours
around the world. Where you been?'

'Growing up, getting my life together and playing my own music.' She takes a generous sip.

'She'll be glad you're not an adoring fan. She puts up with them but they can be tedious, she says.'

'I think I would be grateful for fame.'

'Do you have a name for yourself in America?'

She implies with her forefinger and thumb that her audience is small, but it exists.

'Well, this is where she started, Rayna did,' Terry goes on, wistfully. 'So maybe it can launch you, too.' He abruptly puts down his glass and pulls Nell around the bar, marching her to the piano.

'Woah, Terry, I spilled my drink.'

'Sorry. But I have an idea.' He pulls the cover off the piano and the dust motes make Nell cough. 'Why don't we make it a big special? Don't just play a few songs for a couple of nights. I could publicise to the whole area. Get some of the old punters back to see and hear a new jazz singer, only in town for a limited time. A one-night-only extravaganza. What do you think?'

'An extravaganza? Just for me?' She has a wide grin on her face but she shakes her head at the same time.

'Why not?' he asks. 'It'd go down a treat if we promote the hell out of it.' Terry opens the lid of the piano. 'Your voice and your playing. It'll be stunning.'

'You like my voice?'

'Love it.' He had been mesmerised into stillness when he'd heard her sing. He'd felt she could be the main act, not just the support. He should have complimented her more. He could kick himself, now. Maybe if he'd shown more enthusiasm, she wouldn't be hesitating.

'You say you like my voice, Terry, but it can't be the best you've had in here though, right?'

He looks down and twists his hands, ears reddening as he searches for words. Nell steps onto the stage and touches her hand to Terry's. He looks down at the link between them, again that feeling, that rush of warmth enters his body, takes over him and he looks into her eyes.

'How old are you?' he asks.

'Why would you ask me that?' She puts her whisky glass on a nearby table.

'You look so young ... I–'

'I'm not a child. How old are you, Terry?'

'Forty and a bit. I could be your dad.'

'No way. And don't even say that.' She turns quickly and looks at the piano. 'You want me to play?'

'I'd love it. And sing something?'

'Something Ella sings because I know you like her.' She winks at him and starts the opening bars of *Autumn In New York*.

When she begins to sing, he leans his forearms on the top of the piano. He looks at the shape of her lips curling around the words, how her eyes close at the end of the lines where she holds the notes, adding just the right amount of vibrato. She is even better close up. Much better than when she did her half-hour set earlier, amplified and joined by three other musicians. He could tell she was singing from the heart up on that grand stage. She had added two of her own compositions which the audience had loved. Terry had been gushing with pride to know that out of everyone in the auditorium, the singer, Nell, knew him and had agreed to perform in his humble pub. If only they knew he was meeting her outside after the show.

She weaves another song into the last and Terry has picked up her whisky glass, sipping from it to stop himself grinning too widely because he has always loved the song she has broken into now. He closes his eyes, tapping the sides of the glass and doesn't notice when she stops.

'You know, I have no idea what is happening with the woman you told me about but I'm here now.' Nell reaches one hand and rests it beside Terry's on the top of the piano.

'I – what does that mean?' He stutters, face reddening again.

'You know what I mean, Terry. Right here and now it's just you and me.' She stands close to him, pressing her body along the side of his, linking his arm so that he can't move away. 'And if you don't want anyone else to know, then that's fine with me.' Her eyes flick towards the open door leading to the flat.

'I don't–'

She moves closer still, and he can feel every curve of her and the way she fits into him like a groove has been especially made in his body for this kind of contact. He hasn't felt this wanted, this desired in … well, he can't remember how long. He's been pushed away and ignored for ages, that much he knows. He knows he's lonely and he knows she wants him. Someone wants him. He picks up the glass of whisky, drinks the rest and takes her hand.

When the lights over the bar click off, The Pelican is in shadow again and the strange dancers reappear. Terry leads Nell to his bedroom. He leaves the light out as they undress. He is hungry for her body and she gives it willingly, arching and flowing and pulling him so tightly he feels as if he is being devoured.

'Are you sure?' he says in a hot whisper.

'I've never been more sure of anything.'

Upstairs, above the statues of odd dancers and the smell of nicotine, a young woman's voice moans a new song into Terry's ears.

30

When she gets back from Basing Street at four o'clock in the morning, there is nobody home. Rayna clicks on the hall light and inhales the smell of emptiness, the taste of nothing and the feeling of spaciousness. She has no sense of attachment to the hallway with its high ceilings, white walls and the narrow hall table, on which sits a vacant vase. No one has been here in months and her heels echo on the floor tiles as she makes her way to the living room. She puts her head around the door for a brief second, just to check, but she knows not to expect Terry. He'll be at The Pelican. It's late and he'll probably be fast asleep.

She stayed a long time at the Basing Street address, chatting to Junie into the early hours, sipping strong tea, nibbling on cake and making plans with Junie about where the women's refuge would be situated. They thought about the large houses on Oxford Gardens or perhaps one around Blenheim Road. All the time Junie couldn't stop thanking Rayna for her generosity and all the time Rayna couldn't stop thinking that it was the least she could do. She wanted to believe her kindness, though it would help many women, would somehow absolve her of the kind of woman she had turned out to be. She has lied in the past and vowed to be better, now she has been unfaithful to Terry, a man who has done nothing but love and care for her since the day she was forced onto the street by her landlord.

Was she right to leave Terry after everything they'd been through? He has put up with her trips across the globe, the weeks and months away. He has loved her through her moods, her insecurities about life for a woman in the music business. He has fed her, held the fork her trembling hands could not, bathed her and stroked her back when she doubted herself, grew tired and wasn't sure she could carry on. He had done that, not Eddie. He hadn't been around. He was off surging forward with his own career. Though it could have been Eddie who was there for her, had she not pushed him away. He has always loved her and only now, she comes to realise, she has always loved him, too.

In the kitchen, she runs water into the kettle; she's had so much tea, she's not sure she can drink another cup. She turns off the tap and sees a large bottle of champagne and two of red wine on the kitchen counter and is tempted to open them all and drink herself into oblivion just so she doesn't have to face up to the decision she has made about her and Terry.

In a hotel in the middle of London, she knows Eddie is lying in a large bed. He's probably asleep, too, now that his gig at Ronnie Scott's is over. Her suitcase is there. She had gone straight to see him after landing at the airport. They'd made love in the afternoon before the show and she'd wept in his arms when she told him that she was ready to end it all with Terry and that she would do it straight away. She strokes the bottle of champagne and swallows as if she is thirsty for it, dying to pop it open and drink, but in actual fact, the idea of consuming alcohol turns her stomach as much as the idea of breaking Terry's heart. In her way, she still loves him, too.

How laughable that she manages to love two men at once when she'd vowed never to love another after she left Dominica.

With memories of her mother and her island, she returns to the living room, takes off her coat and covers herself with it as she lies on the sofa and falls asleep, exhausted. Now at last the thoughts can drain away.

*

Showered and dressed in flared jeans and a polo-necked sweater, Rayna pulls on a suede jacket and hooks the long straps of her handbag over her shoulder. She pulls on a hat with a peak, trying to hide as much of her identity as she can as she makes her way to the main road to look for a taxi. She sees one quite quickly and gives the taxi driver directions for The Pelican. As he drives, he looks constantly into his rearview mirror, screwing his brow as he tries to figure out where he's seen this woman before. Before he can start the usual questions – 'Are you really her?' 'When will you bring out your next record?' – the taxi stops by the pub.

The driver calls the fare over his shoulder and Rayna searches in her purse. She hands him one of the notes she finds but is suddenly distracted by movement she detects in her peripheral view. A person, a woman, is walking in the direction of the Great West Road, seemingly in a hurry. But where did she spring from? It's as if she came from nowhere. Rayna follows her progress, turning to look over her shoulder through the back window. She looks young, walks with purpose, her head high. Her small afro bobs away urgently and Rayna's neck hurts as she tries to take in what the young woman is wearing. A coat to her ankles, high-heeled boots and a cheap-looking bag at her side.

'I can't change this,' says the cabbie.

'Keep it,' says Rayna and scoots out of the door.

'It is you, isn't it?' the driver says at last. 'You going back to sing at The Pelican? I saw you there once, you know? Great little show. What you doing back here?'

Rayna doesn't answer but closes the taxi door and waves absently. She stands searching for the key to the flat upstairs, looking up at a window while she feels inside the bag. Her heart begins to thunder and she is losing her nerve by the second. Suddenly, she hears footsteps and the door opens wide with a flourish.

'Bloody 'ell, Rayna. You nearly scared me 'alf to death.'

'I, I'm sorry. I…' she holds the key up, pathetically, then lowers her hand. Terry reaches out into the street, arms not quite sure where to hold Rayna, before he brings her closer to the threshold in a hug. She inhales the area of his neck. He hasn't showered. He smells of Benson and Hedges but of something else, something new. Maybe it's the distance in time and miles that makes him different. Because he is. Different. Somehow. Stepping back, she stumbles awkwardly. Terry helps her right herself and guides her inside. At last. She was beginning to feel as if she wasn't quite welcome. Terry seems strange. She knows that the last time they spoke she had said they needed to talk, so perhaps he's dreading what she has to say, knows that the inevitable is coming. They must go their separate ways. No hard feelings. At least they tried.

'Tea?' he asks as he walks slowly back up to the flat.

'Um, yes, that would be nice.'

'Hark at me treating you like you're a guest in your own home. Sorry.'

'Don't apologise. Sometimes I feel like a bit of a stranger when I'm here.'

He stops dead as he reaches the top landing and swings around. 'Do you? I never knew that,' he says. He looks sad all of a sudden and she wishes she hadn't said that. It was thoughtless and a bit cruel. Considering what they will be talking about.

'Oh, not like that,' she says. 'It's all this travelling. And plus, I'm tired. Look, let me make the tea. You sit down. You look tired.'

Terry sits at the table in the kitchen and she can feel his eyes on her as she moves around it, trying to act naturally in a kitchen she hasn't cooked a single thing in for months. She can smell coffee and toast; Terry must have been up a while. She still has her coat on but she did remember to put her bag over the back of a chair. She undoes her buttons, shrugging her coat off while the kettle starts to boil.

'I was going to ask if you were cold,' Terry says. He lights up a cigarette and yawns.

'Late night?' she asks while pouring boiled water into the pot. She notices Terry's ears redden. He hasn't answered so she asks again. 'Did you have a lock-in last night or were you out?'

'What? No. Well, yes, I went to see a show.'

'What, West End?' She places the teapot on the table and looks around for the tea cosy but has no idea where it could possibly be. That is, of course, if Terry still uses one. The cups are in the same place so that's easy and the sugar is on the table, along with a jug containing a small amount of milk. She sniffs it and gets a fresh bottle out of the fridge. As calmly as possible, she sits down opposite him and shuffles her chair under the table.

'Well?' she says. 'The show?'

'Oh, that. Nothing special. A jazz double bill on at The Lyceum. Something I saw advertised and thought I'd give it a go.'

'You look disappointed. What band, or bands?'

'Couldn't tell you now. I forget. No one big like Eddie Keane. I see he was at Ronnie's last night. Got a week-long run if I read it right.'

Now Rayna is quiet. She pours the tea. They both sit, blow into their teacups and sip. Neither speaks and the silence makes the fabric of her clothes rub and itch, like they aren't her clothes but garments made for a smaller person. She fidgets and pulls on the collar of her sweater.

'God it's good to see you, Ray.' Terry stubs out his cigarette and slides his hand across the table. She hesitates before stretching her arm out, fingers just touching his. He reaches further and holds her hand.

'It's always like a breath of fresh air when you're around. Always has been. From the day you first walked in here and it's the same whenever you come back.'

'My, you make me feel bad about enjoying my shows.'

'Don't be silly. This is who you are now. I accept it. My little Ray of sunshine became the whole sky. The stars and the moon included. Did I ever tell you, my mum used to sing me that song? *You Are My Sunshine*? I whistle it when I think of you because of that line: *You make me happy when skies are grey.*'

'That's a lovely thing to say, Terry. You really are… You're such a lovely man. Good, kind. The best.'

'So why do I get the feeling that you were coming home to tell me goodbye? Why have I been feeling that every time you leave the house, you'll never come back? That I'll get a letter saying, "You're a lovely bloke, Terry, but I'm moving on now." Why do I feel like that's about to happen?'

'Because, Terry. We haven't been getting along.'

'But I love you, Ray. I know that more than anything.'

'Terry.'

He gets up, comes to her side of the table and kneels before her. 'What if we talk about it? Talk about the things that aren't so right and try to make them better?'

'You think it's worth it?' She can't look at him.

He stands abruptly and returns to his seat. He reaches for the cigarette packet but changes his mind about smoking.

'I just know that in the last few days,' Terry continues, 'I've felt like we could just give up. Go our own way. Maybe even be friends. But just before you showed up, I got this feeling, right in here.' He lightly thumps his upper abdomen. 'That I don't want to give up. I don't want to throw what we have away and I think it's worth fighting for.' He looks at her with desperation in his eyes, and hers can barely meet his. The rhythm of her heart is irregular and she feels uncomfortably hot in her sweater. 'Talk to me, Ray. Tell me what's on your mind.'

He gets up again and reaches a hand out for her to take, as if they are about to dance. She takes his hand and stands. Terry sweeps her into a close hug that she is not expecting and he wraps around her body with force. The sound of his breath near her ear sounds as if he's crying, whimpering like a little boy. Her hands, hesitant at first, match his embrace. She strokes his hair and her hands rest around his shoulders. She inhales him again; there's that strange smell she wishes he didn't have because he feels foreign to her. When she realises that, yes, he is crying, she allows her body to sink ever deeper into his until each part of her body has contact with a part of him. She has the feeling of love and safety, the dependable feeling that is always there for her, no matter how overworked or wired she feels when she comes home from a tour. This is the hug she remembers and was always the thing she wanted to rush home to in the early days. How could she think it would be so easy to leave Terry? He loves her with all his might and he can't stop crying.

'Shh,' she says, stepping back. 'Everything is okay. We're okay. We'll be okay.'

'You sure?' He sniffs. 'You promise?'

She nods and touches a kiss to his lips. He pushes his tongue into her mouth and kisses her deeply. She thinks he wants to make love but that's the last thing on her mind. All she wants, right now, is not to hurt Terry, and telling him about Eddie will break his gentle heart. So she mustn't do it.

31

He wakes, hot and confused. Confused about the dry feeling in his mouth, the thickness of his head as if his brain suddenly grew too large for his skull. Confused by the ripple of his bedclothes and the curves they make around the woman lying next to him. It comes back quickly, the show, the walk through Piccadilly, the singing, the kiss and the strong limbs the woman in his bed has and the suppleness of her, too. It comes back in all too vivid a memory, and his body responds to the memory of their love-making and the number of times she demanded that he please her for as long as he possibly could.

She is fast asleep. She has got to be as exhausted as he is. Though he is not too exhausted to think about what he has done. Poor Rayna. How could he have done this to her? The one thing she ever worried about before they got engaged was whether she could trust him. She had been an insecure, frightened young girl. Scared to take a chance on either him or Eddie. But she had chosen him and that came with a promise: that he would never let her down and give her cause to regret her decision.

He rolls onto his back jamming the heels of his hands into his eyes. He rubs at them furiously until they feel sore and he's unable to reopen them. Perhaps if he keeps them closed, he won't be able to see what a mess he's made of things.

'You okay?' Nell is leaning up on her elbows, squinting at Terry, a sideways smile on her face.

'What, me? Yeah, I'm fine. You? Okay?'

She laughs at him. She has laughed at him a few times over the last few hours and he wonders what it is about him that amuses her so much. *Of course*, he thinks as he rolls onto his side to stroke the slope of her back, *I'm old enough to be her bloody dad. Just look at her.* What the hell was he thinking?

'I need the loo,' he says and rushes from the bed with so much gusto he sweeps the covers off Nell's body. Looking back quickly, he sees she hasn't covered up but she studies him, curiously.

When he comes back to the bedroom, Nell is putting her underwear on in a hurry.

'You leaving?' he asks and then tuts at this question.

'Well, yeah. You want me to stay?'

'I suppose you must have a busy day though, right? I don't want to keep you.'

She looks down, sadness in her eyes as she searches for the rest of her clothes. Those and her shoes are on the floor by the door. She walks past him and doesn't look his way.

'Wait. Hold on, Nell. Can't we have a coffee or some-thing?'

'If you're offering,' she says over her shoulder. 'But I'll make it. You guys don't know the first thing about making coffee.'

Her voice is so flat he can't tell what type of mood she's in and whether she might have regretted sleeping with him. He regrets it with every fibre of his body. It wasn't as if he was trying to get back at Rayna for being away so much or leaving the fact that they needed to talk dangling over his head. He was just so attracted to Nell that he lost all control. It was a chance to be wanted, and for all he knew, Rayna was prob-ably intending to break things off with him. He knew he didn't want that, so why on earth would he go and sleep with another girl?

He dresses quickly in last night's clothes and finds Nell in the kitchen trying to light the grill. She clicks the ignition and holds a lit match that will not catch.

'You have to try and … may I?' says Terry, striking another match as Nell shakes hers out.

'Be my guest.'

He lights the grill with ease. 'Toast is it?'

She nods and carries on making two cups of strong instant coffee.

'I wouldn't mind a couple of slices meself. We never did eat anything, did we?'

'I guess we kind of forgot.' She carries two mugs of black coffee to the table and sits, one elbow on the table, her chin resting on her hand.

Terry grins and turns the toast. He puts butter on the table alongside the small jug of milk that might have been there days.

'Help yourself, I'll put another two in for me.'

'We'll go one each of these and one each of the next round,' says Nell. 'Only fair.'

They eat and drink in silence until Nell clears her throat.

'Look, you're not feeling guilty about last night, are you?' she says, looking Terry straight in the eyes. Only problem is, he can't reciprocate, save for a split-second glance.

'Look, Terry, you gave me the impression that you and your girl were more or less over. Didn't you?'

'Well, I'm not sure how things are. But it's…'

'You're a good man, aren't you, Terry? One of the good ones. I like that you feel guilty. I wouldn't respect you if you didn't. But the fact is, I'm not a little girl. I'm old enough to know that if a relationship is good, people wouldn't go straying. How d'you know she's not doing the same?'

He looks up sharply. 'No.' He gives a thoughtful shake of his head, but surely there is nothing to think about. 'Not her, she wouldn't. She's as honest as the day is long.'

'You'd be surprised.'

'I'd be surprised if she did go with someone. I really can't see it.'

'Then you need to open your eyes.'

'What do you mean?'

'I mean, think about why this happened, Terry. You like me. You liked me last night. You liked kissing me, you liked all the things we did. You're not the sort of person to go into something like this lightly.'

'This isn't a "something like this". This was a complete one-off.'

She looks at him with the eyes of a child who is about to start crying.

'I'm sorry, Nell. I'm not a bad person. I didn't mean to use you or nothing. I'm not like that. It's just, you know, in the moment I…'

'You wanted me.' She sits back in her chair, matter-of-factly. 'But what you have to ask yourself is why it was so easy to want me like that, to make love to me as if no one else mattered. There is something going on here, Terry. Even if you don't want to admit it.'

'Don't… Look, I said, I'm not a bad person.'

'I didn't say you were. You're good and that's why I'm not giving up on this.' She gets up and walks towards the living room, returning shortly after to ask what she did with her coat and bag.

'They're downstairs.'

'Don't get up.' She holds out both hands. 'Finish your coffee. I'll let myself out. I hope you still want me to sing here?'

He nods, then hesitates.

'You thought it was a wonderful idea,' she says. 'It's not like I'm going to get in anyone's way. Not the great Rayna Laurence. I don't suppose she'll ever sing here again.' She walks quickly to Terry, puts her arms around his shoulders and kisses the side of his face. 'I'm gone from here. For now.'

She is on her way downstairs and Terry has no time to gather his thoughts before he hears the flat door downstairs open and close shut. He's up out of his seat, carrying their mugs and plates to the sink. Puts the butter in the fridge. Why would he do this at such a turning point in his life? Instantly, he knows he must go after Nell and tell her that perhaps it's not a good idea to sing at The Pelican. What would he tell Rayna? How could he explain anything that has happened between him and Nell without blowing up his chance to be with Rayna? Marry her, even, after all these years of her wearing his engagement ring.

He bolts down the stairs and pulls the door open, only to see Rayna standing right there, her key in her hand.

*

He dries his eyes. 'Should we get over to the house. It's more comfortable there. I've been a bit of a slob. The bed isn't even made.' He can't say anything about the mess and tangle of sheets that he'll need to change before he lets Rayna anywhere near the bedroom.

'Okay, Terry. It is a bit grubby in here. You obviously haven't been entertaining.' She laughs and Terry's whole face reddens.

'My coat is in the bar,' he says. 'Should we walk?'

'I'm too tired. There'll be a taxi on the Great West Road.'

'Shall we?' He hooks his elbow and Rayna links his arm. They walk awkwardly down the stairs, side by side.

*

The taxi pulls up to the tall, lonely house. Terry is keen to pay the driver and leaves him an enormously large tip. He can't stop himself smiling, the weight of this morning's realisation of his mistake lifting from his shoulders. It's still on his mind, though, and perhaps the only way to rid himself of it is to admit to Rayna that he has strayed. He thinks that, being as they haven't officially tied the knot, Rayna might be forgiving. Right now, he doesn't want to jeopardise what could be a pivotal point in their relationship and that what he should be doing is building not destroying. There's a future in which they will be together after all. His worst fears finally out of the way.

Terry waits while Rayna enters the house first. Closing the door, he still cannot contain his smile or how wide his chest swells beneath his jacket. He helps Rayna off with her coat and hangs it up. Pulling his jacket off, he hangs it beside Rayna's coat and the contrast in the quality and age of each garment is striking. Maybe he'll learn to dress better. For Rayna. It's important to her. Maybe if they marry, Rayna might stay home more, consider having a child, perhaps. He's not too old and considering Rayna's age, she might finally agree. A little girl named Ella, Shirley or Sarah. He

217

only hopes she can sing jazz so she can live up to the name. He laughs inwardly, listening to the sound of Rayna's heels soften when she reaches the rich pile of the large rug in the living room.

'Shall I make us a brew?' He puts his head around the living room door. 'Did you even have breakfast this morning? I forgot to ask.'

'Well, you shepherded me out pretty quickly.'

'I'm sorry.' He sits beside her and the sofa makes a light puff. It still smells new, probably because it is. It wasn't long ago that Rayna had all new furnishings put in place. He hates the leather suite, the uprightness of the sofa and chairs, their width and the grandeur. He loves the beaten up couch in the flat, the sunken one Rayna had threatened to throw out though he'd talked about reupholstering it. He'd change it, if she asked. He'd change a lot of things now. Now there was a reason.

'You don't have to apologise. I wasn't hungry but I am now.'

'I'll make something.' Terry shuffles forward.

'No, Terry. You're a lousy cook and I don't think there is anything in that isn't old or mouldy. You haven't been here. The place is covered in dust. I'll have to call Mrs Grady to come and make it look and smell better.'

'Sorry, Ray. I don't like to be here on me own. I miss you too much. The place feels too big for just me.'

She rests her hand on his lap and he is compelled to take hers in his. He kisses her palm and sniffs the inside of her wrist.

'No perfume? That's not like you,' he says.

'I've just come back off tour. The last thing I want is to be all fancy, Terry.'

'I know. But, Ray…'

'What's wrong, Terry?'

'Nothing could be more right. Now. Now that I know it's not over between us.'

Rayna says nothing and seems to be looking through him. She must be tired after her tour and he wonders if this is the best time to ask his question. Before giving it more thought, he blurts it out.

'Rayna, will you marry me? The last time I asked, you said you would think about it. I think I've been very patient so far. So, I'm asking. Once again. Rayna, love, why can't we get married?'

'Terry–'

'Don't think too hard. Just let the answer come from your heart.' He looks at the hand he is holding. Rayna's left hand. 'Where's your ring? Don't you wear it anymore?'

'Of course I do. I must have taken it off. It'll be with my things. In my suitcase. I haven't even unpacked.'

'You should get it. Put it on,' he says.

A strange look passes across Rayna's face and then there is a knock on the door.

'Who the hell…?' Terry says. 'I'm trying to set a date with my fiancée.' He laughs but she does not, looking over Terry's shoulder at the window. A fist rumbles another rapid knock on the door and the couple stare at each other.

'I'll get it,' says Rayna.

'You stay there. I'll go.'

Terry can't believe his eyes. Eddie stands there, as plain as day, a large grin across his face and in his hand is a suitcase. Rayna's case. But why…? The baffled expression on Terry's face turns to recognition. These two have been taking him for a fool.

'You going to stand there all day?' he asks Eddie.

'May I come in?'

'That's what I said, isn't it?' Terry turns his back and strides towards the living room.

'It's good to see you, man,' he hears Eddie say, but there is no sincerity in his words. In fact, his comment is empty of any emotion while Terry feels as if he is going to crack open from his head to his belly and he is finding it hard to calm his breathing.

'Look who's here,' he says to Rayna as he walks in backwards, stops by the sofa and jams his hands into his pockets. 'I don't suppose I should ask why he has your case.'

Rayna stands and Eddie slowly lowers the case to the floor. He puts out both of his hands.

'Terry…'

'No, no, no, no.' Terry shakes his head and walks to the other side of the coffee table so he can see them both, watch for any traces in their body language that will tell him how long this has been going on, who started it, how far it's gone and are they in love. It's obvious, though. No matter when it started, that sod Eddie has always had a soft spot for his Rayna. But didn't she just say he and she, the two of them, that they would be together? How does Eddie fit into the equation?

'Can I say something?' Rayna asks, pivoting her look from Eddie and back to him.

'I insist,' says Terry.

She walks towards him and he is hoping, with all his heart, that she is going to say the right thing. That, yes, they had a fling but it's over now. She loves Terry and she didn't know what she was thinking. He can soften the blow, make her feel less guilty by telling her about Nell. They'd be even and then they could move on.

'Terry, it's a very complicated feeling I have. For both of you.'

'Either you love me or you don't, Ray.'

'I do love you, Terry. I do…'

'But?'

'But I don't want to upset you.'

'Upset me? Upset me? Our friend walks in, a man, carrying your suitcase and you don't want to upset me.'

'Terry, I just need time to sort things out. To talk to Eddie and talk to you so we can … I don't know. Terry, please. This whole thing is breaking my heart.'

'Consider my fucking heart, Rayna. For once. Just once.' He feels his neck burning; his cheeks must look like a flaming traffic light. He can't take it anymore and he'll blow up at them both. The two people he has loved and respected above anyone.

'Terry, man,' Eddie begins. 'You can't just swear and shout at Rayna like that.'

'And who asked you to stick your oar in?'

'Well, this has just as much to do with me as you,' says Eddie in a soft voice. He can't look Terry in the eye, be a man.

'I'm off,' says Terry. 'If I stay a second longer, it'll be more than words and I never hit a bloke before. Not over a woman. Not for anything, and I ain't starting now.'

'I don't need you to fight for me, Terry.' Rayna crosses her arms, advances on him as he heads for the door.

'Don't,' he hisses at her. 'Don't. To think I thought we were finally… Just don't.'

He barges past Eddie, practically taking his shoulder off and hurting his own in the process. He rips his jacket off the hook and Rayna's coat flops onto the floor like a useless rag that he ignores. He slams the door shut behind him and stands on the front step, his shoulders heaving, his eyes filling with tears. He cups his eyes, rubs the tears away and heads for the front gate, stopping first to light a cigarette. His hands shake with rage as he extinguishes the match, tossing it onto the pavement, a pavement he stabs relentlessly with his feet, marching and puffing on his cigarette until he has to light another and then another until he is at The Pelican and he doesn't know how the hell he got there so fast.

32

Terry calls Sandra and tells her that he won't be at The Pelican tonight.

'You what?' She's not amused. After closing, she'd done the whole clear-up on her own, he discovers. And she's not shy about telling him that the daft kid he hired as a part-timer had drunk more than his share of sneaky half pints when he thought Sandra wasn't looking and had made full use of the offer of "have one yourself" by making the one for himself a double or triple. Sandra had wanted to leave urgently because she was having a late supper with her boyfriend and hadn't had a night off in ages. To top it off, Terry had taken a night off on a flipping Friday and left her with the half-wit kid.

'I'm not feeling myself,' he says to appease her.

'But it's Saturday night, Terry, we'll be packed and you gave that twit of a boy tonight off, too.'

'Did I?'

'Yes, Terry, you did. What's up with you these days? I thought Rayna should be back now. You can stop all your moping around.'

'That's not funny, Sandra. Things haven't been good between us for a while. Now it's all got worse.'

'How do you mean?' Her voice grows dark. Terry knows Sandra thinks that his and Rayna's relationship has been waning for a while now. She has more or less told him he should cut his losses and he's sure she's probably said as much to Rayna, too.

'I tried, Sandra. You know I have but something, something has come between us.'

She's quiet on the other end of the line. He hears the bustle of the Goldbourne Road and the greengrocer below her flat calling 'Salad t'matoes!' He's probably standing under the awning, pot belly stretching his sweater, a mucky apron from lifting and loading sacks of potatoes.

'You mean some*one*?' Sandra says. 'Like a tall and famous sax player.'

'Did you know about them?' He's growing cross again. Feeling like an idiot because he's obviously the last to see it coming. He thought Rayna, if she was going to leave him, would at least have the grace to end it first before waving Eddie Keane in his face. The shame of it all. What a fool he has been.

'Took a wild guess.'

'Because you saw it coming?'

'Honestly, Terry, I didn't but it was one or the other.'

'And you're surprised it was me she chose. Everyone must have been. Well, they're welcome to each other. That's all I can say. Look, I'll ring around. See who I can get to help out tonight. I promise I will. I just can't be in the pub tonight.'

'I understand, Terry. I've got the key, I'll let myself in if you've already gone out. I take it that's what you're doing. Going to some seedy jazz club and getting plastered. Make sure you have enough cash on you to get yourself home. I don't want a call from the police at one o'clock in the morning.' She laughs but not with her usual gusto. Sandra must understand how much pain he is in. He doesn't know if he will ever get over this, get over Rayna. Everything about The

Pelican reminds him of her. It's as if the place wasn't his life before she walked into the pub one night. Since then, everything has been about Rayna. Rayna's voice, Rayna's laugh, Rayna's heart, her body and Rayna's secrets. He'll never unravel them. He wonders if perhaps Eddie has and that's why she wants to be with him. Because he understands her better, because she trusts him more and told him about her life before him. He would give anything to know what that was all about. The secrecy.

He hangs up the phone to Sandra and calls Nell straight away.

'You're lucky you caught me. I was on my way to get a late lunch with the guys. They only just got up.'

'That's the music business for you. Bed late, up late.'

'And then repeat.' She sighs heavily down the phone, waiting for him to speak, perhaps, but he's not even sure why he's calling. 'Look, Terry. You left things rather up in the air this morning. Why are you calling me now? To apologise?'

'Something like that. I didn't know where my head was at.'

'And now you do?'

'You could say that.'

'Tell me why you called.'

'I want to see you. Tonight. After your show. I'll wait for you.'

'I'll get you on the guest list. It's the last night and there's a surprise guest. What do you think?'

'I think I've had enough surprises. But, yes, why not? I'd only be propping up a bar somewhere. Some good music would be just the tonic.'

'Good. And then wait for me. We can plan the show at The Pelican so I know when I have to go back home. If I go back home.'

'What do you mean? You planning on staying in London?'

'Well, it wouldn't be a bad thing to try to make a name for myself here. What do you think?'

'I think you can do anything you set your mind on. I'd come see your shows. You've always got The Pelican's stage. Until you make it really big of course. Which won't take long, judging by what I heard.'

'You like to blow hot and cold, Terry. One minute I'm flavour of the month…'

'Look, I'm sorry about earlier. I just … I just need to feel wanted right now. Shoulder to cry on. But I'm not trying to use you. I really want to see you. That is if you forgive me for being all over the place. For being…'

'For being you. I like the you that you are.'

'So, later, then?'

'You bet.'

She hangs up without saying goodbye. He likes how direct Nell is. Not wishy-washy. Says what she means and doesn't hide anything. No hidden agenda. No secrets.

*

It's a small theatre. Tucked down a side road between the Strand and Kingsway. The auditorium is small, intimate but the stage has played host to several prestigious musicians, most of them classical, but other artists from contemporary and now jazz have graced it. Again, Terry's chest swells with pride when the lights dim and he sees someone he knows take to the stage amidst swirls of applause and whistles. It's a fashionable crowd; he doesn't really fit in but he's a real fan of the music, not like this la-di-da lot with their expensive suits and evening gowns. Most of them are there to show themselves off rather than hear good music. They can tell their friends at cocktail parties that they went to see some jazz at the weekend and this will impress them.

He does feel self-conscious about his old blazer now. Maybe he could have made more of an effort for Nell, worn one of the la-di-da suits that Rayna bought for him. But no. Nell won't expect this. She really likes him, though he doesn't know why. He's not well spoken, he's not well dressed. He assumes it's because he's so knowledgeable about jazz, the thing they most have in common. It's not age, culture, dress sense: it's music. And he lets Nell's music flow into his whole body. He already appreciates the precise yet flowing style of her piano playing and the accuracy and smoothness of her voice. She is so well trained and could so be the headlining act on this stage. But she is young, she has time.

Nell had left a note for him at the box office with his ticket. She will meet him after the main act because as it's the last night, she needs to hang around, network, get leads for work going forward. That's the business. Of course he understands and what's so wrong about another free show in the space of two nights? He's blessed. Though he can't wait to see Nell.

To Terry's surprise, Nell is called up on stage to do a number with the headliner, and she sings a beautiful duet while he shows off his complex and captivating guitar style and signature riffs and interpretation of the songs. He hears Nell scat for the first time and he is enthralled. The applause is rapturous; Nell is asked to stay up on stage as the revelation of the surprise artist, just back in town after a run of shows in Paris, is about to be announced. Terry has no idea who it is but he can see Nell is excited. The audience sit forward in their seats. Maybe he got them wrong, maybe they are real jazz lovers; he feels their anticipation rising.

And on walks the special guest, alto saxophone in the crook of his arm. Tall, elegant and cool, Eddie Keane takes a bow and then kisses Nell on the cheek. The band leader counts in the biggest hit of Eddie's career. Nell sings the head before Eddie takes a solo. His rhythms swirl around the auditorium for several bars. Terry has never heard Eddie sound so good. He has tried to keep up with Eddie's career but he hasn't heard him play or bought one of his records in a long time. It has always been too painful. Memories of a happier time at The Pelican, before things got complicated, would always creep in whenever an Eddie Keane record was on. Envy, insecurity and a longing for a simple life again would make Eddie's music sound harsh and would soon irritate him. But now Terry can't deny the magic in this man's playing, the free yet steady way he stands on the stage as if he was born for this. Born to be someone he could never be. Not in Rayna's eyes. Now it looks as though Nell is also taken with him. Her scatting and his riffs and runs melt into the other. This isn't rehearsed: they just feel the sensations of the other's musicianship, and Terry can't stop himself tapping his foot, nodding his head, clapping when one or the other finishes yet another sixteen bar solo. It's incredible.

Then he sits back. Rayna. She might be here watching how absorbed he is in the music. Would she pity him, laugh at him? Does she know how much her betrayal has torn him apart? His back prickles under his jacket as he leans back and looks around the auditorium, scanning the theatre stalls for a glimpse of Rayna, being as subtle as he can as he turns to look up at the balcony, but he can't see her if she is there. Not without drawing attention to himself and that's the last thing he wants to do. Rayna is probably offstage somewhere, waiting for Eddie. He wonders if Nell has introduced herself to Rayna. His ears burn and he can't wait to get out. If he stands now, he might be seen, so he stays stock still and claps his hands in a wooden fashion until the show is over. The curtains close and people begin to file out of the theatre.

*

On the way to Nell's hotel, Terry is agitated and has questions he can't wait to ask her, but she hasn't stopped gushing about Eddie Keane and what a great show it was.

'Didn't you like it?' she asks.

'What? Yes. Of course I did. I was just wondering if you knew Eddie Keane would be there?'

'I knew just minutes before I did my set.' Nell has obviously been drinking, she's that animated. Champagne. He had tasted it on her kiss. 'I saw him walk by me and down a corridor carrying his case. Not that the case was a giveaway. Eddie Keane is unmistakable. I was so nervous about him hearing me play. Did you hear how tight my throat sounded?' She is bobbing beside him, walking sideways like an excitable child. Mind you, he knows what she means. When Eddie walks into a room, he commands it. Very much the way Rayna has learnt to do.

'You sounded fine to me,' he says, reaching for another cigarette.

'Those things'll kill ya.'

'Want one?'

'Please.'

'Watch out for your voice, though.' He strikes a light and they turn against the wind, the ends of their cigarettes forming red tips.

'I don't smoke an awful lot,' says Nell, exhaling smoke up to the sky.

'You drank a lot, though.'

'Well, it was a party. Last night and all.'

'Who was there?'

'What do you mean?'

'Well, more special guests?'

'No, Terry. Jeez. Why are you so uptight, man. Relax.'

They walk for a short while before Nell notices another taxi has passed them by and stops to search for one.

'You still want to come to the hotel?' she asks, waving her hand at an oncoming black cab.

'I am relaxed. Is there a bar in your hotel?'

She nods as the taxi stops and they jump in.

'Good, because I need to catch up with you.' Terry is dying to be in bed with Nell.

In the hotel bar, they sit drinking whisky and eating roasted peanuts while Nell talks endlessly about the number of Eddie Keane records she has and how she used his saxophone solos to form the style of her voice.

'He is the most knowledgable of them all. He should be bigger than Miles or at least on his level. But that's the music business for you.'

'He does okay.'

'I'm not saying he doesn't but…'

Before she can go on any further, he leans into her, thrusts his tongue into her mouth, pressing her closer to him with a hand behind her head, one on her lap.

'What you trying to do, smudge my lipstick?'

'You're not wearing any.'

'Well, I'm surprised you noticed because you've barely looked at me. You've been weird all night.' Their foreheads are pressed together, their intoxication melding into a cocktail of dizziness and drawn-out words.

'Let's go up to your room,' he whispers.

She stands and takes his hand. They wrap their arms around each other, one supporting the other, walking together past the reception desk in a circular movement and over to the lifts. Nell frees a hand to press the button. When they get to her floor and the lift doors open, they empty themselves out into the hallway, then into her room and onto the bed. They shed their clothes with the lights still out. They enjoy kisses, skin being squeezed, stroked, pulled. They moan and tangle on top of the blankets until there is no part of their bodies that has not sparked back to life. Then they are too tired to do anything else but sleep. Their sleep is profound and lasts for hours until the sky is very bright. Neither can lift their head from the pillow, only open their eyes by a slit and grin, no energy to do anything more.

33

The phone rings again. Rayna wishes she hadn't had a phone installed in her bedroom but it was a very modern thing to do, Sol's assistant, Barbara, had insisted. But since seeing Terry over a week ago, she hasn't wanted to talk to anyone, especially not her agent, Sol, nor his assistant. She felt suddenly burnt out and tired from the day Terry stormed out of their house, angry. And who could blame him? One minute she was telling him that they had a future, and the next, Eddie – the man Terry had always feared Rayna would leave him for – walks in carrying her suitcase. She couldn't explain it away. It couldn't be coincidence or by accident that Eddie would come across her suitcase. Terry hadn't given her a chance to explain anything, just rushed out in a fury and she hadn't gone after him.

Now the phone keeps ringing and she knows it isn't Terry. He must be done with her. She knows it isn't Eddie because he is in the kitchen now, making her some tea and probably a sandwich because he's been trying to convince her that she should eat something. She has only nibbled on her food when they've been to a restaurant and sent untouched plates back. She has lost her appetite, guilt filling her stomach, tea and wine quenching her thirst.

'You can't go on like this,' Eddie has been saying in between leaving for the studio to record his latest album and coming home to rub her shoulders and run her a bath.

'I could stay like this, being loved and adored by you.' She had smiled up to him from a bath filled with bubbles and sprinkles of lavender oil.

'It won't be enough. You need to be singing. Most of all you need to be telling Sol to get you some engagements where you're singing your music. Jazz.'

'I can't,' she had said and sank beneath the effervescent water.

Eddie walks into the bedroom with a cup brimming with black tea. A slice of lemon on top makes the contents ready to spill onto the saucer that he places gently onto the bedside table. He sits beside her.

'What will you do today?'

She shrugs.

'Then come with me to the studio. Come and sing on my album.'

She looks at him and sighs. 'I'm not in the mood to sing.'

'Then go and see Terry and have this out, once and for all. You guys have a long history. It can't just come to a stop like it did. You know as well as me that this isn't over.' He takes her hand. 'I have to go now. The room is booked.'

'I'll see you later?'

'Of course.' He kisses her cheek and walks to the door where he hovers for a moment. 'And answer the phone. It might not be Sol. It might be Terry and you owe it to him to talk.'

She looks up at him and nods. 'I will.' She blows him a kiss, and right when she hears him leave the house, she reaches for her tea. She upsets some of the contents. The phone rings again with an urgency that makes her spill even more tea so that it splashes off the saucer and onto the bed-sheets.

'Damn it. All right. I'm coming.' She replaces the cup and picks up the phone receiver, bracing herself. She does not know how to approach Terry if it's him. He will be angry still and she doesn't think an apology will be welcomed. He'll want an explanation.

'Hello? Rayna? Rayna, is that you?' She doesn't need the receiver close to her ear to hear Sol's booming voice on the other end of the line.

'Yes, hello Sol.'

'Hello? Hello? Is that all you've got to say for yourself? I thought you might be dead. I was about to come over. What happened? Why haven't you answered the phone?'

'I'm tired, Sol.'

'Tired? What from? You've been home since Paris. I waited for you to tell me when you wanted another booking sorted and I've heard nothing.'

'It's only been a week.'

'It's been two. And don't think I didn't hear about your little foray onto the stage at Ronnie Scott's with Eddie and his band. You can't just go off and do that kind of thing.'

'Invoice me for your ten percent. Not that I made anything out of it.'

'It's not the money, Rayna. It's your image. Ronnie's is a jazz venue. We've talked about this.'

'No. You've preached about it. I've done everything you've asked of me but, Sol…'

'Don't say it.'

'I want to go back to jazz.'

'Really?' He sounds angry and she can hear him drawing on a cigarette. The long inhale he takes when he's trying not to explode, wanting to be calm so he can talk her round.

'You know I want to.'

'Yes, I know. But I'm afraid you might be a little too late, Rayna love.'

'Late? What do you mean, late?'

'Because, apparently, word around town is that there already is a jazz version of you out there.'

'What on earth are you talking about, Sol?'

'I'll read this for you. It was in the evening paper. The headline says, *A return of live jazz music to The Pelican Public House in Notting Hill Gate.* Then it goes on, *Made famous by the great Eddie Keane and Rayna Laurence, the West London pub welcomes a new voice in jazz to its hallowed stage. With so many of Eddie Keane's band having made a name for themselves in the world of jazz, not to mention the mega stardom of jazz-turned-cabaret singer, Rayna Laurence, The Pelican is showcasing an enormous and long-awaited show with a hot and talented young singer and pianist. Nell Robertson, a beautiful and vibrant musician who hails from Michigan USA, is due to star in a special one-off event ...* Blah, blah, blah, but okay, listen to this. *They are calling Miss Robertson the jazz singer Rayna Laurence would have become if she'd stayed true to her roots in music. The new Rayna is ...* etc., etc. What do you make of that, eh?'

Rayna has no idea what to say. She is stunned. Who is Nell Robertson and how the hell can she take Rayna's place?

'What does this mean?' Rayna is asking herself this question more than she is Sol. 'I mean, how do the papers have the right to print a declaration like that? I've never even heard of her.'

'I think you are missing the point, Ray my girl. This showcase ... it's at The Pelican. Did you know about this?'

'How could I? I've been away and Terry and I have not really spoken.'

'Then, it's time you did speak. Find out what he's up to.'

'Well, it's his place. He can do as he wants.'

'True, but he can't bandy your name around like that.'

'That article makes it sound as if I'm all finished.'

'No it doesn't, Ray. On the contrary. They're talking about a jazz singer. You're not a jazz singer anymore.'

Rayna is quiet for a long time. She moves slowly, getting up from the bed, planting her feet on the floor just so the idea of being replaced by some new star can sink in and she can think about what it means to her. She knows the music business is fickle and that the press is always looking for the next big thing. Someone younger, more attractive. At least that's what it's like for women in her business. She can already feel a wave of resentment for this Nell Robertson creeping up the skin on her back and tensing the muscles of her shoulders.

'Ray? Rayna, you still there?'

'I'm here. I'm thinking.'

'Look, I didn't want to worry you or anything. There will never be another you.'

'Perhaps there should have been?'

'What do you mean, Rayna love?'

'Sol, I told you from the beginning. I am a jazz singer and I let you convince me to walk away from that world.'

'And look at you now.'

'But what if I was wrong? What if I should have stayed a jazz singer?'

'Then who's to say you would have got where you are? I knew what I was doing and it's paid off.'

'I'm not thinking about the money. I'm thinking about the people. They used to love me at The Pelican. They were real lovers of jazz, of the musicians, of me.'

'It's too late for regrets.'

'Is it? I have them all the time, constantly doubting myself. When I sang at Ronnie Scott's, it felt great, Sol. I felt alive on stage for the first time in ages.'

'People love you, Ray. Your fans. I'm getting calls left, right and centre and you've been avoiding me. We need to book you into another –'

'I need to go back to being me.'

'And what was that? A barmaid with a good voice who sang to a bunch of drunk punters who didn't know one thing about jazz music.'

'That's not true, Sol. And if it was, then how is Terry able to bring a jazz musician back to the stage there and for it to be so big it's in the paper?'

'Look Ray, no one can go back in time. You have so much going for you and there's more to come. You've a way to go. Trust me.'

'And what about me? Can't I trust me? I've lived my life doing what other people think is best for me. I can't, I don't want to stop listening to me. Can you understand?'

'All I know is you've got an empty diary and I've got venues calling up all day asking when they can have Rayna Laurence on their stage again. That's calls from all over the world. Believe me.'

'I know. I'm not ungrateful, Sol. I'm very happy with the way it's all gone.'

'You sound as if we've come to the end.'

'No, I just need to step back. For a while. I'm helping a good friend start up a charity. I want to be involved.'

'What are you saying, Ray?'

'I'm saying I need time, and when I know what I want, I'll call you.'

Rayna hangs up the phone even though she can hear Sol still speaking, trying to convince her that he knows best and that she should trust him.

She walks over to the window and looks out into a breezy spring sky, streaks of yellow and white intermingle with grey and move across her view, unseen by her. Her thoughts go to Terry. Their relationship cannot be over in one slam of a door. She should have done more to make him understand her change of heart. She led the man on for so long, it was unfair. She has been unfair, and everything she tried to be – a better singer, a better friend, a better lover, all in an attempt to redeem herself of her past – seems not to have worked. In all these years, she is still a frightened teenager, a thief and a liar who abandoned her poor mother on an island so far away she had forgotten it existed. She will never be able to go back. She does not have the heart to look into her mother's eyes and say sorry for leaving her to field the backlash of her deceit. She is not a good person. Though she is afraid, she knows one day she has to go back. Go back and see her mother and beg for her forgiveness. She doesn't know, after all this time, who stopped writing first, her or Urma. All she knows is that she has let the distance grow painfully wide between them and she pictures herself at seventeen again leaving Dominica days before her eighteenth birthday. If she had stayed, she would not have become estranged from her mother, broken the heart of a teenage girl, stolen money and tried to cover her tracks by becoming as successful as she has. She is undeserving of it all.

It is time to start making amends. With Terry, her mother, Sol. Everything is about to change. She only hopes she can find the strength to apologise. She will do it without the need for forgiveness. She doesn't deserve it.

34

In the heat of the afternoon, Roseau seemed to swelter. Rayna didn't have a hat or even a headscarf to keep the sun off her brow, and she felt hot and sticky from the long ride into town, standing on a packed lorry full of people that juddered on the rough roads and jiggled the jewels in her pocket. She tried to keep them safe by holding her hand around them so that the bumps of the lorry wouldn't allow them to slip out and scatter onto the feet of the passengers all hitching a ride into the capital. Again, the poverty of her family came to mind. If her father had been working, and any job would do, maybe they would have their own truck. If her brother had lived, he would have been making a contribution. Then she would not have had to give up school to take a job. She wouldn't have had to work for the St Jeans. She would not have encountered Mr St Jean on a chilly morning in a gloomy kitchen when everyone in the house was fast asleep. She thought then of Daniella. The poor girl would be on her own with Mr St Jean, a brute who would rape his own child, and a mother who turned a blind eye. While the miles slipped on between her village and the town, she knew that she was going to have to leave Daniella stranded. Rayna was never going back there. The money she made on the jewels would be her escape.

She jumped off the lorry when it stopped in Roseau. She didn't want to run into Mr St Jean. His large grocery shop was there but he was likely in one of the offices above the

240

shop, working on his plans of running for mayor and securing deals to make the whole thing financially viable. She'd overheard Mr St Jean talking to his wife about it one day. She hadn't known what it all meant but it seemed to keep him away from the house for even more hours in the day than usual, which was all the better for her and for Daniella, too.

Rayna entered the first jewellery shop she came across. It sold watches and clocks, gold rings and jewels that shone as much as Mrs St Jean's. The door was heavy and the couple behind the counter stopped mid-sentence when she presented herself in front of them. The woman, tall and elegant, looked down her nose at Rayna. She was conspicuous in Roseau, wearing an old blouse and the tatty skirt she wore to work at the St Jeans'. The man, however, smiled to Rayna and looked over the top of small and round gold-rimmed glasses at her. His cheeks, like sponges, allowed the edges of his glasses to sink into them. His face was shiny and welcoming. The height of the floor behind the counter was a step higher than at shop level, so the couple towered above Rayna. She cleared her throat and took out the treasure from her pocket. She laid it all on the counter, one of the rings sticking to her palm so that she had to brush it off. It rolled across the counter and the man stopped it under a tubby hand.

'Whoops. There you are. Now, what can I do for you, young lady?'

The woman cocked a hip and rested a fist on it.

'Well,' said Rayna. 'My mistress send me to sell these and bring her back the money.'

The man picked up a bracelet and rubbed the stones, looking at Rayna all the time.

'And your mistress is?'

'Mrs St Jean, her husband have the shop.'

'Yes, I know the St Jeans. I just wonder why she send you and not come here herself.'

'My mistress sick.'

The woman kissed her teeth and said, 'That woman always sick.'

'Wait,' said the man. 'With all the money Mr St Jean have, why your mistress have to sell her jewels?'

Very quickly, Rayna had an answer which she had to sum up the confidence to deliver.

'My mistress tell me that she don't want anyone to know her business. Not even Mr St Jean, and if anyone find out she send me, I will lose my job. She say it's for her safety.'

The couple looked at each other and the woman raised her eyes. All the time the man was rubbing the gems of the bracelet.

'Well, give it a value,' the woman said to him. 'And quick.'

The man inspected all of the jewels, slowly, one by one. When he'd finished, he picked up the piece of paper he'd been making calculations on and gave Rayna the figure. When he read it aloud, the amount in British West Indies currency was so high that Rayna had to hold the edge of the counter to stop the ground beneath her from spinning.

'We would have to get a bank draft to pay her.'

'No,' said Rayna. Then, standing up straight, added, 'She say she want it all cash and she want it now.'

The couple looked at each other again. She heaved her shoulders and he shook his head.

'This will take me a day to arrange. You will have to come back tomorrow.'

Rayna reached out and gathered the jewels into her hands.

'What you doing?' the woman said.

'I taking this somewhere else. My mistress tell me not to come back without the money. She say her life depend on it.'

'Hold on a minute,' the man said, palms covering Rayna's hands. 'I'll see what I can do at the bank if you just wait here.'

'I will.' Rayna knew that this implied the jewels were worth much more than he'd suggested and they didn't want to risk her going elsewhere. Rayna was more than happy with the price he'd quoted, her mind already focused on an escape for her and her mother. Off the island, away from their misery and the hard life they were living. They could start again. A new life. Leave her drunk father and the memory of her attack far behind. She could still feel Mr St Jean's hands on her, the pain he caused, the shame she felt and the anger because she could not do anything to punish him. If she took the money, she would really just be punishing Mrs St Jean and Daniella, but she knew the only way she was going to survive everything that had happened to her in that house was to put miles between her and it. Here was the perfect opportunity.

She waited two hours for the money. The chubby man returned from the bank, sweating and breathing heavily, counting dollars onto the counter twice and asking if Rayna wanted it in an envelope: it was a lot of money for a young girl to carry, unaccompanied.

'Yes, please,' she said.

At the door, she tucked the envelope into the bodice of the slip under her blouse, where it pricked her chest. She walked down the road looking at the top button of her blouse to make sure the envelope wasn't peeking out, crossing her arms until she found transport to take her home.

Her mother, Urma, would not arrive home until the early evening and there was no sign of her father. Rayna couldn't eat, drink or rest. She kept counting the money before deciding to hide it. Peering out of her bedroom window every few minutes, she looked out for Urma who finally returned.

'I tell you to go and get what your mistress owe, I didn't tell you to steal from her.'

'After what that family put me through, don't you think I deserve it?'

'What happen to you is a sin but what you doing is a sin, too. Rayna, please, I beg you to go by Mrs St Jean and give her back her money.'

'But, Mum, we have something we never have in our lives, a chance to get away from this place we call home. Where you break your back and you trapped with a man who is good for nothing. I have no work now and goodness only knows when I will find work again.'

'There have work, you only have to look.'

'What I want is to finish my education. I don't want to work for people. I want people to work for me.'

'Stop talking nonsense and go.'

Rayna looked down at her feet. She shook her head and watched the tears already gathered in her eyes splash into the ancient wooden floorboards. How long had this old house been standing in this little plot on the outskirts of a village, so close to the sea they could hear the waves and feel the sand in their shoes purely because of the proximity of the beach. This house had been standing long before it became the home of her family, and if she did as her mother told her, she would be standing in it, looking down at the feet of an old woman, those of one who had worked all her life for the benefit of some rich family, nursed a mother who had worked even longer hours than she ever had and buried a father who drank himself into an early grave. Was that all she had to look forward to?

The dreams she had when she thought about using that money to escape were immense. She saw herself in a big house with large windows and soft beds. Carpets in all the rooms. A piano. A room that opened onto an enormous garden and let in the sun all day. She had a cupboard full of fancy clothes. Her jewellery box was twice as big as Mrs St Jean's and her bed taller and more comfortable. Her old clothes she would have burned in a fire pit by the sea and danced around the sparks, holding hands with her mother who would be able to dance because she wasn't tired or in pain. Where would this house be? Another island? Or would she leave the Caribbean altogether for her new life? Maybe a life in which she fell in love, had children and had so much time on her hands she didn't know what to do with it. Perhaps a life in which she could sing all day long because she was just that happy.

Rayna turned to her bedroom to fetch the money, remembering just in time that she had hidden all of it in the metal bread bin in the kitchen. All it had contained was a stale loaf and she put the cash beneath it for safe keeping, just in case her father went searching for her wages or her mother's in their bedside tables the way he always did.

She was about to go out to the kitchen but Urma stopped her.

'Where you going, Rayna?' her mother asked.

'The money,' she said, pointing over her shoulder. 'I hide it from Dad.'

Just as she said this, a thunder of fists against the door startled Rayna. Urma pulled Rayna behind her and opened the door wide.

'Who coming and knock so loud at my door before I even have time cook my food for the evening?'

From behind her mother, Rayna saw Mr and Mrs St Jean. Mr St Jean's large frame obscured most of his wife's who stood with a handkerchief under her nose, sniffing, eyes puffy and sad. The black sky behind them creaked and chirped with night breezes and busy crickets. Mr St Jean puffed out his chest.

'I come to see that girl you have hiding behind you.' His voice was heavy with anger and rattled the very walls of the house.

Rayna went to step around her mother who moved to block her.

'And what you want with my daughter? You don't already take what you wanted from her?'

Mr St Jean swallowed before he continued and Mrs St Jean turned her head away.

'I want my money back. She stole it and she must give it back. Now.'

'And what money is this?' Urma crossed her arms. Though Rayna knew it must be painful for her and that her mother most likely needed to be lying down for a rest after work, Urma stood with a straight back, looking unblinkingly at Rayna's former employer.

'The money she go and change for my wife's jewels.'

'And what your wife doing sending a child to go and run errands carrying jewels? Is she mad?'

'How dare you?' Mr St Jean stepped inside the house and shook his index finger in Urma's face. 'No one will call my wife mad. You hear me? Now *you*.' Blasting past Urma and rounding on Rayna, he waved an angry finger in her face, too. Before he could splutter another word more, Urma grabbed his upper arm and pulled him with all her might back round to face her.

'If you lay one more finger on this girl of mine, I will kill you, and when I finish kill you, I will go by the police sergeant and tell him I just kill a rapist who come in my house to trouble my poor daughter again, and all his mad wife do is stand up there and watch just like she watch when he doing the same thing to his own daughter.' Urma's cheeks were red and so were the whites of her eyes. Mrs St Jean cried and held out her arms to her husband.

'Please, we have to go. I'll speak to Rayna in the morning. Please, Rayna, come tomorrow and talk to me about the money.'

Urma lunged towards Mrs St Jean. 'What the hell money you talking? You been drinking again? You never even pay my child what you owe after the work she do for you, and you come here accusing her of being a thief. Madame, I think it's time you warn yourself and go.'

'But Rayna,' Mrs St Jean stuttered. 'I was sure I saw you today and give you those jewels. And I thought I…'

'Amelia!' Mr St Jean pushed Urma aside to confront his wife. 'You mean to tell me you come all the way here for money and you not sure the girl even have it?'

'I'm sure. I'm very sure.'

'Well, if you so sure,' said Urma, 'then the pair of you, search this house and find what you come here for.' Urma gathered Rayna by her shoulders and pulled her to one side to give the St Jeans full access to the house. Mrs St Jean was tearful and looked pleadingly at Rayna to support her claims. Rayna looked down at her feet again and said nothing.

'Well?' said Urma. 'What you waiting for? You already push your way into my house, you might as well look into all my private things. Not that I have much, but you are welcome to look. Go on.'

Mr St Jean kissed his teeth, gave one last scornful look at Rayna and her mother and stormed out of the house. Mrs St Jean blinked a trickle of tears down her cheek and followed behind her husband. She left the door wide open and Urma went to slam it shut.

'Mum?' Rayna was tearful. She had tried to be as stoic as her mother but her heart was nearly out of her chest when her mother declared that the St Jeans could search the house. Her hands still trembled even after hearing the St Jean's horse and wagon leading away from the house.

'Why didn't you tell them the money was in the kitchen?' Rayna sat at the table trying to still the quiver in her voice, the vibration of her hands on the table. 'Didn't you say I should take it back?'

'Not after I see the look in that man face. After what he did to you, I decided he should pay.'

'So I did right?'

Urma threw herself into the chair beside Rayna, exhausted. She loosened the knot in her headscarf and took it off. She shook her head for a long time and didn't look at her daughter for what seemed an eternity.

'No, Rayna. You did wrong. So do I. I should have given it back, rid you of the sin, but instead I put it on both our shoulders.' She turned to Rayna and took both of her hands. 'Now, if it's an escape you want, take the money. Pay your passage off this island and go.'

'You mean…?'

'I mean run. I mean get as far away from here as the money can take you. You are a clever girl. Brave and strong. You can do anything. You can train in something. Find work, but only make sure it's not in anyone house. You understand?'

'No. I don't understand. I want us both to go. Not only me.'

'And why not? Everyone leaving here, Rayna. England. America. Canada. You can go to the motherland because they saying there have work and England will welcome you with open arms. They say it on the radio.'

'I can't go on my own. I don't know … I don't know what I can do. And I don't want to leave you.'

'The minute you make this decision to take the money, your mind was already made up. Dominica doesn't have anything for you.'

'You. Mum. It have you.' Rayna began to shake in her seat. She knew her mother was right; she'd known for a long time that if she wanted more for herself, she wouldn't find it on this small island.

'We can write,' said Urma. 'We will write to each other and you can tell me how you doing. Only don't forget.'

'I will never forget and I will send for you.'

'I'm not leaving here. Maybe when you can, you can visit me. Me and the old man.'

'I don't care what happen to him.'

'Hush, Rayna. He may be worthless but he still your father.'

Rayna leapt towards her mother and wrapped her arms around her. She cried into Urma's shoulder, sitting on her lap like a five-year-old Rayna who had fallen and cut her knee.

'You have to be brave, my Rayna. I know you can. You have to be so brave that all you ever do with your life is make it bigger and better. Make me proud. Let at least one person in this house have something they can be proud of.'

'I'm proud of you.'

Urma pushed Rayna back to her own seat. 'I coming with you to find out about a passage to England in the morning.'

'Mum. I'm so scared. What do I know about England?'

'Go in London where there have jobs. Mrs Martin daughter working as a nurse in a hospital. That is a decent and honourable job.' She held each of Rayna's cheeks. 'You will go very far, Rayna. I know you will.'

At the harbour, the women waved so hard when Rayna got onto the boat one of the crew told Rayna to stop before the boat to Jamaica capsized. As the ocean widened further and further between Rayna and her mother, her tears began to dry. Her face grew straight and determined. She couldn't land in England being so weak; she had no idea what life was really going to be like. Between her and Urma she'd arranged a place to stay and there was a training position at a hospital waiting for her. It was time to really grow, to really see how far she could go. She would write to her mother at every stage of her journey and one day she would return to Dominica. When everything she'd done to get herself to England was all forgotten, she would be with her mother again.

<h1 style="text-align:center">35</h1>

It's fresh and bright in London now. Rayna sits in Holland Park wearing a headscarf tied at the nape of her neck and a pair of sunglasses that are dark and enormous on her small face. She has no make-up on and has dressed so casually she is bound not to be recognised. She needed to be out of the house, have the wind blow into her face, freshen her up. Wake her up, actually, as she hasn't slept well for the last two nights. Not since her telephone conversation with Sol about the mysterious new artist that Terry is planning to showcase at The Pelican and who is being hailed as the Rayna Laurence of jazz. Rayna had called a few friends in the industry in America to see if any of them could shed any light on who she might be. No one knew who she meant and Rayna became obsessed with this enigma of a singer until a late night supper with Eddie in a dingy restaurant off Carnaby Street.

'I know that name,' Eddie had said. 'In fact I met her.'

'You what? You didn't tell me.'

'I didn't know who it was you were talking about.'

'Eddie, I told you the name after I spoke to Sol.'

'You said Nell something. I couldn't place the name. But I met her the other week when I did that guest slot.'

'So she was there?' Rayna had replaced her knife and fork. The head waiter had come to refill her wine glass and place another tumbler of rum on the table for Eddie, bowing as he retreated.

'Yes, she was the support act. I caught her act. Well, heard it in the green room. From what I could hear, she was very talented.'

Rayna had picked up her wine glass and held it close to her lips, not daring to say what was just seconds from slipping from them. Instead, she had gulped back some wine and placed the glass down heavily before picking up her knife and fork.

'She is very good.' Eddie had shoved the last chunk of his rare steak into his mouth. So large his cheeks bulged and he seemed to chew endlessly when all Rayna wanted was to hear more about this Nell Robertson. In the end, she had become frustrated.

'You can just tell me,' she'd said.

Eddie swallowed before he'd finished chewing. 'Tell you what?' He sipped some water.

'What she's like. Is it true that she is the jazz singer I should have become?'

'Rayna. Are you asking if she's better than you? There's no one better than you.'

She'd dropped her cutlery and the waiter turned his head.

'Don't feel you have to say that. It's not about ego. I just want to know and I value your opinion.'

'My opinion is that she is one hell of a talented young lady. All this business in the paper and comparison between the two of you is all hype. Like all media. They want to make people curious so the venue packs out and the reporter can claim they discovered her. Make more news. That's all. She's not after your throne. Besides. We're still talking about two very different art forms. You're not a jazz singer any-more.'

As she sits on the park bench, hungry pigeons pecking around her patent pumps, she wishes she was still a jazz singer. Sol keeps on telling her to stick to cabaret, stick to cabaret, but she wants to tell him he's wrong. She wants to show the world that she was always a great jazz singer. She wants to be in that world again and she wants to show every-one that there is only one Rayna Laurence, the jazz singer. Only her.

She realises that the uncomfortable feeling between her shoulders, the one that leads to a constant furrow in her brow, is all about ego. And she is jealous. Jealous that this newcomer is stealing the stage she used to own. Jealous that Terry has found another singer whose voice he has clearly fallen in love with. Is he in love with her?

She picks herself up. Three pigeons flap upwards from the path, their wings making gusts of dusty air circle around her. She blinks and waves them away. She fastens the buckle of her beige Macintosh and heads out of the park in the direc-tion of Holland Park Station. She turns into Ladbroke Grove and walks its interminable length, all the way to Portobello Road where she turns into a very familiar Tavistock Crescent in the direction of The Pelican.

The atmosphere in Tavistock Crescent has changed and the street looks alien. The surrounding ones, too. The people dress oddly and there are no children in the street playing hopscotch or chasing each other across roads in large screaming groups wearing knee-length socks with holes in the elbows of their sweaters. But it's still school time. That's where they'll all be. Looming in the distance is the unwel-come sight of Trellick Tower, altering the skyline she used to know so well. The trains on the Metropolitan line are still present and she feels the rumble despite the rush of traffic on the Westway, whose construction had split their West London streets apart and had created such a furore with the residents when the plans became known to them. Terry still talks about it. At the time, Rayna was on her way to becoming a star and she'd had no time for his talks of protest. It hadn't affected the ins and outs and the comings and goings of the pub. The place that started Rayna's real escape from her past, the place that helped her forget.

Before she reaches The Pelican, she senses the familiar scent it emits into the air that surrounds it: cool cellar air wafting up from the floorboards, laced with the components of beer and lager. Riding on this wave is the nicotine and spirits, whiskies that mingle with each other so you don't know which is which unless it's the really expensive kind. She pictures the people whose clothes and breath were so soaked in The Pelican's fumes they took the very brickwork of the place home with them and returned the next day in fresh clothes, so baked in pub fumes they may as well have stayed the night. She sees them all as she gets closer, ghosts from the past. They'd merged into a cloud of bodies on the first day she entered the pub up until she could, at last, distinguish each face, each flat cap, smell the hair grease and perfume, tripping over the leads of the dogs sleeping under the table or curled around the leg of a bar stool. How the years have flown by and how she has come to experience so many aromas from around the world. But none of them has ever come close to this intimate smell of The Pelican.

Rayna doesn't know if she should use her key for the door up to the flat or if she should walk into the saloon. A man leaving the snug decides for her because he holds the door open and gestures with his arm for her to come in, make herself welcome. He has long hair to his back and reeks of marijuana.

'Thank you,' Rayna says in a thankless way as she enters the snug. She pictures Sol sitting on the banquette with a tumbler of spirits surrounded by a haze of his cigarette smoke. She sees Eddie, the day he was attacked and half dragged, half carried into the snug for Sandra to patch him up. His blood glinting on his cheek. The light above the table he sat at was like a spotlight, everyone focused on him, so much love and concern this great man had evoked. So much joy and entertainment he and the boys, her old friends, had provided.

She hears music now as she slowly approaches the saloon door. The piano, someone is messing around with a tune, making mistake after mistake, learning the song. With her hand on the brass plate, she hears the player get it right. A little blues riff that she can't place. She sees the red varnish on her nails when the door pushes involuntarily under her touch.

Terry is at the piano and turns when he hears the swoosh of the connecting door. The saloon is empty of people apart from him. He stands and leaves a half-played melody in mid-air.

'Rayna. I took you for a punter.'

'Hello Terry. Is it all right if I come in?'

'Jesus. Has it come to that? You have to ask permission to come into your own pub?'

She walks closer to the stage.

'This place was always yours, Terry.'

'Mine and yours. Once.' He puts his hands in his pockets and steps off the stage. 'Well, that's how I always saw it.'

'You play piano now?' she says. He grins and briefly looks back at the upright. It's a new one she realises. Slightly bigger and expensive. She has no idea when it was upgraded because it's usually covered over.

'Nah. Not really. Been messing around on it from time to time. Like first thing or a time like this in the afternoon in the middle of the week when there isn't a soul around.'

'It looks a lovely instrument. Keep going with it. It can be fun to play.'

'You play now?'

'Well, not like Truck used to. I tinkle out the odd tune. Have a go in rehearsals and someone is always happy to teach me the odd tune or two.'

'Nice. What about Eddie?'

'What about him?'

'I mean he plays piano so I wondered if he ever taught you.'

'No. Not ever. He hasn't even heard me. Never had the opportunity.'

'Oh, I thought you and he were sharing lots of musical moments together. When you've been away, like.'

'It's not like that, Terry. It never was a case of us sneaking around behind your back. Not like that.'

'But somehow you two finally got together, eh? The great Eddie Keane and the wonderful Rayna Laurence. Quite a team.' He laughs an empty chuckle and shuffles on his feet. The wrinkles around his bright blue eyes are deeper but he still has a boyish look. The traces of sadness in his face get brushed aside as he goes behind the bar and slams two tumblers on the counter. He whistles, not asking Rayna what she wants but pouring her an expensive whisky over three cubes of ice.

'Want a mixer?' he asks, finally looking up.

'As it comes.' She lifts onto a bar stool. The stools are new, too. How is it she never notices these changes when she comes here? She supposes it's because she's hardly here or perhaps she can't shake the memory of The Pelican back in 1956 when the world was a different one altogether and a moment like the one she is encountering was the furthest from her mind. She thought that was it for her at one time: a job in a bar, a job as a singer, a place to call her own, a man who loved her. Two. She thought she'd finally made it. But it was never enough.

'Cheers.' Terry lifts the glass, sips and leans his elbows across the bar, looking straight into Rayna's eyes. 'You've changed.'

'I'm older. I look older than I am.'

'Rubbish. You're beautiful and you always will be.'

She looks down at the drink she hasn't touched yet. 'Thank you, Terry. You always say the right things.'

'Oh, I'm not so sure. I never knew what to say in the end. To you. When the love ended.'

'It never ended, Terry. It never will. It's just…'

'Not the same?'

'Exactly.'

They both sip now, unable to look the other in the eye. They start to speak at the same time and Rayna insists that Terry goes first.

'I was just saying. I suppose you've heard about the show I'm putting on soon.'

'I heard. Well done, Terry. I'm sure it will be great.'

'You should come.'

She looks at the whisky and shakes her head. Smiles. 'No, I'd be sad and nostalgic to see a show here.'

'Would you have done it if I'd asked? Sung here again?'

'I don't know.'

'The answer is no, Ray. I've asked you countless times over the years. Countless. And you always refused. Said it messed with your image, your schedule, your contract. Remember?'

'I do. So is that why you got someone to replace me? The new Rayna Laurence?'

'I didn't ask for that article. It was some bloke who drinks in here on occasion. Mentioned it to him over a pint in his lunch break. He got all excited. Turns out he knew some journalist or other. The next thing I knew, there's a write-up in the papers. Mustn't grumble, though. We're sold out.'

'Well then, I couldn't have come if I wanted to.'

'Rayna, this is your place.'

'It was. Once. But not any more. You and I are both moving on, Terry. Looks like you are working some magic with this new singer and it's working.'

'So you have, then?'

'What?'

'Moved on?'

'Terry…'

'It's all right, Ray. I get it. If that's why you came here, to make sure I'm getting the message. I do. I get it. I don't hate you. I love you and I want you to be happy.'

For several moments, they drink in silence and Terry refills the glasses. Rayna can feel her head whirring. She could never handle more than just a sniff of whisky before. One glass is her usual limit these days. But she wants to be companionable. She wants to let Terry down gently. To show she still loves him and that she appreciates him and that she wouldn't be where she is today if it wasn't for his kindness.

'Who is she exactly?' Rayna asks.

'Who's who?'

'Nell Robertson. How do you know her?'

'She just walked in here off the street one evening.' Terry tops up their glasses though Rayna's is still unfinished. He fiddles around in his shirt pocket and finds the cigarette packet he is looking for is on a shelf under the counter. He lights up, walking round to Rayna's side of the bar, shaking out the match and dropping it into the closest ashtray. He sits on a stool next to her.

'Just like that?' asks Rayna. 'She's American, right? Wonder what brought her to an old pub in West London.'

'She'd actually heard about the pub before. Was at a loose end and decided to drop in.'

'Seems strange. She didn't come to England from America to visit a pub.'

'No, no. She had a gig here. She was on stage with Eddie on the last show.'

Rayna picks up her glass, keeps her eyes on Terry whose face is a shade of crimson she knows so well. He blushes when he's happy, he blushes when he's embarrassed, angry or hiding something.

'Actually,' she says, 'I knew about her shows. I suppose I'm just so curious about her, that's all.'

'Were you trying to catch me out or something?'

'Catch you out doing what? Terry, you and I know the score here. I don't expect you to have any loyalty when it comes to meeting someone.'

'I haven't met someone. Not like that. She's really young.'

'You won't be the first man who went for a girl who was far younger than him. Some girls like older men. Maybe she likes you?'

'I don't know about that.' The tip of his cigarette glows amber and ash balances close to tipping onto his sweater. He taps the cigarette and balances it on the edge of a bulky ashtray.

'Well, whatever she's here for, I hope it goes well. Her show. Just the one?'

'Yes, originally it was supposed to be for longer. But the idea of a one-off will make it special.'

'I see.'

'You look suspicious of something, Ray. I wish I knew what.'

'Look, Terry, I just came here to make sure that things were all right between us. That we could … well, I suppose I was hoping we could be friends still.'

'Always, Ray. Always.'

'Then that's all I came to hear. I should be off.'

'At least finish your drink.'

'It's so early in the day. I'm tipsy and I haven't eaten.'

'So stay for lunch. Sandra will be in soon. She'd love to see you. Nell is coming to rehearse some new songs.'

'Oh, no. I should go. I've got Sol on my back about new shows. Wants me to record a novelty record. Can you believe that? Anyway, I should go.'

Terry kisses her on the cheek as she is about to leave. He has had a shave, unusually for him, midweek. Normally he spruces up at the weekend. In fact, those are new trousers he has on. More modern, an expensive fabric. His hair is clipped neatly. Hints of Benson and Hedges and talcum powder effuse from him. Nostalgia brushes tender fingers over the place on her cheek that Terry has just kissed. She turns to wave as she walks away. Her feet hurt from all the walking she's done today. Her heart hurts from all the memories that accompany her on her walk.

36

In the week leading up to the big show at The Pelican, the inner walls have seen swells of people. Ones who hardly come to the pub and others whom Terry has never seen before. Sandra seems so giddy with the excitement of it; Terry is worried she might combust.

'I can't believe how many people have come in here since Rayna's interview on that show.' Sandra shakes her head and lifts the pint glass she's just filled onto the bar for the eagerly awaiting punter with wild hair and equally wild eyes. Sandra has a way of asking Terry questions but then answering them herself. She turns to him now. 'That was it, wasn't it? When they asked her how she felt about there being a new version of her. What did you make of her answer?'

'I didn't see the interview, Sandra. You tell me.'

'Well, I think she looked a bit put out. Almost like she was jealous. Which isn't like her.' Sandra plants her fists onto her hips. 'You think it's because she knows you and Nell have something going on or is it something else? You think she wants you back because she can't stand you being with someone else? Oh, no that's not like our Ray. She's so dignified. You should have seen her on that talk show. You wouldn't even know she came from the West Indies the way she talks now. All a bit posh if I'm being honest.'

'She's changed, Sandra. Grown up I expect.'

'Well, she was a young, tiny little thing when she came here. She's so much more now. So famous and rich, I suppose she can't really be bothered by Nell playing here. Can she?'

Terry walks away. He can't stand the conversation. Albeit one-sided. He knows what Sandra is doing, trying to create a drama when there isn't one. He and Rayna are over and he's moved on. With Nell. Nell has spent a lot of time at The Pelican. The pub welcomes her as warmly as it has the new pubgoers and the returners alike. She fills its vacant air with music in the late mornings and early afternoons when only one or two of the regulars show up for a pint and a read of the Daily Mirror. They have no idea that a giant in jazz is about to be born, a famous artist in the making, just feet away on a stage that is about to cast her into the lives and hearts of so many people.

They make love with regularity, Terry and Nell. She has filled the gap in a bed where Rayna no longer belongs. A place he used to lie and dream, wait and wonder. Where the memory of Rayna getting up to leave was always in the forefront of his mind. Now Nell, with an insatiable appetite for sex, walks into his bed, naked, smiling and ready to wrap her supple limbs around him. She eats in his bed, drinks, smokes and sometimes remains there for hours after he's got up and is getting ready to open the pub. She is staying with a friend the rest of the time. She is in London for him, and with every day, he can feel that she wants him that bit more.

Despite all this, there is always a battle going on in Terry's mind. The part that tells him that he still has romantic love for Rayna and the part that tells him that he is falling in love with Nell. He is going to miss Nell now that she has to urgently return to America after the show at The Pelican. Her manager has told her that a recording contract awaits and a record is going to be cut. Her first major recording deal. She can't pass it up. She has promised to come back as soon as she has recorded her album but Terry fears he will never see her again. That is probably why he wants to make love to her so often and so ferociously, to make up for the time they will be apart, be that for months or endlessly. Someone on their way to fame and stardom can't stay in one place. He knows that all too well. He can't entice her to stay. A middle-aged man with a pub, not an ounce of flair, sophistication or talent.

Terry often thinks about going to America with her. Packing the whole thing in. But to leave The Pelican would be to leave half of his body behind. Impossible. Instead he relishes her body, her talent, her good nature and her kind spirit while he can. Her beauty, her laughter and most of all her youth. She makes him young again. There is no denying that.

Now, as he and Sandra prepare the pub for the show tonight, the doors are locked, and beside these two, the band and technicians are setting up, stage lights glinting off the optics. He catches Sandra looking at him and grinning as he watches the band up on his treasured stage getting ready for the performance in about six hours. Terry is motionless behind the bar as Sandra checks the inventory: everything has to be perfect. He wants Sandra dressing fancy and he'll wear a suit. Though the spring day is warmer than any of the others have been.

'What?' he says to Sandra. 'Why are you grinning?'

'You look like a kid in a sweet shop. She's really got to you, hasn't she?'

'Don't be silly.'

*

Rayna wakes with a pain at the side of her neck. It happens when she falls asleep on her back. She'd been talking late into the night with Eddie after the dinner party they'd had. Everyone kept asking her if she was going to see the new Rayna Laurence, did she feel threatened by her and when on earth would she be performing again. You know you have to stay in people's minds or they'll forget about you. At some stage in the evening, she had forgotten why she'd even invited these people to her house. Industry types, would-be actors and singers who claimed to love Rayna and spent most of their time trying to sleep with Eddie. Including the men.

The couple had retired when their guests had gone and Rayna had talked non-stop to him about Nell Robertson.

'Do you think she's pretty?'

'In a way.'

'What do you mean "in a way"? Either she's pretty or she isn't.'

'You've seen her picture, can't you decide?'

'I think she is.' Then minutes would pass and Rayna would ask another question just as Eddie began to kiss her neck or slide the strap of her nightdress off her shoulder. 'What about her voice? Now be honest, is she a better singer than me? I can take it.'

'Rayna, you are the best singer I've ever met. I've said it before and I stand by it.'

Eddie had given up trying to make love to her and their voices had drifted into silence with only the echo of late night footsteps and the occasional thrum of distant cars as a lullaby. Eddie had fallen asleep far earlier than Rayna who lay awake looking up at an invisible ceiling.

This morning Eddie's attempts to make love to Rayna are reciprocated. She enjoys the sleepy smell of him and tries to ignore the pain her neck gives her as she holds him very tightly.

'Coffee?' he asks minutes after they have finished. Rayna nods.

She rolls onto her side and pulls the blankets up over her shoulder, sleepy and cosy, until the conversations from the dinner party filter back into her mind. Perhaps she should go to the show tonight at The Pelican. She'll see for herself if Nell really is pretty, judge for herself how well she sings and plays the piano. Perhaps then she won't feel so threatened. *Jesus*, she thinks to herself, *I am threatened by her, this virtual stranger.*

Nell Robertson has come from nowhere, a woman who is still such a mystery to her and whom she never needs to meet, but yet she can't help feeling fascinated. It has puzzled her for weeks as to how Nell would find herself at The Pelican of all places. It seems like too much of a coincidence. Rayna feels suspicious. Who is this talented jazz performer? Terry will be blind to anything sinister and Rayna is convinced something sinister is going on with this girl.

'Coffee in bed.' Eddie bursts the cloud of fury and frustration that Rayna feels any time the thought of Nell comes to mind. She sits up, smiles sweetly at Eddie and reaches for her coffee cup.

'I hope this is nice and strong. I need it. So tired.'

'We were up late, it's not surprising.' Eddie slurps his coffee. She can never understand how he manages to drink it while it's that hot. She smiles. Eddie looks at her and smiles back. 'So, what do you want to do today?' he asks.

'Oh nothing. Well, sort of nothing.'

Eddie laughs and puts his cup on the table beside the bed. 'How can you do sort of nothing?'

'Well, I sort of want to go to The Pelican tonight.' She doesn't look at him, only at the dark brew in her cup.

'Are you serious?'

She nods.

'But why?'

'I suppose curiosity got the better of me and I don't want people thinking that I'm bitter or envious of her or anything.'

'Maybe the best way to prove any of that is to stay away.'

'And I want you to come with me.'

'No way.' He turns to pick up his cup.

'Come on. By now you must be sick of me asking all these questions about her. I can find everything out for myself and then I can move on.'

'If you want to move on, get on the phone to your agent and tell him to book you a jazz gig. Cut a record and let the people decide who is the real Rayna Laurence.'

'It's not a contest.'

'Then why do I feel as if you're staking out the competition?'

'That's just unfair, Eddie. It's nothing like that. I like the idea of calling Sol and telling him about the change of music. I feel as if I'm stagnating. I want to bow out and leave the whole cabaret circuit to Shirley Bassey. Besides, I get sick of the papers calling me London's answer to Miss Bassey. I want to be … well, I just want to be me again.'

A slow smile spreads over Eddie's face. 'At last.'

'Before it's too late.'

'You're probably right on time. Promise me the first record you cut will be with me.'

'If you promise you'll come with me to The Pelican tonight.'

*

It's just two hours until the show. The band is up in Terry's kitchen eating fish and chips from the shop on All Saint's Road. Terry went personally to get them and came back with enough battered fish, chips and pickled onions to sink a ship in enough chip paper to make bunting for the whole of the pub. Sandra brought a Victoria sponge and brewed several pots of tea.

'You guys and your fish and chips,' Nell says, leaning against the sink with Terry as she sips some black tea. Terry has already started on a tumbler of whisky though he'd promised Sandra he'd watch it because he had to be on his toes tonight.

'You've got to love the British cuisine,' he says to Nell.

'Yeah, I do except both fried fish and chipped potatoes came from Europe.'

'Who told you that?'

'The history books. I guess you guys can take the credit for putting the two together and frying it all in the same pool of oil.' She grins at him in her usual way. An intelligent and su- perior way that he has got used to and doesn't mind in the slightest. She can be as condescending of him and the British as she wants. At this point, she is a queen in his eyes and Nell can say or do anything she wants. Though it's unspoken

and not something the papers have said to him, Nell is the
new Rayna Laurence in his life.

*

Rayna knows as they sit in the back of the taxi that Eddie is
annoyed, that she has dragged him out early, far too early, to
see Nell's show. It doesn't start for another hour or so and
the doors will all be locked, the place empty.

'Maybe we won't stay,' Rayna had said. 'Maybe I might
just go and wish Terry luck, say hello to this girl and then
you and I can go to dinner instead.'

She knows Eddie had been dying to tell her that he wished
she could make her mind up. Did she want to see this girl
perform or not? Why make such a big deal of it all? It's just
The Pelican.

The taxi pulls up outside the ageing pub and Eddie pays
the driver. The place is in darkness apart from a lonely red
spotlight that doesn't allow a visual of the interior. Eddie
looks at Rayna with an 'I told you so' reflected in his eyes.
She tries to ignore it and searches for the key to the flat.

'We can't just go in,' says Eddie, shocked and still a bit
peeved.

'It's okay. Besides, I can't knock on the door. Terry keeps
saying this is my pub as well as his and he might feel of-
fended if I don't make myself at home.'

'I think you should give that key back.'

She isn't listening and Rayna has already unlocked the
door. She hears laughter and excited voices from above and
assumes a big band is up there having fun and relaxing before the show. This is a part of the business she always enjoyed. Bonding with the band members, especially if they

are only booked for one show: it's good to know they are supporting and understand how their front person likes them to play. She wonders how many are in Nell's band as she moves slowly to the stairs. She stops for a brief moment to poke her nose around the door of the saloon. From behind the bar she can see the red light is beaming onto the bass drum of the kit. The rest of the instruments and stage equipment look abandoned, a scene that is alive but has not yet come to life.

'Rayna,' Eddie exclaims, exasperated.

'Rayna?' a voice calls from upstairs. In seconds, Terry is plodding down the steps, his cheeks reddening as he sees the couple poised at the foot of the stairs.

'Terry.' Rayna smiles widely. She reaches to touch his arm and plants a tepid kiss on his cheek.

'Ray? Eddie? What are you doing here?' He reaches to shake Eddie's hand.

'Oh, we were going to dinner.' Rayna's voice stumbles. 'And I wanted to wish you luck for tonight.'

'We could have called,' offers Eddie.

'But there's nothing like the personal touch,' says Rayna.

'I suppose.' Terry's sentence is drawn out. He puts his hands in his pockets. The colour in his cheeks returning to normal. 'Good of you to do that. I thought I heard something. I was expecting the security people.'

'Oh no, sorry. It's only us,' says Rayna. 'Me. I had the key on me. But here.' She dangles the keys between them. 'I suppose I should give it back.'

Terry hesitates before taking them, fiddling with them so that they jangle and then puts them and his fists back into his pockets, cheeks red again. There is silence for several minutes.

'Did you want to come up and say break a leg to our star personally?' asks Terry. 'Eddie, I believe you've met Nell.'

'Briefly.'

'Well, she's a big fan of yours. You might make her day if you came up.'

'Terry?' Another voice from the landing upstairs. Young, female, American. It's Nell, and before Rayna can decide what to say, she is already on her way downstairs. Rayna freezes. With every step Nell takes, the mystery begins to unravel. She knows this person. This Nell. Although her hair, her accent, her figure and even her confidence have changed significantly, she is definitely known to Rayna. When Rayna first knew her, all those years ago, Nell was a teenager: uncouth, rude, emotional, sullen, overweight, insecure, afraid. Her name wasn't Nell then. It was Daniella and she was an angry girl who had been crying her eyes out the day Rayna last saw her. The only thing that remains of the Daniella she once knew is the small scar on her forehead that appeared after one of the many games they played in and around the grand house of the St Jeans.

'My God,' Rayna whispers.

'Hello,' says Nell putting out her hand. 'Nice to finally meet you.'

Rayna reaches out but grabs the girl by her outstretched wrist. She drags her into the saloon and Nell doesn't resist being pulled by her arm, even after the thud of Rayna's foot on the door as she kicks it open. Eddie and Terry follow but Rayna is blind to their existence as she spins Nell around so they are facing each other. Rayna stares into Nell's eyes. Oh, she recognises them all right, even if they are not behind the round glasses of her adolescent years.

'What … Why are you here?' Rayna's voice has a rasping quality that she hadn't intended. Nell shakes loose the grip on her wrist and wanders into the gloom of the saloon, her hips swaying. The only light is the red one that shines onto the drum kit and the scant glimmer of the street lamps that fall onto the pub. Incensed, Rayna follows Nell and they stand, motionless, in the middle of the bar, neither blinking, neither speaking.

*

The chatter is lively in the kitchen as the band, the sound engineer and the man operating the lights sit around the table. Marijuana and nicotine cloud his vision and makes Terry's eyes red, but he can see Nell smiling and grinning, glowing, he would say, with enthusiasm and anticipation of the gig. Sandra rushes around as if everyone in his old kitchen is royalty, like the queen came to visit or something. As for him, he doesn't have much of an appetite, too excited about the show. It's not that long to go and the man who is supposed to be doing security is coming soon, as well as his wife who is collecting the tickets. He'll set up a table for her when he goes back down. When this lot have finished eating, he and Sandra will get the kitchen and living room back in order while the band does a quick line check before the punters come in.

His suit is making him feel hot and scratchy – it was probably too early to put it on but he wanted to look the business. He'll go to the bedroom, take the jacket off at least. He winks at Nell as he leaves the kitchen. She looks at him curiously.

On the landing, Terry imagines he hears a sound from downstairs. No, it isn't imagined that he hears footsteps. Have the security people been able to find a way in? He laughs at the idea of the security bloke breaking into the pub and telling Terry he needs to be more careful about locking the doors. But he's sure they're locked. He stands at the top of the stairs and listens. He hears Eddie Keane calling Rayna's name and on impulse he trots down the stairs. He's surprised to see them and Rayna muddles over her words as if she regrets coming, offers to return his keys and he's not sure how he feels about taking them back.

The hardest thing for him to fathom is how Rayna reacts when Nell comes down the stairs. What the hell is going on and why are these two women staring daggers at each other? He and Eddie stand dumbstruck in the doorway until Terry has the sense to turn the light on over the bar. It illuminates the fierce look on Rayna's face and the look of distaste in Nell's.

*

'Why the change of name?' Rayna tries to find calm, aware that the trembling in her body from anger might be miscon-strued. She isn't nervous, she wants answers.

'Rayna, we've all had to make adjustments in our lives. Listen to your accent. You sound like an English princess.'

'And you? Why do you sound so American now?'

'Because that's where I was sent for school. I was glad to see the back of that island.'

'Your parents did the same for you as they did your brother?'

'Not exactly. It was my aunt who suggested it.' Nell crosses her arms and circles Rayna who follows her movements. They are like slick animals, prowling, waiting to see who will attack. For now, their voices are even, slow, calculated. 'You see, when my so-called parents returned from your house, after they tried to get back the money you stole from them–' her eyes dart over to the men, 'my mother was in hysterics. She blamed him. Told her husband that if he could have kept his hands to himself, none of this would have happened. That if word got out, she'd look like a fool, along with all the other things they said about her. All of them true of course.'

'Then what?'

'Then what? Then I sat on the top of the stairs. I had managed to stop crying. I knew you were never coming back. I was just wishing, hoping and praying that somehow you'd see what you'd done. Pay them back the money you stole. Come back to work. Come back to me.'

Here, Rayna looks over at Terry and Eddie. They must be so confused. They now know she is a thief. That's already too much of her past for her to explain. She swallows hard but it's difficult to swallow shame in one gulp.

'How could I go back there?' Rayna asks. Her voice so soft now, it's as if she is talking to the thirteen-year-old girl she used to care for, play with, confide in. 'You know what he … you know what happened to me. And those people, they were not fair to me. I didn't have a choice but to leave and you *knew,* you *knew* I couldn't take you away from there, that you could never come with me.'

'As you say, Rayna. Anyway, they were happy to send me away. They probably wouldn't have cared if I'd gone with you. She didn't trust him to leave me alone. Told everyone that I was going away to school but all she did was make her sister take me. Told her sister everything that my father had done to me and that he'd done it to another girl. She was horrified, only too happy to take me out of that house, and at last I found someone who actually cared about me. My future. My aunt took care of everything that has made me what I am. The piano lessons, the school she found for me in America to further my education and my training.'

'And your parents?'

'Who cares? I don't know what became of them, or my brother, and I really don't want to know.'

'So you made up a false name and came to find me. Tell me how much you hate me.'

Nell's laugh is tight and slaps at Rayna's cheek.

'I wanted to tell you that. Yes. I wanted to say to you, see, I got out and I made it. But then I saw you had become someone yourself and I worked even harder. I wanted to be better than you. I wanted what you had.'

'Including Terry? You came here to take him from me?'

Nell looks at her feet. Someone knocks on the flat door and both women look at Terry. He excuses himself and goes to the door but Eddie stands behind the bar, eyes watering. Rayna can't tell if that's because of anger or sadness. He doesn't know the whole story but he must feel something, though she can't tell exactly what. Terry returns.

'It's the people doing the door tonight. I showed them upstairs. Look, do you two want privacy?'

'No,' says Rayna. 'You should stay.'

'Aren't you afraid of what he'll hear about you?' Nell adds.

'No, he needs to hear about *you*. I'm very sure that you came here to steal him away from me, to make me suffer.

You learnt jazz because you knew I was no longer singing jazz so that you could replace me.'

'Don't flatter yourself, Rayna. You and I always loved big band music and then it became jazz. You deserted it and looks like you deserted Terry, too.'

'So it was easy to swoop in.'

'I came here to mess up your life. Yes, it's true. I didn't know the whole situation and I wanted to find out.'

'And cause trouble for me.'

'It's not all about you, Rayna. How did you get so big-headed? Is that the cost of fame? You sold out. You didn't stay true to yourself.'

Rayna advances on her but stops herself from blurting out something she will regret. Nell's words have hurt her more than she'd like to admit. Perhaps she sold out but which young girl wouldn't be attracted by fame and fortune. Especially the fortune. It was all that mattered to her ten years ago when she was a nobody. Came all the way from Dominica to make a better life but it didn't come easily. Then she got lucky. She saw an opportunity and took it.

'But you changed your name as a disguise so that you could come for me,' Rayna says.

'I changed my name to disassociate myself from the St Jeans. That name was a curse. My life was cursed until my aunt came to my rescue.'

'Well, all's well that ends well. You got what you wanted. Got your career, Terry, and maybe this bar, too.'

'My God you're materialistic, Rayna. Is that how you always were?'

Rayna can't deny how ashamed this eloquent young woman is making her feel. Like nothing, like a fraud. Nell,

Daniella, was never this assured. No matter how she started, Nell's life hasn't worked out so badly.

Nell shakes her head. 'Of all the questions you're asking me, of all the things you now know, there is something that you haven't even bothered to ask me about.'

'What did I forget?'

'Your mother, Rayna. Have you forgotten about your mother?'

A lashing wave of silence strikes them all, and for a moment, no one can move. Rayna feels something rising in her throat. Words, nausea, she can't be sure. All she can do is swallow and the sound echoes in the saloon.

'Not so vocal now,' says Nell. 'When did you last speak to your mother?'

It was a long time ago. Years. Rayna can't remember now. The exchange of letters fizzled out and she doesn't know who is to blame. Life took over and the weeks of not writing extended to months and then there were no letters. She'd promised herself and her mother that she would go back one day. Or at least send money to help Urma. As a young girl training to become a nurse who then became a seamstress and later a barmaid, she never made enough to do that: she had always struggled. But that struggle finally ended and by then her mother had been far from her mind. How cruel of her, how selfish. Every now and then, she'd told herself she must get on a ship and go back to see her mother. Rayna was, after all, finally making money, but when that began to happen, the time was never right. She had left it so long the shame of never keeping her word stopped her from acting on it. What sort of daughter does that to her mother? She pictures Urma now and she knows if she boarded the plane, Urma would forgive her everything and cradle her in her arms. Just like the day she left, the day she made all those promises.

'You know your mother looked out for me, too?' says Nell. 'Came to the house to check I was all right. I visited her for weeks and then I went to stay with my aunt. Then I continued writing to her. *I* continued to write.'

Rayna can't meet Nell's eye. She can't look at anyone. She turns instead to the red-soaked drum.

'Are you still in touch with her?' she asks Nell.

'Rayna. Your mother is dead.'

Rayna's head jerks back towards Nell. She searches her face. Surely she wouldn't lie just to hurt her.

'When?' Rayna stutters.

Nell moves towards her as if she wants to reach out but Rayna steps back.

'Tell me.'

'Four years ago she became frail. Just overnight. Developed a cough and no one knew why. I begged her to come to America. The medicine is better and I offered to pay, but…'

'But what?'

'She refused. Said she was waiting.'

'To die?' Rayna shakes her head and the trembling in her body returns.

'She was waiting for you, Rayna.'

The tears fall from their eyes. Rayna can't stop shaking her head, saying no, over and over. She won't accept this as truth. Won't accept what she has done. She has killed her mother. Leaving her out there alone was the worst thing she could have done.

Eddie races around the bar to hold her, catch her before she collapses to the floor – her grip on the edge of the bar won't last.

'Rayna, my Rayna,' Eddie says and leads her over to a chair. Nell is sobbing like a child. The door opens and Sandra appears.

'What's happened?' she ask and runs into the saloon. Of the two women crying, she doesn't know which to comfort. She looks at Terry who steps towards Nell.

'We can't do the show,' he says in a small voice. 'Not like this.'

All that can be heard are the stifled sobs of both Rayna and Nell until Rayna clears her throat.

'Yes, you can.' Her voice is small, weak. 'You can't cancel now. It must be less than an hour to go.'

'Where do you want me?' The security guard and his wife come in now.

'Could you leave us for a bit, mate?' Terry holds up his arms as if to shield the unfolding scene. 'Just wait for me upstairs. You, too, Sandra. Please. Keep 'em all up there. If you don't mind. Ta love.'

When the door closes behind the bar, Rayna stands.

'Nell, you've worked hard for this. I wish I didn't come tonight. I don't want to … I can't spoil this, too.' She rushes to Nell, wraps her arms around her. Nell holds her just as tightly and looks up to the ceiling, blinking away tears. Rayna whispers into her ear. 'Please forgive me. Please try. I never wanted to hurt you. I loved you like a sister but I made a mistake. I made many and I'll regret them for the rest of my life.'

'More than anything, I just wanted to see you again,' says Nell. 'I couldn't hurt you if I tried. I did want to but then I met Terry. I didn't mean to get in your way.'

Rayna pulls back and holds Nell's upper arms, sniffing and looking through a gloss of tears. '*I* got in my way. I did that.

I am not angry with you. Only myself. I'm going now. Going home. I wish you the best night of your life. And so many more.' She pulls Nell to her again and then guides the girl into Terry's waiting arms.

'Look after Nell. She's a special person.' Rayna looks at Eddie who nods, puts an arm over her shoulder and leads her out of The Pelican.

By the pub door, people have already begun to gather. They smoke cigarettes and talk loudly, forming a swirling queue as more appear to join them. Once upon a time, this audience would have come for her. The last thing Rayna wants to do is sing for anyone.

*

Rayna walks blindly, passing several streets and turning into ones she hardly recognises. A hand reaches out and grabs her arm and she shrieks.

'Are you going to slow down?' Eddie is at her elbow, looking furiously at her. She realises she isn't actually on her own. She came to The Pelican with Eddie and has barely acknowledged him since seeing Daniella, or Nell, come down the stairs. How calm, beautiful, how self-assured she'd looked, only for Rayna to reduce her to tears. Something she'd become expert at.

'Eddie. Eddie I'm sorry. You don't have to stay. I just need to walk.'

'And you think I'm just going to leave you on your own out here?'

She shakes her head. 'No, but, I wouldn't blame you if you did.'

'What are you talking about?'

'Eddie. You know it all now. You know my secrets. Everything I've kept from you. You must hate me.'

'You sound as though you want me to. But I never would. Not ever.'

'Eddie.' She clenches her fists against his chest. 'Didn't you hear what she said? My mother. My own mother. I abandoned her. Had no idea she'd even died. What was I doing with my life all this time that I could forget her?'

'I don't believe you forgot her. Look, I haven't been in touch with anyone back home in so long.'

'But not as long as me. What kind of person is that? Why are you with me?'

'I'm with you because I love you. Always have, always will.'

'But that's my mother. A woman I loved. How can I just ignore what I've done? How can I go unpunished for that? How?' She softly beats his chest and Eddie takes her wrists. He lifts her hands to his lips and kisses her knuckles.

'Not one of us is perfect, Rayna. You had a lot to run away from. What that man did to you. You were a child. So you ran and you kept on running. You stopped here and made this your home.'

'I don't have a home,' she says. She looks into his eyes. 'Except with you.' She breaks away from him and looks around to see where her feet have led her. She hears music playing. Someone is playing reggae from a top floor flat. 'Where the hell are we?' she asks, still looking around.

'Near the Portobello. We can get a taxi home from Ladbroke Grove. Come.'

*

About half an hour after Rayna leaves, Nell washes her face again in the bathroom sink. No one has been able to get through to her, not Terry and not Sandra. Her manager called from New York where he has been securing more engagements for her. A run of coffee shops and small theatres with what he claims is the hottest group of young musicians on the scene. Nell wasn't able to exchange more than a few words, only to say thank you and I'll see you soon.

'Are you definitely sure you don't want me to call this off?' Terry stands like a lost child in the bathroom doorway. He's taken off his jacket, loosened his tie. One hand in his pocket, the other holding a lit cigarette between his thumb and forefinger.

'I'm sure. I need my music right now.' She pats her face dry and looks in the mirror. 'God, I look like a horror show.'

'No you don't. Come here.' Terry flicks the half-burned cigarette into the sink and puts his arm around Nell. He cradles her head against his chest.

'Careful you don't mess with my fro.'

'Sorry,' he raises his hands. 'I'll find your afro pick.'

'And ask Sandra if she has any lipstick.' She looks in the mirror again and pats her cheeks. 'I need something to bring all of this to life.'

*

The saloon is completely full when the band enters via the snug and make their way down the centre of the room to the stage. The platform is as it always was, though Terry had toyed with the idea of making it taller. Nell had said to keep it authentic. She always seemed to say the right thing and he is falling for her more each day. He has no idea what he'll do without her.

He watches as the music transforms her from the angry young girl who stood up to Rayna. She had been so calm to start but by the end of a heated confrontation, Terry could see that Nell has loved and missed Rayna. Rayna is an easy person to love but has always been a difficult one to fathom. With Nell, it's so much easier. Name change, that was all, but this woman has a heart of gold. At the very end of the evening when her adoring audience has left, when the band has gone home and Sandra and the other two members of staff have cleared away the debris of the evening, he lies in his bed with Nell's cheek against his chest. He strokes her arm as rays of moonlight tinge the wall above them.

'When you go, I'm closing this place for a while. And I'm coming with you. That is, if you don't mind.'

She kisses his skin and rests her head back onto his chest.

'If you hadn't suggested it for real, I'd be imagining that you did. Imagining you were with me up to the moment I could see you again.'

The Beginning

Autumn comes back around and the warmth of the last few months are nothing but a wistful memory. It's been a busy time. Meeting new musicians, adjusting to new venues, adapting to many changes as a new era begins. New doors open, new songs are learnt and aspects to her character are changing, too. She is growing; she is blossoming. She is happy to have the man that she loves so close by. He's like a tonic. A boost to her ego and oh so encouraging. He has put his life on hold so that she can find her way and she will never let him down. Her musicality has never been as good and her performances get better with every rehearsal. She sings her jazz music with more confidence than she ever had and she has been able to let go of the past and grow into a future that has all the potential to give her lifelong bliss and happiness. She can appreciate what she has, she won't waste any opportunities and she will always be open and honest.

On this small stage, where the audience is so close the rustle of their clothing risks being heard on her microphone, she scours each face for the ones she knows personally and looks over at the one who has followed her all the way here. The one she will never keep the truth from. Ever.

With a few opening bars to the first song, the applause, once again, is deafening. She lifts her lips to the microphone and Rayna sings to the people she loves and all the people she has ever loved.

Thank you for choosing

When Skies Are Grey

I really hope you enjoyed it. Your thoughts mean the world to me, and I'd love to hear what you think. If you have a moment, please consider leaving a review—it makes such a difference in helping new readers discover the book.

You can share your review at your preferred retailer.

I also love connecting with readers on social media, so please do follow my journey and say hello on Instagram and TikTok. @franclarkauthor

Thanks so much for your support!

Fran x

Connect: Hop onto my *website* for links & info!
franclarkauthor.co.uk

And: Join my *mailing list* for a Free Read! And be ahead of
all my offers, news and updates!

Also by Fran Clark

Lovers

Other books in The Island Secrets series:

Holding Paradise

A Prayer For Junie

The Long Way Home

The Hope series:

Wherever You Will Go

However Far We Fall

About the author

Fran Clark is an author of emotive women's fiction, whose stories are deeply rooted in the connection between London and the Caribbean. Born to Dominican parents and raised in West London, her work explores themes of identity, resilience, and the strength of women—often inspired by the vibrant storytelling of her mother.

Her first novel, *Holding Paradise*, was published in 2014 and later reimagined as the first in the *Island Secrets Series*. Fran holds an MA in Creative Writing from Brunel University and lives in the English countryside, where she teaches vocals and leads a local choir.

She also writes contemporary fiction under the pen name Rosa Temple.

www.ingramcontent.com/pod-product-compliance
Lightning Source LLC
Chambersburg PA
CBHW031254120726
47906CB00003B/735